The House
that Wouldn't Go Away

PAUL GALLICO

The House that Wouldn't Go Away

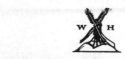

HEINEMANN : LONDON

William Heinemann Ltd
10 Upper Grosvenor Street, London W1X 9PA
LONDON   MELBOURNE   TORONTO
JOHANNESBURG   AUCKLAND

First published in Great Britain 1979

© 1979 by Mathemata & Anstalt

SBN 434 28065 8

Printed and bound in Great Britain by
Morrison & Gibb Ltd, London and Edinburgh

for
GINNIE
with more than love

CONTENTS

AUTHOR'S NOTE

I will never forget the impression my first house made upon me. True, I was born in what was known as a house – a New York brownstone – but we only had a set of rooms going through it from front to back on the top floor. At an early age – say nine or ten – I was taken ill and for my convalescence was sent out to a house in Westchester of a pupil of my father's, to stay for two weeks. This was a real house in the country with woods and garden, bright chintzes, fireplaces, and the room I was given was beneath the roof and had a dormer window. I can still see my bedroom with its crazy quilt bed cover and the view from the dormer. As an ardent reader of fairy tales, I was for the first time living in an enchanted place. It was a house.

P.W.G.

The House

Perhaps it all never would have happened had not the Easter holidays begun so inauspiciously for the three Maitland children, Michael, Miranda and Roddy. It was their second day home, and for a second day it was raining. How it was raining.

As they stood together, dolefully dressing-gowned, staring at and staring out the swirlings and lashings on the boys' bedroom window-pane, they could hear the rush of the overflow down the pipes from the roof, seven floors above, to Hallam Street below. Down there passing cars were throwing up spray like the bow waves of ships, and occasional, early, soaked passers-by hurried along the pavement rivers until they were washed from view.

'Would you believe it?' said Michael, at twelve the oldest of the trio. A slim, dark-haired, neat boffin of a boy, he wore his seniority easily and benevolently. Sinking his chin into his crossed arms on the window sill, he brought himself down to Roddy's eye level. 'Of all the rotten luck.'

Roddy, only weeks away now from his eighth birthday, scratched his carroty curls and circled away chanting to himself, 'Raining, raining – cats and dogs, bats and frogs . . . rats and hogs . . . sprats and mogs . . .' until the rhymes ran out.

'You're repeating yourself,' Michael checked him without turning around.

'Why? What did I say?' Roddy returned to his side indignantly.

'Mogs *are* cats, aren't they?' Michael started on.

'Well? So? What if they are? The rain's repeating itself all the time, isn't it?'

'What are you talking about?' Michael asked wearily.

'Well, it's not like snow, is it? No two snowflakes are the same, are they? But I bet raindrops are. All the same. Boring, boring. Same old rain.'

'Why don't you go down and make sure?' Michael half-smiled to himself.

'I don't need to. I just know. And I'm right, aren't I, Miranda?'

But Miranda, gazing silently still, said nothing. Elegantly tall for her eleven years, though poised less gracefully between childhood and adolescence, she had a delicacy and a fragility even that served only to intensify her concentration now.

Unanswered by his sister, Roddy turned back and rallied, 'Anyway, I've got a better idea. Let's all go down and play "Blast Off" under the lift-shaft.'

'That's your game,' Michael shuffled dismissively.

'So?' Roddy queried. 'What's your game then? Rain spotting?' Ignored, his pun either missed or not appreciated, he moved closer. 'Surely you're not just going to stay there all day, waiting for it to stop, are you?'

'It's not going to stop,' said Michael.

'What, never?'

'Not for a long time at least. The weather men are predicting a record rainfall over the next few weeks.'

'How do you know?' Roddy was too brought down by the news to believe it.

'I heard it on the radio this morning.'

'When? I didn't hear any radio.'

'Of course not, stupid. I had my transistor on under my pillow.' Then, half-turning, Michael asked, 'Did you hear it on yours, Miranda?'

But there was no reply. Still Miranda stared in silence.

'Miranda?' Michael tried again. And again: 'Miranda?' as she slowly looked askance.

'Sorry?' she asked.

'I said did you –' But then troubled by the glaze in her eyes he stopped. 'Miranda, are you all right?' he asked instead.

'Yes, I think so,' she answered, looking back again out at the rain.

'You don't seem very sure,' Michael persisted. 'Really? Is there anything the matter? Anything else, I mean?' resting a hand on her shoulder and looking round into her face.

Miranda swung aside her long brown hair and brightened for him.

'Really. I'm all right. I just . . .'

But it was no good. She had to sit down. She perched on the bottom of Michael's bed, and both he and Roddy dropped to their knees beside her.

'What is it?' Michael almost whispered, anxiously.

'Shall I get Mummy?' Roddy offered.

'No,' Miranda shook her head urgently, then looked from Roddy to Michael and down again.

'Well, can't you tell us?' Michael took her hands in his, and watched in a shared silence only she could break now.

Slowly she prepared to, while Michael and Roddy tried not to distract her as they waited. Then softly she began. 'I must have woken very early. I seem to have lain in bed for an hour or more without stirring – sort of awake and asleep at the same time. I don't know. It was very strange.'

Michael glanced an order of silence at Roddy as he shifted on his knees – but too late.

'Did you have a nightmare?' he asked.

But Miranda again shook her head. 'No, Roddy. No nightmare. No dream really either, that I can remember.' She continued, 'It was more like a vision I had. Just lying there. I don't know . . .'

Michael's hands closed around hers with a comfort he himself was without.

'I just lay there with my eyes wide open, staring at the

ceiling – but not seeing just the ceiling. All the time I kept seeing more and more of the House.'

'What house, Miranda?' Michael asked slowly, in pace with the trance she seemed to be in still.

'The House that was here. That *is* here.'

'You mean Melton Court?'

'No,' she shook her head again. 'Not this block. The House that was – is – where the flats are now.'

'What kind of a house?' Again Michael tried to draw her gently.

'A very grand house. With beautiful grounds and beautiful – oh, beautiful everything.'

For the first time she looked into their faces, and watched them watching as if even now it was not her own voice speaking. But there was a boldness and certainty as she confided to them at least, 'We are living in somebody else's house.'

Bewilderment vied with forbearance in Michael's eyes as he waited for her to go on.

'But this is our flat. Nobody else lives here – only Mummy and Daddy,' Roddy frowned. 'And no one has lived here before. This is brand new –'

'Just like all the others – I know,' Miranda nodded. 'But there is another house here – a real house. It's much, much bigger than this. Our flat is only a part of it, on the first floor.'

As Miranda seemed to drift silently into her trance once more, Michael felt too curious to reproach Roddy for intruding as he had – and as he longed to now.

'Do you mean a house that must have stood here before Melton Court was built, then – or what?' he shrugged.

'Yes, I think so, I think that's it,' she nodded, almost apologetically. 'They had to tear it down, of course – to make room.'

'Well then,' said Roddy, 'it's gone, isn't it? If it was torn down it couldn't be here any more – so they came with a lot of big lorries and carted all the stuff away.'

'The stones and the bricks and the beams and everything,

and the windows and the chimneys and fireplaces, the walls and the roof, I suppose,' Miranda agreed. 'But they couldn't take away the place where it was, could they? That would always be here, wouldn't it?'

Michael caught fire. 'And we are in a part of it?'

'Yes,' she replied firmly. 'In quite a bit of it, I think.'

Roddy regarded his sister out of the corner of his eyes. He had been minded again to retreat behind that unanswerable question, 'How do you know?' but desisted, because Miranda quite often just knew things, and the things she knew or felt had the strangest way of turning out to be so. Not that there was anything odd or funny about her. It was just that she seemed able to feel things, or if not feel think them or imagine them so hard that they would be like feeling – which perhaps was why they so often came true.

It wasn't anything you could put your finger on, or even remember. It was just that Miranda seemed to be moving, at times, in a slightly different world from his own, and sometimes she would open the door to that world. Michael, being one year older, and more used to her now, was able immediately to slip through the opening and join her there, but Roddy, whose boundaries were still fixed by what he saw, could only peer inside.

Well, the door was open again, and Roddy looked and felt the sudden longing and determination just for once to pass through that door.

What was there in his world but rain and wind and boredom of nowhere to go and nothing to do? And so, asking, 'Can you still see it?' he joined her there.

'Oh, yes, Roddy.' Miranda smiled. 'I'll always see it. Because it's here – now – all around us.'

Just then Michael rose up and plunged his hands deep into his dressing-gown pockets, and walked back to the window. He stared out again, then turned back, and leant thoughtfully against the sill. He looked across at Miranda as Roddy rose too, to sit at the bottom of his own bed, across the rug from her.

'I'm sorry you –' he began.

'Oh, don't be sorry, Michael,' Miranda smiled up at him. 'There's nothing to be sorry about. I think we're very lucky. We've never lived in a proper house before, have we? It's what we've always dreamed of. Only this time it's no dream. I don't know what it is.'

Michael and Roddy swapped swift looks before each in turn addressed her.

'You say you can see it all?' Michael enquired.

'All of it, yes,' Miranda beamed. 'Every room and every stair.'

'Will we see it?' Roddy asked, uncertain whether he really wanted to, or could believe in it even.

'I don't know,' said Miranda. 'But I can tell you all about it.'

'Could you really describe it?' Michael asked.

'Oh, yes. Better than I could describe Melton Court, I should think.'

'Enough for me to be able to draw a plan of it?'

'Oh, yes. Yes. Would you, Michael?'

'I think a plan would help us all,' he smiled, then glanced across anxiously as the bedroom door opened and Mr Maitland looked in.

'Come on, you three,' he chided fondly. 'Breakfast is ready.' Then, as they prepared to join him, he added, 'Rain stopped play again, has it?'

'Oh, no, Daddy,' they chorused.

'Started, more like,' Michael almost whispered, with a private smile for Miranda and Roddy as they trooped out.

CHAPTER II

The Plan

Breakfast was an anxious time. Anxious for Miranda, who couldn't really be sure she would be able to remember afterwards all that she had seen of the House on waking. Anxious for Michael and Roddy, who couldn't wait to hear much more from her about it. Anxious for Mr Maitland, with a water-logged drive to his office at National Motors ahead of him. And anxious for Mrs Maitland, who was hoping the new char lady, Mrs Prume, would still turn up despite the rain. But together, in early morning comfort, they quietly ate their scrambled eggs and bacon, and, by finishing first, Roddy was able to pour himself a second glass of orange juice – the last in the jug.

Then, with kisses all round, Mr Maitland prepared for his day. Like his wife, a handsome and young forty, he stood immaculate and tall in his pin-striped suit, picking a hair from one lapel and darting her an intimate smile as he reached down his raincoat, buttoned and belted it in readiness, took his umbrella from the stand in the hall, made a last-minute check of his brief case, and was off.

The children joined their mother at the door as she waved him to the lift, then they were free once more to return to the playroom-bedroom where the spell of the House was all about them.

With a brother who spent so much of his time – and pocket money for materials – on drawing and designing everything from motor cars to launching pads (and those not just for Roddy), Miranda knew that in Michael she had the readiest of architects for her vision of the House. With a sense of urgency almost, he was soon turning over and tearing off pages of his own devisings from his latest and largest sketch pad, with a pot of sharpened pencils beside him on the floor, ready to take down whatever Miranda could tell of the House.

She was silent again, on her knees beside him, and looking no longer than Michael expected.

'Maybe you ought to go into a trance,' he suggested.

'What's a prance?' Roddy asked.

'Don't be stupid, Roddy. A trance, not a prance,' said Michael. It's sort of like – well – I don't know – but I've read about it. You look into a crystal ball or maybe a bowl of water or a ring or something, and then you're sort of half asleep and see things.'

'I don't think I could do that,' Miranda said. 'I don't think I'd like to do that.' Then added, 'But I could close my eyes.'

She did so, and immediately the House was standing nobly behind its red brick wall – she on the outside peering through the iron gates of the drive. It stood as it would have in its day on a spacious plot of ground surrounded by elms.

Michael looked up at her from his sketch pad and asked quietly, 'Are you seeing it, Miranda?'

'Yes. Oh, yes,' she assured him.

'I can draw a house,' said Roddy. 'With a chimney and smoke coming out of it.'

'Not now, Roddy,' Michael sighed. 'Where do we begin, Miranda? How big is it?'

'Start with the outer wall,' she replied, 'with twin iron gates which you can look through, then a drive leading up to the House. It's three floors, with a roof part. But the windows are funny. They aren't like our windows – just square – some are very long and thin. Can you draw those?'

'I think I know what you mean,' said Michael. 'Isn't there a house on Ashburn Road like that? Mummy said it was Victorian.'

'I wouldn't know,' said Miranda. 'But there are four sweet little windows in the roof, each with its own peaked roof. Can you put them there? And those tall – very tall – chimney stacks that you don't see any more. They're sort of flat. There are two on the right side of the House one on the left, so we will be able to tell where the fireplaces are.' She paused, then asked, 'What do you call the funny little fancy roof over the front door?'

'The portico, I think.'

'Well, there's one there. The windows on the ground floor and the first floor are taller than those at the top. You could actually walk out of the windows into the garden.'

Michael sketched furiously, moving from roof to ground floor level as Miranda's attention switched.

Roddy, leaning over his shoulder, asked, 'Can you put a dog in?'

'Not yet, Roddy,' Michael snapped. 'Is this what it looks like, Miranda?'

She opened her eyes. 'Oh, yes. I wish I could draw like you, Michael. We can colour it in later, but it's all grey and white, with a dark red door, and the roof is slate. The chimneys are red brick –'

'Oh, could I colour those?' Roddy interrupted again. 'I really am very good at chimneys.'

'We'll see,' said Miranda, thrilled with the way the House had turned out – or at least the way Michael had managed to draw it from her description, almost as if he had seen it too. It served all the more to firm her conviction of its presence.

'We really should make a plan now of the inside as well,' Michael was saying. 'And then we could see exactly where we are in it. Can you close your eyes again and look?' He turned a page of the sketch pad to a fresh sheet.

'Yes, of course,' said Miranda, and did so. 'Two of the roof windows are maids' rooms, and the other two are the attic. The attic is huge, and shaped like a U, with the biggest part in the front, and a long hallway leading to the stairs in between.'

Michael again tried to keep pace with Miranda's detailed recital, but almost involuntarily interrupted her now.

'Why are you starting from the roof down?' he asked.

'I don't know. Why not? What's the difference?'

'Well, usually architects start from –'

But now Miranda interrupted him. 'Well, this is a very *un*usual house – and I'm just describing it to you, not designing it.'

Michael was properly contrite. 'I'm sorry, Miranda. Go on.'

'Well, there are two more staff bedrooms at the back –'

'Still in the attic?'

'Yes. With just ordinary windows. Oh, and there's a bathroom too. It's between two of the servants' rooms.'

As Michael completed his drawing of the attic floor, he said, 'I suppose we ought to make one of these large bedrooms into a staff sitting-room. Three bedrooms are enough. Nobody has that many servants, except in castles.'

With a nod Miranda allowed him this artistic licence, then he flipped over the page of the sketch pad again and said, 'Next floor. Which would that be?'

'The second floor – which would have been ours. With bedrooms all along the front.'

'Ours?' Roddy queried.

'The children's floor in the House, I mean,' Miranda explained.

'Would I have my own bedroom then?' he asked excitedly.

'Of course you would. We all have our own bedrooms in the House,' said Miranda. 'And then there's Nanny's besides.'

'Nanny's?' Roddy frowned. 'Who is Nanny?'

'Well, I don't actually know,' Miranda conceded, 'but we would certainly have a Nanny. So then there's our and Nanny's bathroom at the back – and a big playroom which was called the day nursery where we'd have our meals, and Nanny's little kitchen where she'd cook them.'

'All in a row, like that?' Michael asked.

'Yes, I think so – with the stairs in the middle.'

Michael carefully laid out these enclosures, then, not quite looking up, said, 'Right,' to signal he was ready for the next floor.

'Then there would be the first floor. Lots more bedrooms and bathrooms – so nobody would ever have to wait,' Miranda smiled, her eyes closed. 'And Mummy could have a boudoir and Daddy a dressing-room.'

As Michael turned over to yet another fresh page he asked, 'How do you spell "boudoir" and what's it for?'

'I'm not quite sure about the spelling,' Miranda replied. 'I think it's b-o-o-d-o-u-r – and it's where Mummy could keep her clothes and her mirror and make-up and have her scents and bottles and things.'

'And where do I put that?' Michael asked, pencil at the ready.

Miranda squeezed closed her eyes even more tightly. 'Well, there'd be a big main bedroom on the front, and then a really big bathroom, and then off that Mummy's boudoir and then Daddy's dressing-room. That's where he'd keep all his suits and shoes and things.'

'He's only got four pairs of shoes,' said Roddy.

'Well, in our House he could have more,' Miranda retorted.

'What about on the other side of the passage here?' Michael asked.

'Guests' bedrooms and baths,' Miranda replied immediately. 'They're known as "the Yellow bedroom", "the Green bedroom" and "the Blue bedroom" from the way they are decorated – the curtains and the cushions, and the colours of the walls and the bedspreads. And when a guest came you'd say to the maid, "Daisy, show Mr and Mrs Trimble to the Blue room".'

'Who are Mr and Mrs Trimble?' asked Roddy. 'When are they coming? And will they bring presents?'

'Of course not, Roddy. They're just imaginary people,' Miranda explained.

'Like the House?'

Miranda reacted sharply. 'Certainly not, Roddy. The House is real.'

'I'll say it is,' Michael agreed. 'Take a look.'

He had finished blocking in the entire plan of the first floor now, which, although it might have been an architect's nightmare, from the children's point of view had both a logic and a longed-for clarity.

Miranda took a look indeed, her eyes shining with excitement as the House became more and more real and *there* with every pencil stroke.

'Michael,' she cried, 'where are we now?'

'Where?' he frowned.

'In our House, I mean.'

It took a few seconds for the thought to crystallize, but then he said, 'Oh, I see. Wait a minute.' He went to a cupboard and produced a sheet of tracing paper and a ruler, then drew well enough to scale, by eye, the plan of their flat in Melton Court: the drawing-room/dining-room at one end, the kitchen across the hall, the master bedroom and bathroom, and the two smaller bedrooms with their bath between at the far end. Then he placed the tracing paper over the first-floor plan of the House.

Miranda gave a delighted cry. 'We're in the main bedroom and Mummy's boudoir. Look, it's huge. We could play anything there. I could play dressing up.'

Michael scoffed, 'Ho! You could. But what would I want to be in a boudoir for?'

'Ah, but don't you see?' Miranda pointed out. 'You've got Daddy's dressing-room too. You could keep all your things there. We've got the best rooms in the House – right on the front.'

'Well, where am I then?' asked Roddy, feeling even more left out of it all now.

'Right between us here in the bathroom,' Miranda first pointed and then laughed with Michael. 'Only it's so huge you wouldn't know it was a bathroom. In fact the bath you could use as a submarine base or something.'

'Whooppee!' Roddy was well pleased at the suggestion.

'That's all your part there, where you can do anything you like – where we all can.'

After that Miranda's House ran riot on the ground floor, with everything that flat-confined young people could wish, from the wide entrance hall and the curving main staircase to the library, the study and the drawing-room. To this had to be fitted in the dining-room and breakfast room, joined by double doors, the butler's pantry, the big old kitchen, coupled to the larder, then the scullery, and next to that the laundry room.

Michael was called upon to use his rubber a great deal, and occasionally protested in vain that a certain room couldn't be there, or a wall would have to be at this point, or the kitchen was too far from the dining-room. But none of this worried Miranda, who refused to argue, merely standing her ground with 'I can't help it. That's the way it is,' until in some manner, using his ingenuity, Michael fixed it.

'There,' said Miranda, when it was finished, and looking upon it with satisfaction. 'That's just how it is.'

But another frown came to Michael's forehead as he regarded his own handiwork. 'What about the cellar?' he asked.

Miranda closed her eyes again, and while they were shut said, 'It's dark down here. I can't see anything.' Then she opened her eyes and said, 'You do the cellar, Michael.'

'Can I? Any way I want?'

'Yes,' Miranda assented generously. 'That is, the way it ought to be. I mean the way it really is.'

'I was wondering if there could be some kind of workshop for me down there.'

'Oh, *that's* all right,' she said, even more generously. 'Every big house has a kind of workshop in the cellar, hasn't it?'

Michael smiled, nodded, and then tried Miranda's method of concentration, closing his eyes tightly. It worked partly – not that he saw anything extraordinary or definitely placed, as Miranda seemed to do, but it helped him to

visualize and adapt what he knew of what went on below
the ground floor of Melton Court.

After a while he opened his eyes again and pencilled in a
boiler-room, trunkroom, a huge wine cellar, storage
space for coal and wood, and his workshop, complete
with bench, lathe and tool repositories.

As he knelt back then, and returned his pencil to its pot,
Miranda and Roddy came closer to gaze with him upon the
sheets of finished drawings with excited animation.

'Oh, Michael,' Miranda cried. 'Isn't it beautiful? You've
done it exactly as it is. That's the way it was, wasn't it?'

'Have I? Was it?' hesitated Michael. 'That's good.'

Roddy declared, 'I want to start living in it now. Can I?'

'Of course – we all can,' said Miranda, 'since it's here,'
stretching her arms wide and spinning with elation.

But Michael, who was still studying his drawings, said,
'I suppose in a way, though, we ought first to find out who
is living with us and whether we like them.'

And so it was borne in upon the children that they would
not be occupying the House by themselves, or indeed solely
with their own family. There were others all around them.
But this did not worry them – if anything it added a sense of
shared excitement. What would other people in Melton
Court think if they knew they were living in somebody
else's house as well as their own flats?

CHAPTER III

All Around

The irritable weather gods of late March hurled more buckets full of violent rain against the windows, but by now drew not so much as a glance from Michael, Miranda and Roddy, who were wholly and blissfully engaged in exploring on paper the House which encompassed the first three floors of Melton Court.

'What are you doing, children?' Mrs Maitland called suddenly from the dining-room area.

She was busy herself with Mrs Prume, the new char lady, who had come after all, and on time – explaining to her the layout of the flat, the nature of her duties, the hours she would be needed, and problems that might be encountered, while at the same time trying to make the whole thing sound like the happiest romp imaginable, and the kind of job where just a few merry wipes with a duster would see it done in a matter of minutes. From the children's quarters, however, there emanated a silence that might very well prove ominous and result in a sudden outburst that would ruin all her endeavours.

Michael's answering shout penetrated through the intervening rooms. 'Drawing.'

This came as some relief to Mrs Maitland, but not entirely, for Michael was usually drawing when he had nothing else to do, and so she called again, 'And Miranda and Roddy?'

'They're drawing too,' the answer came back. 'They're helping me.'

'You see, Mrs Prume? You'll find they are very quiet children – not always running about, getting in your way and upsetting things.'

In fact the three of them were particularly quiet just now. They were thinking hard about others in Melton Court whose flats would be occupying part of the House. But the harder they thought the more they came to realize and had to admit to each other that all together they really knew less than a lift-full.

Even their nearest neighbours were virtual strangers to them. Much more familiar were Mr Biggs, the handyman, and Mr Thompson, the Superintendent – but they were more or less fixtures of the basement and the ground-floor offices. On their own floor and the two floors above the children were hard pressed to put a name to anyone. Anyone at all.

Their inability, therefore, even to begin to draw up the list of occupants threatened temporarily to fragment their vision of the House. Except that it was no longer just a vision now: they had Michael's wonderfully real plans of it – just as Miranda had described.

If she had seen the House in such detail, Roddy reasoned to himself at first but then aloud, surely Miranda must have seen the original inhabitants too.

'Oh, yes, I did,' she was quick to confirm.

'Well, what were they like?' he asked.

'Curiously, very much like us really.'

Michael looked across apprehensively. Just as when Miranda had given him the run of the cellar to plan so now he was conscious again of a more than possible mix of the imaginary and the real in her picture of the House. She had convinced him that there was indeed a house intruding into Melton Court, but whether she could really be so sure of so many details of the interior he did not know.

Sometimes she seemed so definite in her pronouncements, at others less certain. But again she spoke with such conviction. 'Three children – two boys and one girl – all about the same age as us, or perhaps slightly older. A mother and a father and a nanny, and lots and lots of servants, living-in maids and other staff indoors and for the garden.'

'Just one family in all that huge place?' Roddy was incredulous.

'Oh, yes,' Miranda assured him. 'That was how they lived in those days.'

'Was the nanny a very old nanny?' he asked, curling his legs under him at the foot of his bed again.

But this time, before Miranda could answer, Michael sought to return them both to the present with a question of his own.

'Surely,' he began measuredly, 'isn't it the people that are in the House here and now that we should be considering?'

Miranda gave a look of indignation and almost protest as he gazed steadily, reasoningly, at her, then at Roddy and back again, in silence for a moment.

'I think what we should really do now,' he went on, practical as ever, 'is find out just who is living where in the House within the block – though, of course, they won't know that – and what they are like.'

With less reluctance than even she had felt at first Miranda slowly nodded in assent. Still it was easier for her to begin by addressing Roddy rather than answering Michael directly.

'Michael's right, of course,' she began. 'But' – and now her eyes sought help from both of them – 'how do we begin?'

'Well,' said Michael, taking the initiative more now, 'there is, of course, the key-board in the lobby. Mr Thompson has all the names of everyone in the flats on his pigeon-holes. But they are just names. Though I am sure we could get all those from him, first he'd wonder what on earth we wanted them for, and secondly they would, as I say, be no more than names. And names don't fill a house, do they? They'd hardly even add much to the plans we have now. We'd be none the wiser, really, would we?'

'Mr Thompson knows everybody, though, doesn't he?

It's part of his job to know everybody,' Roddy began to argue. 'I bet he's the only person in Melton Court who knows everybody by sight. And not just by sight either. He seems to know all about them – who they are, where they live, what family they have, and *how* they are too. Have you never heard him asking Mrs So-and-So how her back is? Or Mr What's-his-Name if his whizz-bang waste disposal is clear again . . . ?'

'But, Roddy,' Michael half-sighed as he stopped him, 'as you said yourself, that is Mr Thompson's job – to know everyone who lives here. He'd be a pretty poor Superintendent if he didn't. But knowing who's who isn't the same as really knowing what they are like, is it? And he mightn't tell us anyway,'

'No, Roddy. Michael's right.' Again Miranda agreed. 'We don't just want to know who is who and who fits where. We want to get to know them better than that.'

'And how do you think we can?' Roddy challenged.

'Well, I'm not suggesting we hang around the lobby and get to know anybody that way. No,' Michael said firmly. 'Nor am I suggesting we go round systematically ringing on every doorbell from the ground floor to the third.'

'Oh, no. I couldn't do that,' Miranda shook her head.

'And nor could I,' Michael added.

'I wouldn't mind,' said Roddy.

'You wouldn't?' Miranda smiled indulgently. 'What, going round introducing yourself, a complete stranger, to other complete strangers, with a ring at the doorbell?'

'Yes. Why not?' Roddy was almost swaggering now. 'It would be great fun.'

'And you would actually be prepared to do it? 'Michael asked again.

'I said I would, didn't I? You just say the word.' Roddy stood as if ready for the off.

'I think the word is "No",' Miranda reproved.

'Oh, trust you,' Roddy glared.

'I'm not sure it's right – or that we should presume – to go bothering people in their own flats,' she went on.

'Well, they're not going to be bothered. I'll be very polite, and if they don't want to talk to me then that's up to them. But they are not just in their own flats, don't forget. They are in our House too. You said so yourself,' Roddy countered.

'Yes, I know,' Miranda acknowledged, then was silent for a few moments. They all were, as they each weighed the pros and cons of such a procedure. Then it was Miranda again who took the initiative. 'All right then,' she allowed.

'You mean I can?' asked Roddy, as surprised as he was excited.

'But I think we need to organize things more first,' Michael joined in now, and Miranda and Roddy looked up at him together.

'We all agree,' he addressed them both, 'that with her unexpected vision of the House Miranda has shown herself to be some kind of diviner – someone sort of sensitive, who can see and smell out things that other people can't. Almost a witch, if you like.'

'I think I'd rather be a witch than a diviner,' Miranda smiled, altogether more delighted with the concept.

'All right, then I think we should nominate Miranda Chief Witch,' he suggested.

Miranda accepted the title with appropriate dignity, and waited for Michael to confer similar honours upon Roddy and himself.

Roddy was impatient for his already. 'Can I be a witch too, Michael?' he asked.

'Don't be silly,' Michael scoffed. 'Whoever heard of a boy witch? A wizard, yes. But –'

'Well, a wizard then. How wizard to be a wizard!' Roddy chuckled, whirling round as if casting a spell, then stopping to ask, '*Chief* Wizard, is that?'

'No,' Michael said firmly. 'I don't think wizard would be right for you at all.'

'Right for you though, I suppose,' Roddy jeered.

'Wrong again,' Michael swept the suggestion aside. 'Since I shall be coordinating all our plans and enquiries and things I thought I should perhaps have a title like Chief Investigator or something.'

'Oh, yes,' said Miranda. 'Chief Investigator would be a splendid title.'

'Well, what about me then?' Roddy looked from one to the other indignantly. 'Don't I get anything at all?'

Michael was smiling and shaking his head almost teasingly now. 'Miranda will be Chief Witch, I shall be Chief Investigator, and you, Roddy, I propose, in view of the mission you have volunteered for, should be Chief Intruder.'

'Wow! Yes, please!' beamed Roddy.

They all laughed together, and Miranda agreed it was another very appropriate name.

Then, with a sudden salute, Chief Intruder Roddy stood before the Chief Witch and the Chief Investigator, proud and ready.

But just when it seemed that things were really getting under way all three children were startled off course by a call from their mother for lunch.

CHAPTER IV

Roddy's First Visit

Mrs Prume had clearly impressed. Michael, Miranda and Roddy heard all about her from their mother over lunch, which, as always, was so much better than the school version.

It was a warm and loving time – home time at its best – and Mrs Maitland did all she could to brighten the prospect of the next few weeks with promises of trips to friends, to the cinema, museums and exhibitions, even some special treat with their father one weekend over the Easter break.

Still she assumed it was the rain that was subduing them so, and refused all offers of help with the washing up, suggesting instead, 'Why don't you all try that giant jigsaw Miranda had for Christmas? I do believe it's never even been opened.'

'Perhaps we will,' said Miranda, more out of appreciation than deliberate pretence.

'Would you excuse us, anyway, Mummy?' Michael asked.

'Of course,' Mrs Maitland smiled, and with that the children were off once more.

Alone again, Mrs Maitland wished so much that she could suggest they invite some of their schoolfriends over to play. But where could they? There was just not enough space in the flat. And a rained-in day like this only served to emphasize the confinement all the more.

In the playroom, as Roddy slipped on and zipped up his

windcheater in preparation for his first expedition as Chief
Intruder, so Michael settled down to redraw, properly this
time, the plans he had sketched all too freehand before
lunch. Miranda was at his side, sharpening his pencils for
him, and feeling rather like Dora helping her 'Doady' in
David Copperfield, which they had all watched when it was
the Sunday serial on television a few months back.

'I'm off then,' Roddy announced.

'All right,' said Miranda, still apprehensive for him.
'But take care – and don't be too long.'

'Look upon this as just a reconnaissance mission, if you
like,' Michael urged. 'Stroll around and take it all in – but
don't go making a nuisance of yourself.'

'I know. I know.' Roddy assured them both, well into
his part now. 'I'll report back in a hour or so. All right?'

'All right,' Michael and Miranda chorused – and as
Roddy stepped out he whispered with just a trace of
nervousness, 'If I leave the front door ajar will you close it
quietly for me?'

'Yes, of course,' Michael agreed, and rose to follow.

'Good luck,' Miranda called.

'Yes, good luck,' Michael echoed.

Then Roddy was gone – not just on his first mission but,
though he would never admit it to the others, to try to
make more sense of the whole business than he had been
able so far.

It was all rather discouraging to begin with. The first
four doorbells he rang – and rang – went unanswered:
each flat hypnotically quiet in its owner's absence.

Guessing then that probably many of the occupants of
Melton Court were still at work, or perhaps, in some cases,
had gone away for Easter already, he took the lift from the
first down to the ground floor, intending to go on down the
back stairs to old Mr Biggs in his basement quarters. He
at least was bound to be in.

However, as the lift doors opened and he stepped out
Roddy was suddenly splashed by the umbrella of a rain-
soaked young woman hurrying in. On an impulse he

decided to join her, and, stepping back into the lift, asked her, 'What floor, please?'

'Three,' she answered breathlessly, concentrating on gathering together the folds of her dripping umbrella.

Roddy pressed the proper button, the lift doors closed, and they ascended in silence. In fact the woman ignored him completely as he did his best to avoid further splashes from her umbrella. Then, at the third floor, as the doors opened again and she hurried out, she quite failed to notice him following her from the lift and along the corridor to her flat: 3B.

She thrust her key in the door, opened it, and made straight for the bathroom with the umbrella, calling on the way, 'I managed to get some pastilles, Tom. Antiseptic, antibiotic and anaesthetic, the label says – so even if they don't clear your throat maybe you'll forget you've even got one.'

It was only when the dressing-gowned man came into the hallway to greet her gratefully that he noticed Roddy still standing at the open door. A young but balding man, of medium height, he looked very pale to Roddy, but paled even more at the discovery of him. At first he just stared, and Roddy looked back with an apologetic smile.

'What do you want, young man?' he asked. Then called back, 'Who's your friend, Amy?'

She came out of the bathroom even faster than she had entered, and stopped as she removed her headscarf and shook her blonde hair back into shape. 'Why, you're the lift boy, aren't you?' she asked.

'Well, I was in the lift when you came in, but actually no,' said Roddy. 'I live here too. Roderick Maitland, Flat 1A,' he introduced himself, extending a hand.

The woman stepped forward and shook it. 'Oh, I am sorry. I'm Amy Anderson, and this is my husband, Tom.' Tom nodded and shook Roddy's hand too. 'You must have thought me so ungrateful,' she went on. 'I really was very wet, and all I could think about was getting up to our flat and drying off.'

'That's all right,' Roddy smiled. 'It is a rotten day, isn't it?'

'It is indeed,' said her husband, smiling too. 'But what are we all doing standing in the hall? Come on in for a warm drink or something.'

'Yes, do,' his wife urged too, holding the door open wider for Roddy, then taking her keys out of the lock and closing it again.

'What would you like? Hot chocolate? Warm milk? Tea? Lemon and honey?' her husband asked, ushering Roddy into the drawing-room and indicating a choice of two facing Chesterfields for him to sit on.

'A warm milk, please,' said Roddy, sinking into a corner of the nearer Chesterfield like one of the buttons.

'One warm milk,' he nodded. 'And tea for you, darling?' he called.

'Please.'

'All right then. One warm milk, one tea, and one lemon and honey I think. I've got this burning throat, you know.'

'Yes, I heard,' said Roddy – then quickly corrected: 'I mean, I heard your wife say she had some pastilles for you.'

'That's right. Whenever I get a cold it goes straight to my throat. Why, first thing this morning I could hardly speak,' he explained, with no such difficulty now. 'Anyway, let's have those drinks.' And shuffled off into the kitchen.

Left alone for a while, Roddy tried to take in as much of the flat as he could see from his soft, sunken seat. With one levering arm over the side of the Chesterfield he craned his neck to peer into the dining arbour and the bedroom, the door to which was open. The bed was made, but crumpled; he guessed Mr Anderson must have been resting on it.

He tried hard to visualize the plans Michael had drawn, and where the flat fitted in to the House. It was at the top, certainly, but just which roof space it occupied he could not be sure. He closed his eyes as Miranda had done, but before he could concentrate his thoughts he felt the breeze of Mrs Anderson passing by, and opened his eyes again to see her settling composedly opposite.

She smiled appealingly and leant forward to push a small silver dish on the coffee table towards him. 'Sweet?' she asked.

'Thank you,' he nodded, and chose a twist-wrapped one – always a safe bet in his experience: either a nut or a toffee centre.

'Have you been here long?' Mrs Anderson asked.

He was right: it was a hazelnut.

'In Melton Court, you mean?' he asked as he crinkled the wrapper and dropped it in an ashtray at the far end of the coffee table.

'Yes,' Mrs Anderson watched.

'Oh, no,' he shook his head. 'Not quite a year. We moved in last summer.'

Mrs Anderson nodded. 'We've only been here since January. We were negotiating for a house in Drewsbury Road, but the owner suddenly decided he didn't want to sell.'

'Oh, I know Drewsbury Road,' Roddy settled back a little too far, then slid himself more upright. 'We pass it every day on our way to school.'

'Where's that?' Mrs Anderson asked.

'Canfield.'

'Oh, that's a very good school, I hear.'

'It's all right.' Roddy swallowed the last of his sweet.

'Do you have any brothers or sisters?'

'Yes – one of each. Michael and Miranda. They're both just a bit older then me though.'

'But you all go to Canfield, do you?'

'Yes.'

'Well that must be fun.' Mrs Anderson offered another sweet, but he declined with a polite nod of thanks.

'Sometimes it is,' he conceded.

Just then Mr Anderson reappeared with the tray of drinks, which he set down before joining his wife opposite.

'There we are,' he gestured. 'That should warm us up.'

'We were just talking about Drewsbury Road,' his wife explained, and Mr Anderson's smile faded.

'Oh, yes. The house we nearly had,' he grimaced, taking the first pastille from its tube and sucking it quietly.

In fact, for a moment they were all quiet, and Chief Intruder Roddy glanced over them both at the window beyond, trying to figure out which side of the block it was on.

Mr Anderson turned as if to follow his gaze. 'Yes, this weather's a real washout, isn't it?'

'I'm sorry?' said Roddy, snatching himself back.

'This rain. It's worse than ever today, I'd say, wouldn't you?'

'Oh, yes,' Roddy agreed. 'I was just wondering, do you look out on to Hallam Road from here?'

'No.' Mr Anderson stood up again as if to make sure for himself. 'This side is the Square. But our box room, as we call it, looks out on Hallam Road – if only you could get to the window. I'm afraid it's still piled high with tea chests and cartons at the moment. We just don't seem to be able to settle here at all. It's very difficult to put down roots in a flat, isn't it?'

'Very,' Roddy agreed again readily.

'Quite. So we've really come to look upon this as all rather temporary until we can find another house in the area.'

'Yes, we're hoping to buy a house too next time,' Roddy volunteered.

'Oh, there's nothing to beat it,' said Mr Anderson, settling back now with his lemon and honey. 'In fact it's funny you should mention the windows. I've always had a theory about windows, haven't I, darling?'

Mrs Anderson nodded over her tea.

'There seems to me such a striking difference between the windows in a house and the windows in a block of flats,' Mr Anderson launched in. 'The windows in flats always seem to be no more than square holes cut into the outer wall to let the light in – such light as there is,' he smiled, with a backwards nod at the dull afternoon outside. 'Windows in houses, on the other hand, are quite another thing. They are more like eyes to let those inside look out to see who and what is passing by. You can imagine them as very watchful eyes—wary, not suspicious, but reserved. Wide open during the day, lidded at night when the shades are pulled down, but still regarding you silently and thoughtfully from underneath those lids.'

Roddy was by now engrossed, and, finishing the last of his milk, settled back to listen intently, almost unable to believe his luck at the way the talk was going.

'Very often,' Mr Anderson continued, 'I don't know if you've noticed, but a house even seems to have a face of its own, made by the windows and the front door. Then those eyes really do seem to be watching you, and even following you as you pass by. Sometimes it's a jolly face, sometimes a stern one, and in some cases just a blank one, but still it gives a house a life which you would never find in any block like this.'

Both Roddy and Mrs Anderson were silent still, and so Mr Anderson went on.

'Then what about having a roof over your head? You must have heard people using that expression.' Roddy nodded. 'Well, there's no roof overhead here, is there? Only a ceiling – and on top of that another ceiling, then another and another, until eventually you come to the great flat space at the top of the building. Still not a proper roof though. A sloping roof is the thing – with shingles or tiles on which you could actually hear the rain drumming or the hail rattling.

'Only people in real houses have a roof over their head – and the eyes of their windows go on watching for them long after they have closed the front door.' Mr Anderson paused abruptly. 'Oh, give me a house any day and the sooner the better, eh, darling?'

His wife smiled wistfully, but Roddy was so stirred by all that he had said that almost involuntarily he offered some immediate consolation: 'You're in the attic of our

House – so you not only have a roof over your head but special windows too.'

Mr and Mrs Anderson exchanged looks of confusion.

'I'm sorry?' Mr Anderson leant forward.

'In the house that was here – the House that Miranda saw this morning. This would be where part of the attic was. The servants' quarters.' Mr Anderson sat back uneasily, then, looking carefully at Roddy, began: 'I'm not sure I understand . . .'

'I wasn't either, at first,' Roddy confided. 'But Miranda was quite sure about it – and now so are Michael and I too.'

'Well . . .' Mr Anderson looked again at his wife then back to Roddy. 'It would be very interesting to meet your brother and sister, sometime, wouldn't it, Amy?'

'Yes,' Mrs Anderson agreed hesitantly.

'And I'm sure they would be interested to meet you,' Roddy smiled then rose. 'They'll be delighted you're in our House, I know. I'd better be getting back to them, I suppose.'

His hosts rose too, both still half-wondering just how and why they had come to be entertaining him at all.

'Thank you for the milk and everything,' Roddy smiled. 'And I hope your throat is better soon.'

'Thank you,' Mr Anderson nodded, as his wife showed Roddy to the door.

'Goodbye,' he beamed, and with a brief wave walked off down the corridor. The door closed behind him, and, thrilled by the way his first intrusion had gone, he decided not to wait for the lift. Instead he ran down the two flights of back stairs to Flat 1A, to report.

CHAPTER V

From Attic to Cellar

One muted flap of the letterbox at Flat 1A brought Michael padding to the door to let Roddy in. With a quick shared smile they marched back into the boys' room, where Miranda was crouched over the redrawn plans of the House spread out on the floor.

Roddy unzipped his windcheater and immediately slumped in exaggerated exhaustion on the foot of his bed once more. Both Miranda and Michael stood watching and waiting anxiously for him to begin. But for a few brief moments he could not resist the savour of their attention and anticipation, and just shook his head in bemused silence.

'Well?' said Miranda at last.

'How did it go?' asked Michael.

'If everyone's as nice as Mr and Mrs Anderson this is going to be a very happy place,' he beamed.

'Who are Mr and Mrs Anderson?' Michael frowned impatiently, twirling the pencil tucked behind his ear.

'They live in 3B, and –'

'What on earth were you doing up there? I thought you were going to check our floor first,' Miranda broke in.

'I did,' Roddy protested, 'but there didn't seem to be anyone in. Not one answer anywhere – I promise.'

He then reported in full the unexpected course of events that had taken him up to the third floor with Tom and Amy Anderson. Michael and Miranda listened without interruption to each and every twist in the tale – told with none of Roddy's usual embellishments – then, as he finished and fell back, Miranda hugged him and whispered, 'Oh, well done, Roddy. It's as if the House is really beginning to open up to us already, thanks to you.'

Michael smiled and added, 'Congratulations, Chief Intruder. That was a first-class report.'

Roddy accepted the commendation with a nod and a blush, while Miranda stepped carefully across to the third-floor layout.

Without looking up, she said, 'Let's fill in the Andersons right away, shall we? They would be *here*,' pointing to the second of the front attic rooms.

Michael picked his way over to her, knelt alongside, and pencilled in the surname in capital letters.

'While you were out,' Miranda said turning to Roddy, 'Michael was telling me he thinks he remembers seeing some wall-charts and plans of Melton Court in Mr Biggs' basement office the first time we went down there. Did you notice any?'

'No, I don't think so,' Roddy shook his head.

'Neither do I,' said Miranda. 'But we were just saying, before you came back, perhaps we should all pay Mr Biggs a visit.'

'You mean you don't want me to go by myself?' asked Roddy, with an injured look. 'I told you I was on my way to see him when I bumped into Mrs Anderson.'

'I know, Roddy,' said Michael, 'and it's not because we don't trust you. It's just that I'd really like to look at those plans myself. So we thought perhaps you could ask Mummy if you could go down to play "Blast off", and –'

' "Blast Off"?' Roddy almost shrieked with delight at the suggestion.

'Yes,' Michael smiled, ' "Blast Off". And then we'd go with you, and all see Mr Biggs, if he's not too busy.'

'Busy Biggs. Busy Biggs,' Roddy chanted excitedly.

'Roddy,' Miranda stopped him with one look. 'Don't be silly. Now are you going to ask Mummy if we can go, or aren't you?'

'All right,' he sighed. 'But are we really going to play "Blast Off"?'

'Really,' Michael answered for her. 'But there'll be no time for anything unless you hurry.'

With that Roddy was out of the room like one of his imaginary rockets, and Michael and Miranda started to laugh. Michael then began to roll his plans up, and reached to the top of his wardrobe to slide them back, out of sight.

'He really deserves a game after his discoveries this afternoon,' Miranda said as she picked up Michael's ruler and pencils and put them back on his desk.

'Don't worry,' Michael nodded, 'I meant it. If Mummy lets us go, I'll even do the countdown for him.'

Miranda smiled, and smoothed down the bedcovers.

Mrs Maitland followed Roddy, who raced ahead to announce excitedly, 'Mummy says we can!'

'Only if you promise not to make a nuisance of yourselves down there,' Mrs Maitland qualified. 'And remember, don't touch anything.'

'Of course we won't,' Roddy hastened to assure her. 'We'll see Mr Biggs, anyway,' he added, then winked at Miranda and Michael as he took his space helmet from the shelf.

'Thank you, Mummy,' said Miranda, as they all went into the hall.

'Off you go then,' Mrs Maitland smiled. 'And be sure you bring me back some Moon rock.'

They laughed as they kissed her, then wandered waving to the lift.

Dorothy Maitland's smile slipped away as she closed the door and stood for a moment looking into the playroom: so much a bedroom still, for all the toyshelves, bookcases and cupboards; so compact, so confined, so makeshift. She glanced across at the rain-splashed windows, and the tears of rain reflected her own inner sadness. Sadness and longing too. As everyone longed for the downpour to relent so she longed more than ever for a real home for her family, with room for her children to live and grow. Not venture off to an apartment block basement to play. Not billeted in boxes that seemed to shrink every day they grew. A house, with room for expanding minds as well as bodies. And space. Space to move freely, to develop and to flourish.

She turned from the room at last, the longing almost too much to bear, but about one thing at least this Easter she was now determined: whenever or wherever her husband's design work at National Motors uprooted them next, they must somehow try to afford a house. Far greater than any debts they would incur was the debt they already owed – that was overdue even – to Michael, Miranda and Roddy. She could wait no longer. She resolved to broach the subject with her husband that same evening. For all the promise and the prospects of his position at the car plant now, this was something he could neither dispute nor disregard any more.

The children, meanwhile, were weaving their way carefully but enchantedly through the cavernous warrens of boilers, pumps, pipes, electrical circuits, and workshops that were Mr Biggs' exclusive domain, underground at Melton Court. Here too was the base and all the intricate mechanism of the main lift – better than the end of a rainbow for Roddy.

He looked up the shaft as, out of sight, its cabin locked and descended slowly at the behest of some tenant's finger on the button. His eyes sparkled through the visor of his helmet, and Michael and Miranda stood by as he tilted his head with its unsteady weight to inspect the ramp in readiness.

His voice came through muffled, and the visor clouded as he addressed his brother and sister in anticipation. 'Ready for Blast Off?' he asked, standing upright with legs firmly astride now.

'Thirty seconds and counting,' Michael smiled down at his watch, his wrist held high across his chest, and nodded each second away in silence until the final moments. 'Ten, nine, eight . . .' his voice rose with glorious sonority in the basement corridor.

Miranda stood poised and silent beside him, looking from her own watch to Roddy and back again – listening all the while for the next movement of the lift above.

Michael's counting slowed with the sound of the lift doors opening just above them now. As the doors locked once again, he intoned the final seconds of the countdown: 'Three, two, one . . .' Then, after a timeless pause as anxious as any at Cape Kennedy, with the rumble and the draught from overhead, he pronounced, 'Lift off. We have lift off.'

Out of a pause of concentration, Roddy responded, 'Roger, Houston. All systems go.'

'Roger, Roddy. You're looking good,' Michael continued the unscripted recital, until the lift itself suddenly jogged to a halt several floors above.

The spell, if not broken, was at least suspended, and Roddy ceremoniously lifted his helmet over his head and stepped forward to rejoin Mission Control.

'That was terrific,' he beamed. 'Can we have just one more go before –'

But Michael was shaking his head already. 'No, come on,' he urged. 'We really must find Mr Biggs now.'

Roddy had no choice: either he stayed behind on a deserted launch pad or he followed Michael and Miranda as they turned to go. So he followed, imagining the menacing 'DANGER', 'HIGH VOLTAGE' and 'KEEP OUT' portals along the subterranean passage as airlocked hatches in an orbiting space station.

Mr Biggs was indeed busy in his office, sorting through drawers and files of old papers, most of which seemed to be going into the wire basket on the floor, destined ultimately for the boilers no doubt. But as always he greeted the children heartily, with his weather-beaten smile and the usual instant offer of biscuits and lemon barley water.

Now a spry stocky sixty or so, Mr Biggs, like Mr Thompson, the Superintendent of Melton Court, was a Royal Navy veteran. He had spent more than half his years below decks, as wiper, oiler, donkeyman, boilerman and, finally, skilled engineroom rating. At Melton Court, still below decks, he was an engineer once more, in well-worn civilian clothes now, charged with tending there the three great boilers that provided all the main heating for the block, as well as the mains connections for water and electricity, including emergency generators and the machinery that operated the automatic lift.

In addition he was general handyman for minor repairs, plumber, carpenter and electrician.

His basement domain, and in particular his workshop, was a kind of forbidden paradise to the children of tenants unless by a special invitation or authorization of Mr Biggs himself or his wife. The area was full of danger spots, as the signs marked in red on the many doors indicated.

Mr Biggs' own quarters were also located in this nether region, down one of the long iron and concrete passages that rabbit-warrened the vast space beneath the edifice. He and his wife, Agnes, having no children of their own, were the warmest of hosts – quite literally, in such surroundings – and seemed almost grateful for the visits of their young friends from the flats above.

'Come to give me a hand sorting out, have you?' he joked, as he cleared a space for the tray of drinks and biscuits, and regarded the piles of papers, old receipts, brochures, outdated equipment, plumbing and wiring plans. 'How rubbish does accumulate. I'll be glad to get rid of it. Papers are always an unnecessary fire hazard is what I say.'

The children agreed as they looked for room to perch on a bench near the table – and Michael signalled with a nod of satisfaction the plans of Melton Court pinned on the walls and cupboards around them.

'Some of this stuff has been here as long as I have – right from the time when Melton Court was going up, in fact,' Mr Biggs went on.

There were two piles of papers on his workbench: a large and a small. A square wire basket stood on the floor next to the seat presided over by the three children. When Mr Biggs said that something was to be chucked they chucked it, taking it in turn.

All this was to the accompaniment of those exciting underground noises: the clanking thump of the lift motors as they stopped and started, the roar of the boilers, the hissing of steam, and the clicking of automatic switches.

Gathering a sheaf of receipts for various supplies, all long out of date, Mr Biggs handed them over, saying, 'Chuck 'em.' He paused for a moment and smiled. 'Captain of a destroyer I was on in 1943 once said, "It won't be the enemy that sinks this ship but the accumulation of paper-work".'

The children chuckled, then looked up for the next sorted item.

'Here's a diagram of the original lift installation, though it's undergone some modifications since. Still, I think I might hold on to that. You never know.' And added it to the smaller pile on the workbench.

'Now here are some more of these,' he went on, holding up a set of blueprints – the front elevation of an old-style Victorian three-storey house, all bedecked with rabbits' ear chimneys and roof dormers. There were successive sheets of architects' plans of the interior floors, the cellar, the attic, as well as another of the drive and the layout of the garden behind, coupled with potting-shed, greenhouse and gardener's hut.

Michael, Miranda and Roddy, leaning forward together over their wire basket of discards, came to attention, and strained neck, head and body to see better.

'What are they?' Michael asked as controlledly as he could.

Mr Biggs shuffled the papers thoughtfully, and held the first sheet up for them all to see. On it was imprinted in rather old-fashioned lettering the legend 'Bennett, Magruder & Griswold, Architects, 15 Crossburn Lane, London E.C.2.' and then a date: 'July 26, 1873'.

'That,' said Mr Biggs, 'is the house that stood here before.'

The children could hardly believe what they were seeing. For Miranda particularly it was an almost frightening confirmation. But for them all shock, incredulity and curiosity were emotions they strove hard to suppress at this amazing discovery. Whether sheer coincidence or good fortune, it astonished them, though Miranda felt deep inside that it was somehow *meant* to be – a continuation even of her vision that morning.

'Just over a hundred years ago. What about that then?' Mr Biggs puffed.

'Gosh,' said Michael, still not daring to release the pent-up excitement all three of them were feeling.

'The architects who put up Melton Court must have left all these here. This is the third set I've come across,' said Mr Biggs. 'Something to do with where the drains were. But they were all changed last year when the Council put in new pipes for this area. Chuck it.'

Michael took the papers from him, but instead of doing as he was instructed this time stared closely at them, with Miranda and Roddy craning beside him.

'What was it called? Did it have a name?' Miranda asked seemingly calmly.

'I think so. Let's have a look,' Mr Biggs nodded for the return of the papers.

There was indeed a name on the first of the prints, the one with the façade, but time and dirt had almost eliminated it.

'Something "Hall", is it?' queried Mr Biggs, straining his eyes in an attempt at deciphering. 'No, look, there's one "Hall" all right, but then there's another. Oh, I know what it must be. Hallam Hall. Look. That's it, isn't it?'

As he passed back the papers this time both Michael and Miranda reached for them.

'Hallam Hall! Yes!' said Michael. 'On Hallam Road, where we are now. Of course!'

'That's it,' said Mr Biggs, offering the biscuit tin to the children and taking one himself in this interruption in the sorting.

They each accepted with a quiet 'Thank you' under their breath as they went scrutinizing.

'But what happened to it?' Miranda asked, still clutching the plans.

Mr Biggs replied matter of factly, 'Oh, they tore it down and carted it away, I suppose when the grounds and property were sold to Lord Truciman and became part of the Truciman Estates – and eventually Melton Court.'

'May we keep these?' Michael asked suddenly, nodding at the plans in Miranda's hands.

'Well, I don't see why not,' said Mr Biggs. 'I've kept two sets already. They're no good here any more.

But by now he was curious himself about the children's own curiosity.

'What's it for then?' he asked. 'Some school project for the holidays?'

'Oh, no,' Michael shook his head, watching Miranda still leafing through the sheets, and checking glances with her and with Roddy, who seemed unusually silent for once.

'You see, Mr Biggs,' Miranda leant forward slowly. 'I know it sounds silly, but although we've never seen any of these plans before – never even knew about Hallam Hall – I actually saw it –'

'Saw it?' Mr Biggs almost choked on his biscuit. 'But how could you?'

'In a sort of vision, when I woke up this morning. It was as clear as clear – and *just* like this. As if it's still here, and we are all occupying a part of it.'

'Now hang on.' Mr Biggs rose as if to call them to order. 'This is all a bit fanciful, isn't it? Maybe you had a dream or something, and imagined –'

'I didn't imagine. Really I didn't. And I didn't dream it either. The whole thing just came to me. I told Michael and Roddy all about it. I described it in detail, and Michael even did some drawings from my descriptions. And seeing these plans now doesn't seem funny to me at all. It sort of fits in with everything else. Though the actual building may have gone and Melton Court is here now, the original house hasn't gone away. It's all about us. We live on part of the first floor of it, in fact – and everyone on the first three floors of Melton Court is occupying some part of it.'

'Mr and Mrs Anderson are in the attic,' Roddy interjected.

Miranda nodded, 'And your basement is the cellar. The whole of the cellar is yours really.'

Mr Biggs took his pipe from his jacket pocket and fumbled as he filled it from his old tobacco tin. 'Well, I've heard some rum stories in my time,' he began, 'but yours surely beats the lot.' Feeling slightly uneasy, he said, 'Now hadn't you better be getting back home – if you are quite certain you still know where that is?'

'Gosh! A quarter past five!' Michael checked his countdown watch. 'But thank you, Mr Biggs, for these drawings.'

'Not a bit.' Mr Biggs pretended to resume his sorting. 'And don't forget your space helmet, Roddy.'

'And thank you for listening and not laughing about the House,' said Miranda as she followed Michael and Roddy out.

'Oh, I'm not laughing. Believe me, I'm not,' Mr Biggs assured her. In fact he was rather too baffled at the moment to know just what he was doing.

CHAPTER VI

One Room

It was almost suppertime when Michael, Miranda and Roddy arrived back at Flat 1A, and Mrs Maitland brightened at the sound of their spirited calls echoing from room to room once more. Roddy's space helmet, deposited on the hall floor like a beacon off its pole, amused her with its special potency for him. She heard all about the 'Blast Off' game, and was reassured to learn that far from bothering Mr Biggs the children had actually been helping him in his sort-out.

What she was not prepared for, however, was the incredible story of the House. She had to be told – this was not something they wished to keep from her any longer – and it came out quite casually at first, when Michael was looking for an elastic band to put round the Hallam Hall plans Mr Biggs had given him. Miranda did most of the explaining, Michael rolled out the plans for her to see, and Roddy marvelled all over again at the mystery and the history they were uncovering, and kept looking at Miranda, who had brought it all about.

Mrs Maitland listened attentively and without comment until she had virtually the full story, then, after she had served their meatballs and spaghetti, sat down with them at the kitchen table, and reacted for the first time.

She was not sceptical, as Miranda was afraid she might be, and was genuinely intrigued by the Hallam Hall discovery. She believed Miranda, which was the main thing, though she seemed cautious in her attitude to the explorations already begun with Melton Court.

'I'm not sure that you should really involve strangers in your investigations,' she frowned. 'After all, you don't know how they will take to being told they are really occupying two homes – or at least a part of one old one as well as their flat here. They might just laugh in your face, or they might be extremely upset by the very idea of it. You must understand that most people here positively prefer living in a flat to a house. They won't thank you for suggesting they are a part of anything else. No, I think this is something you should keep to yourselves as much as possible. Keep it as a game. I know it is really very exciting to you – I can see that – but to others it could seem a most unwelcome intrusion. It could make them very angry – and I don't want you getting into any kind of bother. Big as Melton Court is, it's too small a community for that.'

'But, Mummy,' Miranda came in quickly, 'it isn't a game. It's real – and a community is just how we see it. A community *together* in one glorious big house. It's a *sharing* thing. We're not trying to take anything from anyone. We'd just like them to know they are sharing with us something extra – something that *is* here, after all, and is theirs as much as ours.'

But Mrs Maitland was already shaking her head. 'I still think it would be unwise to involve others in something they know nothing about – and in most cases would probably not believe or like to hear.'

'You believe us, though,' Michael checked.

Mrs Maitland paused, and nodded reassuringly, 'Yes, I do. But then, like you, I'd love a house. I hope next time we move it will be to a house and not another flat again.'

'Really?' cried Miranda.

'Oh, yes,' Mrs Maitland smiled. 'But that is some way off yet, and, of course, depends very much on Daddy and his career.'

Just then the sound of a key in the front door and a call from the hall signalled the return of Mr Maitland himself. They all called back to him, and Mrs Maitland rose to welcome him, with a warning look of silence about all they had been discussing.

The evening's greetings over, Mr and Mrs Maitland settled to an early cocktail, and the children went back to their supper in the kitchen.

After he had gone through his established routine of office grouses and personal pats on the back, John Maitland at last got around to asking his wife what kind of day hers had been, as he mixed them both another drink.

'Quite a strange one really,' she began.

'Why? Mrs Prume?' he asked, looking over his glass as he held it to his lips.

'Oh, no. Mrs Prume is fine – I think so, anyway. No, it's the children.'

'Have they been difficult?' John Maitland could mix sternness with sympathy as well as any cocktail.

'No. Heavens, no. Just very strange. Rather worrying really.' Then Dorothy Maitland gave her own version of the day's developments and the children's extraordinary obsession.

'Well, what's wrong with that?' John Maitland sat back in relief. 'Shows a perfectly healthy imagination – and I should think you'd be pleased they've made up something of their own to occupy themselves. What with this weather they're having a rotten start to their holidays, aren't they?'

'Well, they've certainly not been bored,' she sighed. 'It's just that it's all so real and vivid to them. I mean, Miranda says she knows all about it, or she thinks she does, and Michael has drawn up plans of the whole thing. They keep referring to them and what rooms they are living in. Then, of course, coming upon those copies of the original Hallam Hall plans was an extraordinary coincidence – if coincidence it was – and that has just sealed it for them. They believe it is still here – or, as far as I can gather, the space where it was still here. Only children would think of something like that. According to them we are all living in a part of that space, where the old house was, or where they think it was.'

John Maitland's masculine mind was now well switched on, and he enquired equably, 'Well, what's wrong with that? Two for the price of one, I gather. Why should that worry you?'

'Well, it isn't just us living in it – it's other tenants in the block.'

'Why? Where do they come in?' Mr Maitland asked.

'Because the children seem so set on trying to identify them all and where exactly they fit in to this other house.'

There was a moment of silence while her husband digested this information, but then he shrugged and, sinking back in his easy chair, said, 'I honestly don't see what you're fussing about. They're grown people with their own business to mind, and if they can't look after themselves I can't help them. You can stop children from making a racket, or playing football in the corridor, but you can't stop them thinking.'

Everything that was said triggered some kind of picture or phrase in Dorothy Maitland's mind, and the one that came to her now was 'Or stop them from being lonely in a block.'

But John Maitland could not involve himself with any of it as she did herself, and rose up slowly with a stretch, saying, 'And you can't stop us eating. Come on. What's cooking?'

Resignedly for now, she rose too. 'A rainy day ragout. All right?'

'All right,' he gleamed, and put his arm around her as they made for the kitchen.

Their own supper over now, Michael, Miranda and Roddy had returned to the playroom at the double. There, once again, Michael unfurled the plans of Hallam Hall, setting them side by side in a row, then, beneath them, and so nearer to him as he knelt with Miranda, his own drawings from earlier in the day.

Though Michael blushed at the amateur construction of his plans beside the architects' originals, Miranda pointed excitedly to the many corresponding features. They were alike in so many details that the Hallam Hall plans seemed to complement rather than correct Michael's own of the House.

Roddy was particularly curious about the attic. As the only one of the three who had been there so far, on his visit to the Andersons, he took a proud, almost proprietorial interest in it now, and looked from Michael's own, with the Andersons already pencilled in, to the Hallam Hall originals where they would have been.

Michael carefully lifted his adjustable bedside lamp on to the floor to illuminate each section under scrutiny, and, deep in thought, suggested that from now on perhaps it would be best if they used the professional plans as the true guide and his own for filling in the Melton Court occupants, as they were identified by Roddy on his excursions as Chief Intruder.

Miranda and Roddy both agreed, and together pointed out that Mr Biggs should certainly be entered in the cellar section at once.

As Michael pencilled in the name, Miranda's eyes strayed back to the attic section, and looking from one plan to the other she warned with a pointed finger, 'You know, this room here must be empty still. It was always kept locked.'

Michael and Roddy looked up suddenly at her rather than at where she was pointing, and even Miranda chilled at the realization of what she had just said. What made her say that? Why a locked room, she asked herself as Michael and Roddy asked her too. She closed her eyes in a bewilderment that was soon concentration once more.

'It was the baby,' she almost whispered. 'Always kept shut off in a room by itself.'

Her brothers watched anxiously as she screwed her eyes shut even more tightly.

'Was it a boy or a girl, Miranda?' Michael asked softly.

She did not answer at once, but fell silent for a considerable time, frowning as though trying to remember something.

Michael saw that a shadow cast by some mysterious illumination from within seemed to have crept behind her eyes as they flickered open and closed again. He was getting used to this by now, although he did not know the cause of it – except that when it happened it seemed to remove her a little distance from them all.

'Neither,' she answered at last.

'Neither?' Michael gasped. 'What do you mean, neither?'

'Well, both,' Miranda tried to explain, opening her eyes once more. 'It was just a baby.'

'Oh, come on, Miranda,' said Michael, 'It can't be both. It's got to be one or the other.'

'They only had to look to tell,' Roddy dropped in. 'We had diagrams at school, and –'

'They *did* look,' Miranda insisted.

'And what happened?' Michael asked.

'They couldn't tell.' The shadow went away from behind her eyes. She had seen what she thought she had seen, and was confident and firm now. 'That's how it was,' she shrugged.

But Michael was anxious to question her more. 'You mean,' he said, 'it was something – some kind of –' he groped for the word he had once heard in connection with a statue, but, failing to find it, said, '– a changeling? Like in the stories I used to . . .'

Miranda nodded. 'Perhaps. I think it must have been a changeling. They kept it in a separate room by itself anyway, so it didn't sleep where we would have slept.'

Roddy turned away, as reproachfully as fear would allow, and announced, 'I don't think I want to play this game any more.'

'But this is *not* a game,' Miranda countered sternly. 'It's all part of the House.'

'Rubbish!' scoffed Roddy, sitting back on his bed and kicking off his shoes.

Seeing Miranda and Michael crouched over the plans even more intently now, he felt suddenly excluded by his reaction. He longed to join them again, to be one with them, and in an anxious expression of apparent concession asked, 'Where is this room supposed to be, anyway?'

'I've told you already,' said Miranda, tapping both sets of plans. 'In the attic here.'

'So it's not actually near us,' Roddy checked.

'No, of course not,' Miranda assured him. 'It's the last door on the left, right up where the third-floor flats are now. Don't worry.'

'I'm not worried,' Roddy protested.

'Well, good,' Michael said, lightly pencilling round the room on his own set of plans. 'Because I think tomorrow our Chief Intruder ought to go up and call there, don't you, Miranda?'

CHAPTER VII

The Tringhams

The buzzer, signalling that someone outside was demanding admission to 3E, whirred spitefully. Any doorbell activated after half past nine at night manages to inject an aspect of malice into whatever its mechanism.

Inside, in the small drawing-room of the Tringham flat, Martin Tringham, a gaunt, nervously pallid man in his mid-thirties, raised his head from a company report he had been studying, and his wife, Ellen, a year or two younger but no less sallow, looked up from a copy of the *Library Journal*. The unusual and unexpected sound had so startled them that they were caught for a moment in one another's eyes in full gaze, something which for several years now they had been at pains to avoid.

Martin Tringham gazed irritably at his wrist-watch, and murmured, 'Who the devil can that be at this hour?'

His wife put her magazine aside and rose, saying, 'I simply can't imagine.'

Martin Tringham said, 'We don't know any poppers-in, do we?'

Ellen Tringham shook her head. 'They would have been announced from downstairs. Perhaps one of the men from the building wants to look at something. The heating hasn't been as it should be. I'd better see.'

She went to the door, unbolted and opened it, to look down upon the unexpected and astonishing apparition of a small boy, clad in blue pyjamas, blue flannel dressing-gown, and blue felt slippers with a white rabbit imprinted on the top of each. An attempt he had made to lay flat his unruly, flaming hair had not been entirely successful, so that he gave the effect of being tousled and sleepy. The slightly too prominent ears and the young mouth with parted lips distracted Mrs Tringham from noticing that the only thing which did not match up with the child recently awakened was the ingenuous alertness of a pair of bright blue eyes.

'Hello,' she exclaimed. 'What do you want?'

'I've had a bad dream,' said Roddy. It was the first thing that came into his head, but its effect upon Ellen Tringham was stupendous, as though he had penetrated to and knew her innermost secret.

Instead of bewildering her or putting her out, the apparition of a small boy whom she could not remember ever having seen before, upon her doostep, announcing a nightmare, released such a rush of maternal emotion that she felt herself ridiculously on the verge of falling to her knees and gathering the child to herself.

Her husband, from the drawing-room, broke the spell.

'Who is it?'

'Somebody's child.'

'Well, tell it to go away.'

'Please can I come in?' asked Roddy. 'It was an awful dream.'

The situation had no precedent. There were any number of questions to be asked or things to be considered. Where were the child's parents? Why wasn't somebody looking after him? Where had he strayed from? Why had he come knocking at their door? But the presence of Roddy precluded any of these: he was there, physically, in the grip of a problem, and had asked if he could come in. And so she simply said, 'I suppose so,' and held out her hand. Roddy put his into hers confidingly, and walked at her side, the white rabbits preceding one another firmly.

Mr Tringham looked up as they paused in the doorway for a moment, and said, 'What the . . .?'

'He's had a bad dream,' his wife explained. 'He asked to come in.'

After a fierce staring pause, Martin Tringham swallowed and looked from Roddy to his wife and back, stood up, cadaverously tall, sat down again uncertainly, then clearly no less bemused himself now, said, 'Well, old man, I suppose you'd better tell us about it. A stout fellow like you oughtn't to be frightened by a little thing like a dream.'

Having felt the bait taken, Roddy now set the hook firmly. 'I wasn't frightened by the dream. I frightened it.'

This new twist threw Mr Tringham completely. '*You* frightened it? How does one frighten a dream?'

Roddy had seated himself on a red damask chair – a combination which caused Mrs Tringham suddenly to think of Renoir, and then, inevitably, what she did not wish to think about.

'I dreamed back,' Roddy explained.

'Oh,' said Mr Tringham, lured by now into a more than equable temper. 'How does one do that?'

'Well,' Roddy answered, and spoke in the manner of one who is looking back on a past experience and choosing the proper words to describe it, 'I made myself bigger – bigger than an elephant. Twice as big. And I had claws and teeth like a tiger. And I could fly. And I gave a terrific growl and the thing went away.'

This time it was Ellen Tringham who enquired, 'What thing?'

'The thing that was after me.'

'Oh,' said Martin Tringham. 'What was it like?'

'It was awful,' said Roddy. 'But I was awfuller, and it went away.'

'But then if you weren't frightened,' Ellen Tringham began. 'I mean, if you frightened the thing away . . .'

'Well, *I* was still there,' said Roddy, with unassailable logic. 'I didn't want to be like that and frighten everyone else, and I wasn't sure. I thought if I talked to someone else and they weren't frightened, then I'd know. You weren't frightened, were you?'

'No,' replied Mrs Tringham. 'We weren't frightened.'

But it was not strictly true. They were – or rather suddenly uneasy.

'Where are your mother and father?' she asked.

Roddy threw them again slightly by replying matter of factly. 'They decided to go to the cinema.'

'But aren't you afraid to be alone? I mean, aren't they afraid to leave you alone?'

'Oh, no. We're used to it,' said Roddy. 'I have a brother and a sister, and my brother is very strong and not afraid of anything. He's twelve.'

'Well,' said Mr Tringham, 'what are they doing? Do they let you just go wandering about –'

'They were asleep,' said Roddy, and felt the virtue that comes with being able to tell a lie that is not a lie because of the wonderful things that words can come to mean without really meaning what they say. It was true. 'They were' – past tense of 'are' – that is to say, had been asleep – as indeed they all had been until some giant double-coupled lorry thundering by in the street below had awakened them to a conference.

The chance nocturnal board meeting had dealt with the particularly delicate mission originally lined up for Roddy in the morning. Who was it that occupied a certain bedroom in the House as Miranda had seen it, along with its strange occupant? It had seemed an opportune moment. Their parents were safely out of the way for a few hours.

The Maitlands had trained their children not to be frightened of being left alone, since they were safe from outside intrusion thanks to Superintendent Thompson's stringent night-time security arrangements, and should anything go wrong, such as a sudden onslaught of illness, Michael had the calmness and the maturity that comes with responsibility to cope. There was a list of telephone numbers for practically any contingency, and the Maitlands further made a point of never staying out too late. But they were of the modern breed which felt that having a family should not confine them to quarters or expose their children to the possible eccentricities of babysitters.

The upshot of the conference had been that if one wanted to know something about that bedroom, bedtime, or other people's near bedtime, was a good time to embark upon such an investigation. Michael, Miranda and Roddy had consulted both sets of plans once again, and, as closely as might be determined, had decided it was the people who occupied Flat 3E. So Roddy was briefed and despatched.

The three, through Miranda's eyes, knew what the room in the House, their House, looked like, plus the mystery of its occupant. Now they needed to find out and know what it looked like today, and who might be living in it.

'I sleep with my brother, Michael. My sister, Miranda, sleeps in the room just along from ours,' Roddy further revealed. 'Can I see where you sleep?'

This question, coming upon the innocent revelations of the child's own living quarters, at first appeared to be merely an extension of the subject, until both the Tringhams became suddenly aware that it was nothing of the kind. It was a request, and Roddy back on his feet, with the white rabbits all prepared to take off on the expedition in fulfilment of it.

Mr Tringham felt all the charm and whimsy drained from himself and replaced by an irritation with small boys who went about at night ringing doorbells and demanding to see one's bedchamber.

'Look here, old fellow,' he said, 'that's quite enough. I think we'd better return you where you came from. What's your name and flat number?'

'Roderick Maitland. Flat 1A.' And then he added, 'It's all right. I know where it is.' And before the astonished couple could so much as move went tripping off purposefully through the door that led to the main bedroom and beyond.

The moment Roddy had looked into the mirror to ascertain ostensibly that he was no longer two sizes larger than an elephant, with snaggle teeth and other frightening appurtenances, he had seen through the open door of the drawing-room into a bedroom beyond, another open door leading to a bathroom, and a third at the very end to a second bedroom. That was 'Target for Tonight'.

The Tringhams were still caught in the paralysis of shock and outrage as Roddy passed through the first bedroom, and did not linger there, for the simple reason that, first of all, he was not interested in it, and, secondly, there was nothing unusual in it that might have caught his interest.

Anybody's bedroom: two beds, night clothes laid out, woman's dresser, chairs, pictures on the wall – not exactly like Mummy's and Daddy's, but exactly enough, and what one might expect to find in most of the flats in Melton Court.

Through the bedroom then, and opening the door into the second bedroom, which he had only seen distantly via the mirror.

Now Roddy received a surprise, verging upon a shock – the kind one is subject to when one had definitely expected one thing and arrives upon something totally different.

The room was empty – and no more forceful word could describe it. No bed, no furniture, no chairs, not so much as a single stick, not a picture. An uncarpeted floor, four grey painted walls, a white ceiling, with one unilluminated bulb hanging from a piece of wire.

All this Roddy saw by the light reflected from the bathroom before he felt himself collared violently from behind, and heard the man's roar. 'Goddamn you, you beastly little brat! How dare you open that door! Get out of here! Get out of here I say!'

Mr Tringham was dragging Roddy backwards and away from the empty chamber. And he *was* being dragged, the rabbits pointed straight up towards the ceiling.

'No, no, Martin. Don't,' Mrs Tringham cried. 'He's only a child.'

But Mr Tringham, now blindly angry, went on: 'Who the devil sent you spying on us?'

His wife again cried, 'Martin!'

But he persisted: 'Come on now. Say.'

He had, of course, no inkling of the processes of Roddy's mind and what the panic and terror brought on by his enraged and intemperate behaviour had evoked there. Roddy did what any normal child would do, which was burst into tears. But as he did so he screamed, 'Where is it? Where is it?'

Mr Tringham, tall, towering, menacing, overwhelming, his face empurpled, yelled, 'Where's what? What are you talking about?'

'The thing,' said Roddy. 'The thing kept locked away so that nobody can ever see it.'

'Oh, my God,' cried Mrs Tringham.

It had not yet hit her husband as it was going to, and he was still at the bellowing stage. 'Thing! Thing! What are you talking about? What I ought to do is . . .'

The apparition of the looming man and the threat of what he ought to do was sufficient to drive Roddy further into his retreat, and between sobs, as the first explosion of tears abated, he said, 'There was a house here once. Miranda said so. Where we are. Michael drew it. It's not here any more, but Miranda says all the places where it was haven't gone away. And there were people in it once, and now there are other people living where the House was. And I just wanted to see where the locked room was where nobody ever went in except to give it some food.'

Mrs Tringham fell to her knees, for the simple reason that her legs would no longer support her, but in doing so she was close enough to enfold Roddy in her arms, wipe his tears, and give him some comforting protection from the terror of her enraged husband.

'Come,' she said. 'I'm sorry you've been frightened so.' And then, 'Was there a house here before? Of course, there easily could have been.' But the thought did nothing to assuage the soul sickness that gripped her and which made her somehow hold the child tighter and closer to her.

'What was in the locked room that no one went to see?' she asked. 'People don't keep things in locked rooms unless they are very valuable. Was . . . was it a child?'

Roddy, his sobs subsiding, nodded an affirmative.

'Was it a little girl?' she asked.

He shook his head.

'A little boy then?'

But again Roddy shook his head in denial.

The word and the thoughts connected with 'hermaphrodite' never crossed Mrs Tringham's mind. She had other and greater troubles. As her husband had been before, she was now driven on to insistence that had been better let be.

'But it must have been one or the other,' she said. 'Either a little boy or a little girl.'

'Miranda said no,' Roddy explained with a frown, his breathing regular now. 'Miranda is Chief Witch and knows. Michael said it was a change-thing.'

A thrill of the sheerest horror ran through Mrs Tringham. 'Do you know what a changeling is?' she asked.

In honesty, Roddy shook his head that he did not. But she did. For she was not only a library consultant but a lexicographer who had once collaborated on a dictionary, and the words which she had researched came back to parade across the screen of her mind like one of those illuminated progressive advertisements where the letters chase each other across the building: '*Changeling*: a popular superstition; a child secretly exchanged for another in infancy was supposed to have been exchanged for another by fairies or elves; the elf child was supposed to be recognizable from its deformity, ill-temper or impish behaviour; a baptized child was thought to be immune from such molestation.'

But she had to ask the final question: 'Why did you come here? What has that to do with us?'

'Because that's where it was kept locked in,' said Roddy, without looking up. 'That was the room. Don't you see? The House came up to here, and there were servants' rooms and an attic under the roof and a special room where it was kept locked away so that nobody would ever find out. I don't think it was pretty.'

This finished off Martin Tringham. Raging through a

burst of tears, he cried again, 'Get out! *Get out!* A curse on
your infernal house! Get out!' Then just as desperately,
all the anger and menace drained out of him, he collapsed
into a chair and buried his face in his hands, shrivelled inside
his clothing and inside his soul; exposed, defeated. 'My
God,' he groaned. 'They know. These people *know*. How
do you suppose they found out? Everyone will know now.'

The sorrow in Mrs Tringham's eyes would have made an
angel weep. She feared for her husband in his violent
anguish. 'Yes,' she said. 'Perhaps. But one cannot be sure,
and so I suppose it will never be quite the same again.'

Her sorrow communicated itself to Roddy, who said,
'You're not angry any more?'

'No,' the woman replied. 'But I think we'd better get
you back to bed. Come along.'

Then she arose and took him by the hand, and Roddy,
once more returned to the normal world of his nocturnal
invasion, took it confidently and went with her.

Ellen Tringham pushed the ivory button outside Flat 1A,
and heard the chain rattle into its slot on the door which
opened a crack through which two faces peered: a boy and a
girl. Then the chain was removed and the door flung wide.
Both had dressing-gowns thrown over their night clothes.

'Is this your little brother?' Mrs Tringham asked.

The boy who was presumably Michael, whom Roddy had
mentioned earlier in the evening, replied, 'Yes, it's Roddy.'

'I think perhaps he's been sleep-walking or something,'
said Mrs Tringham.

The girl, who would be Miranda, replied, 'Oh, dear, has
he? Yes, he sometimes does.'

'Then perhaps,' Mrs Tringham said, 'you had best keep
the door locked or at least a better watch over him.'

'Oh, dear,' Miranda said again. 'I hope he hasn't done
anything wrong or been bothering you.'

Mrs Tringham made no reply to this except to let her
sorrow once more break through in the saddest of smiles as
she said, 'Goodnight. And I hope no more dreams,' then
walked away.

Michael closed the front door and said immediately, 'Roddy, what did you *do*?'

'Michael, don't,' said Miranda, for it was obvious to her that her small gallant brother was deeply in trouble, frightened and upset, like someone who has been lost for a long time and in danger, has suddenly found the road back to safety and security, but for a long while after remains shaken by memories of the experience.

'What happened, Roddy?' she asked.

Roddy began to cry again – not in terror but in reminiscence – and softly he said, 'The man screamed and yelled and he choked me.'

'He choked you?' queried Michael, and balled his fists. 'I ought to go up there and . . .'

He had, of course, not the slightest intention of doing so, but by looking fierce he brought some comfort to Roddy.

'Why?' Miranda asked.

'I went into the room,' said Roddy.

'*The* room?'

Roddy nodded.

'And?'

'There wasn't anything there.'

Michael suddenly scoffed. 'Well, of course there wouldn't be. You were only supposed to see where it was.'

'I mean, really,' said Roddy. 'There wasn't *anything*. No beds or chairs or anything at all.'

'And that's when the man screamed and yelled and choked you?' Michael asked.

'Yes.'

'And what did you do?' Michael continued. 'Couldn't you kick him? What was the matter with him? Was he drunk?'

Roddy was silent for a long time before he replied. 'He was so angry he frightened me. I told.'

'Oh, dear,' said Miranda. 'You did? Everything?'

'Well, not everything, but –'

'About the House? About the room?'

Roddy nodded. 'They wanted to know,' he explained in extenuation. 'They kept pestering me.'

'And then what happened?' Miranda continued her questioning.

'The man wasn't angry any more. He fell into a chair, and I thought he was going to cry. Do men cry? And then the lady brought me back here.'

'Oh, dear,' said Miranda for the last time, for she had seen the woman's face. 'I'm afraid there's going to be trouble.' And then she added, 'Well, it won't be our fault. It's the House, isn't it? We can't help that, can we? I think we'd best all go to bed. Roddy, would you like me to read something to you?'

'Yes, please,' he said. 'The part where Piglet gets lost.'

Mrs Tringham disdained the lift but dragged herself slowly up the stairs back to her flat and her husband, the empty room, and now what had to be faced once more, in the light of what had happened.

The reason why they had originally rented the two-bedroom flat was an expectation of their first child, and from the moment of its first shockingly hoarse cry life had been a horror. They had kept his birth, which, as they accounted it, fortunately had occurred in Switzerland, and his condition a secret to the point where almost but not quite it had even become a secret from themselves.

One of the results of the secret, however, was the loathing with which Martin and Ellen Tringham regarded one another – a loathing never expressed in words or actions – a loathing compounded of a hatred of self as much as of each other. They suffered the true and veritable torture of the damned, except on earth and behind the closed door of Flat 3E instead of hell. As in the old wood cuts, the little devils pricked and prodded them with the pitchforks of conscience and roasted them over the slow fires of guilt.

If only in good truth each might have been able entirely to blame the other for the catastrophe which had wrecked them, love, pity, even forgiveness might have been a survival and an end to it. But this was not the case. They were trapped in a partnership of guilt where neither could shift the whole of the conscience upon the other but must accept and share the blame.

It never occurred to them that they were victims of a tragedy beyond the control of either and for which neither was in any way responsible. It was one of those punishments visited upon two harmless, decent human beings that had no rhyme, no cause, no reason, spiritually or morally. No god of any persuasion had cause to have grudge against either.

They made do by never referring to the matter, by behaving towards one another and that world on the other side of brass letters 3 E affixed to their door as though it had never happened. They abolished it with small talk and by busying themselves with the trivialities of living in a world so grotesque that only by adherence to these trivialities could they survive.

But in their looks when they met full or crossed one another before they could turn their heads aside, and in their thoughts, it was always there.

Innocents, they had been born, grown up, met, fallen in love, married, faced all of the world their times could fright them with bravely and honestly, until what had happened turned them to cowards and drained them of any and every kind of love that animates the human heart.

With their one child hidden away in Northumberland in a home for the incurably defective, they had never once been to see him. None of their friends knew about him. But now all this was to be changed, for it was not to be believed that such an exposure could occur: that this room had been reserved for a changeling of deformity, ill-temper and violent behaviour, and that its discovery should result from the imagination of children at play. People must have been talking, and the children had heard.

CHAPTER VIII

Mrs Prume Spills Over

Mrs Prume was that anomaly, a non-chatty London char. A faded, skinny woman, with tired eyes, and tufts of hair growing from her face in places which made it hard to keep one's eyes off them. By only her second morning she had proved middling efficient and clean, and had at least one virtue which recommended her to Mrs Maitland: she understood children, and apparently had a brood of her own. This understanding extended to Miranda in particular when the young girl chose to play the little housewife and padded after her with duster or broom.

Mrs Prume accepted this as part of the journey through the Maitland flat, just as she accepted Roddy's personal questions which elicited all that the Maitlands knew about her: that she had the usual husband who was usually out of work, and, when he happened to be in, spent money on drink, and that she was the mother of a quintet consisting of three boys and two girls, ranging from the age of six to fifteen.

She had progressed to the drawing-room part of her beat with Miranda as a small shadow in tow. Leaving her two brothers playing trains, she had donned one of her mother's aprons, which dragged around her ankles, and tied a towel about her head in the approved fashion for the well-dressed char lady. She carried a feather duster, as being the least likely implement to inflict any serious damage. Mrs Prume herself wielded a dust cloth, but in a manner that was strictly ritualistic. That is to say, she would pick up various articles such as an ash-tray, a piece of bric-a-brac, one of those multi-coloured glass Victorian paper weights, a vase or an ornament, give a flick at the spot where it had been, replace it and move on to the next. Miranda worked her feather duster with a sense of power and satisfaction of having an extension of one's arm so that one could do the necessary without getting too close to it.

The woman and the child worked in the silence of a communal project that required no conversation, the doing of it being sufficient satisfaction and giving time for having one's thoughts simultaneously without affecting the physical effort.

At that particular moment Miranda was thinking about Mrs Prume, for as they passed one of the windows the rain, driven by a gust of wind, sluiced against the pane with an audible thump, so that both stopped and looked at the water running down in a wide rivulet.

'Oh, dear,' said Miranda. 'It's getting worse, isn't it? Will you be soaked going home?'

The question was thoughtful and relevant, since, when she came to the end of the drawing-room, it marked the finish of Mrs Prume's labours – at least at the Maitland flat. But the effect upon the cleaner was both startling and un-expected, as though, while proceeding automatically on her round, something in her subconscious had been churning, to be triggered by one word in this innocent question. For earlier that morning whilst cleaning the play-room, she had been fascinated by the children's drawings and incessant talk of the House that wouldn't go away.

Now Mrs Prume's mechanical actions ceased as though the power had been cut off. She turned to face her satellite and said, loudly and clearly, 'Home? You'd understand – I've got no 'ome.'

'Oh,' exclaimed Miranda, indeed surprised at this com-pletely unexpected outburst, and through her mind flashed anxieties over what sudden disasters might have overtaken Mrs Prume, who, since she had begun to come and go each day, must obviously have somewhere to go to spend the

night with her family. Fire? Flood from this unceasing
spring deluge from the skies? Or, worse, dispossessed? But
she could merely echo, 'No home?'

A trickle had found egress from the pent-up dam of Mrs
Prume. The aperture widened. 'I never think of going 'ome
any more. I 'ad a home once – me own, bought with our
own money. Then the council condemned it. We've been
re'oused – one of them new estates.'

The protest, apparently so long walled up, now dug a
wider hole. The trickle turned into a stream, and the stream
into a torrent.

'Flashy tiles in the bathroom, hot and cold running
fawcets, and me still reaching for the geyser what was good
enough for us and never let us down. Kitchen full of mod.
cons. – blinkin' coloured plastic, and 'ang all your pots
neatly on a hook, Mrs Prume, and don't leave your dishes
stacked up. Gaw! Who wants all that? Who asked for it?
They even put a picture on the wall. Silly looking kids with
a dog. We never 'ad no need of pictures. Photograph of
when me and Fred got married, and the babies, along with
the calendars from the coal merchant and the grocer to make
it look nice and homey, and what else do yer want? All
them what they call pickshoor windows looking out on to
nuffink except somebody else's windows. All that glass to
clean and tiles to scrub and shiny stuff to polish. I've got
more work to do when I leaves 'ere than I 'as for you and
your Mum – and 'oo pays me for it? Not the flippin'
council or the inspector who comes sniffing around with
"Mind you don't leave your dustbin by your door, Mrs
Prume", or 'Can you keep them kids of yours from racket-
ing in the hall? There's been complaints", or "You've
been blockin' up your toilet again, Mrs Prume, and it's
leaking down through number 22".'

'When we had our own 'ome what we bought and paid
for we could do what we liked, and anybody who stuck his
nose in where it wasn't his business I could take a broom to,
as long as we paid the rates and didn't bovver anyone.
What right 'ad they to take our own 'ouse away from us?

It wasn't all that bad, what with Fred being a 'andyman for repairs when he wasn't too busy. A menace to 'ealth, they said, and moved out the whole blessed street without so much as a by-your-leave. "We're going to give you one of the best flats in the building, Mrs Prume. You and your family are going to love it." Love it, my foot. Might as well be in gaol. Can't have no animals, can't have the radio or the telly on without someone banging on the walls. No place for the kids to go except running up and down out in the 'all. Come in off the street, go up in the blinkin' lift, shut the door and where are you? Nowhere. And your 'usband, when 'e's out of work sitting around all day and under your feet, grousin' and complainin'. When we 'ad our 'ouse and he 'adn't no job he'd at least be out most of the days and nights with the boys, even if he come home late. Like we live now, he figures he got no home to come 'ome to, so he just don't go out.'

With the rising tenor of her complaints, the pitch of her voice, rarely heard above a murmur before, rose and penetrated to the kitchen, where it reached the ears of Mrs Maitland, who had been draining vegetables, so that she turned the water off and listened.

'Neighbourly is what we used to be,' complained Mrs Prume. 'Always time for a friendly chat. Now we might as well be living on a desert iling. Yer never see nobody and nobody ever sees you. A house meant having a doorstep that you'd got to clean, with a bit of the pavement in front and the back yard with a fence or two the kids could scramble over, with all of the street to play in and nobody complainin'. And there'd be your neighbour on '*er* doorstep of a morning or coming home from shopping and suggesting you come in for a cup of tea and a natter. And of a hot summer's night you'd all be sitting out the front with maybe the men gathering in a knot to talk over the strike and us women holding our babies. It was our street and our roof over our 'eads and our own doorstep, just like every-body else had theirs; and you might have an argy bargy with one or a set-to with another, but you knowed where you

belonged and who they were and they 'ad the same problems
like you did. Slums, they said. A danger to 'ealth. Danger to
whose 'ealth I say? Our kids never 'ad a day's sickness,
but only last week my Johnny got his fingers caught in the
doors of the lift, and we burn ourselves on the blinkin'
electric stove which you can't tell whether it's on or off.'

Her voice rose another decibel. 'Re'oused, we are, with
everything you could ask for, and I hate it. I hate it.'

'Oh, dear,' said Mrs Maitland to herself, and then
repeated, 'Oh, dear,' waivering, uncertain whether she
ought to go in and become involved or not. And even as
she waivered Mrs Prume augmented her complaint.

'No place to go! Nuffink to do. Nobody to talk to. 'Ow
would you like to be cooped up in a flat with five kids and
a 'usband out of work, and nowhere you can call your own
and make a bit of a muck?'

It was not remarkable, nor did Miranda find it so, that
Mrs Prume did not see the Maitland flat as equally confining
as her own, or think her employers in a sense, as far as their
dwelling was concerned, as under-privileged as herself. For
the Maitlands were to her 'rich', and hence had it better, no
matter where or how they lived. The very fact that they
could afford her to 'do' for them made it so. With her last
accusing query Mrs Prume drew her first breath into which
space Miranda intruded her discovery.

'But we don't mind, Mrs Prume, because as we told you
this morning, we *do* live in a House.'

This clashing thought, coming up against hers, already
off the track, startled Mrs Prume into a suspicious look and
sniff. 'House? What, that one what's on them drawings?'
she asked.

'No, not just there, Mrs Prume,' Miranda frowned. It
was difficult for her to explain. It was all so clear in her
head, and she felt that, almost more than herself and her
brothers, Mrs Prume needed to know that houses and their
influence could never be totally destroyed.

She told Mrs Prume much more about the House that
was there before, and how not all of it could be taken away

– 'So that part that stayed we are living in' – and the same was probably true of Mrs Prume's block.

'If you could think of it that way, if you're not living too high up, I mean, you see, if they tore down houses to put up new blocks, well, there's got to be something of those houses left – and you could be living in a part of one of them right now.'

'I don't understand a word you're saying,' Mrs Prume shook her head. 'I saw me 'ouse knocked down with me own eyes, and I nearly cried them out too. They took away everything we'd ever been or 'ad or was. Do you know what all them new blocks is full of? Grief and tears of women crying for the 'omes they once 'ad.'

'But some things must have been left over,' Miranda insisted. 'The good things as well as the bad, and you could think of those. Of course, it wouldn't be your house you'd be living in. Somebody else would be living in your house, and they might never know unless they could feel. What floor are you on?'

'Two flights up,' Mrs Prume replied, and thought nothing strange of it that she was standing by a rain-drenched, window of the Maitland drawing-room clutching a duster holding converse and, with a curious kind of desperation, trying to penetrate what others would call 'the chatter of a child', but what she, with her strong primitive instincts, felt might be some sort of salvation.

'Well, then,' said Miranda, 'you'd be living in their top floor.'

'Whose top floor?'

'Why, the people who had the house that was there before, don't you see? Who probably had theirs pulled down just like yours.'

Mrs Prume had not yet crossed the threshold of the door that Miranda was trying to open for her.

'Would I know them?' she asked.

'But of course you would,' explained Miranda. 'If you thought about them and wondered, or just before you went to sleep let yourself feel. They would be like you, wouldn't they? If they'd lived in the same kind of house like the people next door? Or you could make them up to be anyone you liked and could have them for friends, and when you put the light out at night they would come and you would be together and could talk to them, and they would make it seem just as if the old house was still there and you were living in it.'

'Oh, you kids,' said Mrs Prume. 'You don't arf come up with some notions, you do. Like living in two places at once . . .'

At this moment Mrs Maitland thought it best to put in an appearance. A char woman was, at best, a tenuous creature, a Will-o'-the-wisp who might vanish at any time she took it into her head to do so. A confused or befuddled char could be that much closer to a vanishing one.

'You mustn't annoy Mrs Prume with your nonsense, Miranda,' she said. 'Besides which she wants to get on with her cleaning, so that she can finish up and get back to her family.'

Mrs Prume bristled. 'Nonsense, is it?' And then added, 'Sometimes out o' the mouths o' babes . . .' taking Mrs Maitland's remark as an implication that she was slacking in her work, standing there nattering with the child instead of getting on with her dusting.

'I was only telling Mrs Prume about the House,' Miranda said, 'and how –'

Mrs Maitland was finding the position invidious, and wished to bring it to an end. 'Oh, come now, Miranda,' she said firmly, 'don't be silly. You can play amongst yourselves, but you must stop worrying others.' Then she turned to Mrs Prume and, with an apologetic smile, began to explain, 'It's just a game the children are playing, but of course as far as there being any truth in it –'

''Ow can you tell?' said Mrs Prume, on the defensive, as always with an employer, yet simultaneously aware of some kind of a strange glimmer of what the child had been driving at – something glimpsed through a door momentarily opened a crack. 'Maybe the kiddie knows something we

don't. My youngest is always talking like to someone that
ain't there. What's 'e need to do that for when he's got a
room full of brothers and sisters? But 'e does.'

'He's lonely,' said Miranda, and it seemed to both the
startled women that her voice had come from very far away.

Mrs Prume gave a snort. 'Him lonely?' she said. 'And us
on each other's 'eels all day long?'

But Mrs Maitland found herself shocked into silence.

'If he knew about the House,' Miranda went on, 'and
could live in it the way we do, he wouldn't be lonely any
more. People who live in houses don't get lonely.'

Mrs Maitland blinked as though Miranda had turned on
the full glare of a thousand candle power to reveal what had,
once again, only the day before, been at the back of her
thoughts but which she was still reluctant to bring forward:
of the millions and millions of people tucked away in little
boxes of flats who were lonely, lonely, lonely.

Mrs Prume suddenly turned upon Miranda as though for
a consolidation of all those strange and vagrant ideas which
had been thrown at her, and asked, 'Well, and what's your
house like?'

'Old and beautiful,' Miranda replied.

'Where is it?' Mrs Prume continued her probe.

'You're in it now,' said Miranda. 'Except we're not in the
drawing-room. We're really in a bedroom.'

Mrs Prume's head was turning with Miranda's, and if she
was not able to see what Miranda was seeing she was
learning how to look. She was filled with sentimental
sadness for her own loss and her memories.

'I'll be getting on 'ome now,' she said. 'I was near as
finished.' And she gave a slap at the small bronze figure of
a lion on the drawing-room table, then, without realizing it,
touched the corners of her eyes with the same yellow flannel
duster, before she shuffled out.

Mrs Maitland noted this, and wondered whether her
daughter had too. She should have known that children
miss nothing.

'She was crying, wasn't she, Mummy?' Miranda said.

'Perhaps she won't be feeling so lonely now – if she can pretend a little. But she did say she'd better be getting on home.' And then, suddenly, with an overwhelming feeling of fear and doubt, she burst out, 'Oh, Mummy, *is* it wrong to talk about our House to other people?'

Mrs Maitland for a moment wished that she might cry herself but could not in front of her daughter. 'I don't know,' she said. 'I just don't know, Miranda. Such things can be dangerous if they get out of hand. They help some and hurt others.'

Miranda looked deeply into her mother's eyes. 'Are you hurt, Mummy?' she asked.

Mrs Maitland could not find the strength to lie. 'Perhaps a little,' she said. And then broke it with, 'Come and help me with the lunch.'

She put her arm around Miranda and they went into the kitchen together.

CHAPTER IX

The Birdman

However mixed or confused her feelings just before lunch, by the early afternoon Mrs Maitland had decided she simply must call a halt – and at once – before any further upset. Then, as the door closed behind her, Michael, Miranda and Roddy looked at one another silently, pondering on the prohibition and how it would affect their investigations of the yet unexplored portions of the House.

Finally, Miranda asked, 'Do you think Mummy meant it?'

'Oh! She meant it all right,' said Michael.

'How do you know?' asked Miranda. 'Sometimes she –'

'By the way she shut the door,' Michael replied. 'And that look. Didn't you see it?'

'Yes,' said Miranda. 'I know.'

Orders had been firm and brooked of no arguments. Mrs Maitland had said, 'You are not to go bothering anybody, anywhere. You've worried people enough already. Look how disturbed Mrs Prume was this morning. You are not to go ringing anyone's doorbell or even go near them. I shall be out for about an hour. Now make sure you stay *in* while I'm gone.'

Michael had tried to salvage something: 'Can we go belowstairs and talk to Mr Biggs? He doesn't mind us being around. He likes us.'

'Perhaps when I get back. We'll see,' Mrs Maitland had said. 'But for now you are to stay here, do you understand?'

Thereafter she had departed and the door had closed with quite audible vehemence. She wasn't usually that sharp. And as for their query about being allowed to go down and play in the basement, the three had been further depressed by her 'We'll see.' As expert conspirators and diviners of adults they knew that 'We'll see' meant either an indefinite postponement of the matter or 'Don't bother me about that.'

If they were to be cut off not only from the residents in the block but from their three most promising sources of information – Tim Ryan, the head porter, who knew everything about everybody, Harry at the switchboard, who heard over the telephone anything that Tim hadn't through gossip, and Mr Biggs, who at one time or another had been called in for repairs to almost every flat – their investigations were over before they were even half completed. They were not prepared to concede this.

It was Roddy who was the most stricken. 'Can't I intrude any more?' he asked.

'No, you can't,' Michael replied firmly.

'Then what am I?' Roddy enquired plaintively.

'Nothing at the moment,' said Michael.

Roddy turned away so that they wouldn't see the tears that had begun to gather in his eyes, but they knew the gesture well, and Michael soothed, 'We'll have to think of something.'

Miranda had been thinking hard, and through her sensitive and strange little mind there suddenly appeared a phrase she did not know where from or why – 'Curiosity killed the cat' – and she found herself saying it out loud.

Michael repeated it: 'Curiosity killed the cat? What's that got to do with anything?'

'I know now,' Miranda replied, because it had come to her that the operative word in the funny pop-pop phrase had been curiosity. 'Never you mind,' she added. 'Just wait and see what will happen when Roddy stops intruding and we don't visit anyone any more.'

Roddy brightened at the mention of his name. 'I know,' he said. 'I can stand on my head. If I do it outside someone's door and they come out and speak to me it wouldn't be –'

'Don't be silly, Roddy,' said Michael. And then to

Miranda: 'What do you mean "what will happen when we don't visit anyone any more"?'

'They'll start visiting us,' said Miranda.

Michael stared at her, uncomprehending at first. He would always be more concerned with actions than the reasons for them or the thoughts that lay behind them. For him, people *did* things and one had to adjust to them rather than what they might be thinking or feeling.

Miranda elaborated: 'People are curious. I am sure they have all heard about the House by now. If we don't come and tell them where they are living they'll want to know, won't they? Well, we're the only ones who can tell them.'

The penny dropped for Michael. 'Of course, Miranda,' he said. 'That's right! I'll bet some of them will. And then it wouldn't be our fault, would it? I mean, if they come around bothering us instead of us bothering them, nobody could say anything, could they? Look, Roddy, instead of Chief Intruder you could be Chief Contact Man.'

'Could I?' Roddy beamed, and then was compelled to add, 'What does a Chief Contact Man do?'

Michael explained, 'Well, you know, like in an office you never get to see the person you want to speak to. First you have to see a whole lot of other people who find out if you're *important* enough. Well, before they get to us they'll have to see you, and if you say they're O.K. then we'll meet them.'

'I liked intruding better,' Roddy said flatly.

'But this is much more official, Roddy,' Miranda joined in. 'Don't you see? "State your name, age and business . . ." Of course, what we really want to know, if anyone should come, is what floor they live on, the number of their flat, and why they want to know about where they live.'

Roddy was considering the nature, dignity and responsibility of this new position and whether it was any better than that of Harry at the switchboard downstairs, who, when someone came into the lobby and wished to visit someone upstairs, enquired, 'Who shall I say is calling, please?' when suddenly the doorbell rang.

They all started a little, and flashed looks one to the other, but then Miranda said, 'I suppose it's the butcher. Mummy said he'd be coming.'

'No, it isn't,' said Michael, 'It's the front door. I'll go.'

'You can't,' declared Roddy firmly, for he had reached the decision that the position of Chief Contact Man gave him considerable powers. 'You said I was to be Chief Contact Man,' he reminded them. 'Maybe it's someone.'

He marched off towards the hall before they could stop him, so that Miranda could only call after him, 'Keep the chain on the door the way Mummy always tells us, and don't let anybody in we don't know.'

Michael and Miranda stood perfectly still, listening. They heard the door open to the limit of the restraining chain and the murmur of voices. They waited. The murmur continued.

Miranda whispered to Michael, 'You should have gone.'

Michael whispered back, 'Well, Roddy's got to have some kind of job, hasn't he? He can find out as well as any of us what anybody wants. And if it should be –'

The murmur of voices ceased, and they heard the chain rattle as it was being unfastened, followed by footsteps in the hall, and then Roddy went to the drawing-room. He was leading by the hand a tall, bony old gentleman with tufted, grey eyebrows standing on alert over a pair of lively blue eyes which were crinkled with amusement. His features and his expression were gentle and confidence-inspiring. There was nothing alarming about his presence. There was an aura about him of someone who was embarked upon an adventure which immediately registered. Roddy dropped the old gentleman's hand, stood to one side, and announced as if in recitation to his brother and sister, who had followed, 'His name is Merrily Fraser. He is seventy-eight years old. He lives in Flat E on the ground floor. He isn't married, and has no children. He's writing a book about some birds. He wishes to know where he is living in our House because of a lovely curiosity.'

Having finished, Roddy drew a long breath to replenish his lungs, and the old gentleman murmured, 'Merriman Fraser, and I think what the young man meant to say was a "lively" curiosity.' Then he added, 'I did enquire first whether your mother was in, for, naturally, I should have asked her permission before speaking to you. But it seems that this young man has been endowed with certain powers to act on behalf of . . .' And here he ran down.

Miranda put him at his ease by saying, 'Oh, that's all right. It's perfectly all right for you to visit us. Won't you sit down?'

Mr Fraser did so somewhat creakily, and in the manner of a folding ruler. Since he had sat on a rather low chair, his knees stuck up almost touching his chin, and he looked over them with his bright and amused eyes, rather wondering how to begin.

It was Roddy who made it simple. 'He wants to know where he's living,' he said again.

'Exactly,' nodded Mr Fraser. 'I couldn't have put it more succinctly myself.' His face had a pleasant and confidential quality. Like so many old people, he was at ease with himself and hence made others feel at ease. 'The notion that I might be living in two places at once struck me as quite fascinating. I had heard about the house, of course' – then quickly correcting himself – 'your house, that is to say. But the idea had never struck me before. There must be hundreds of blocks of flats all over that contain ghosts of houses long departed, but nobody has ever thought to bring them to life. It seems to me a splendid idea.' He tilted his head towards Roddy and added, 'I gather that you are guardian of the portals.'

'Chief Contact Man,' Roddy exclaimed proudly.

Mr Fraser smiled upon him fondly. 'A more practical way of putting it. If it will help my *bona fides*, when I was a boy I lived in a big old house in the Cotswolds in Gloucestershire. We had a beautiful garden that ran right down to a small stream, and there was a bit of woodland there too which framed the house and brought many varieties of birds to us. Some to nest and others in passage, and those that stayed with us all winter, we looked after.'

Michael asked, 'Are you an ornithorol . . .? I mean, are you writing a scientific book?'

'Ornithologist?' smiled Mr Fraser. 'No. I'm writing a book about birds remembered.'

Nothing that the old gentleman might have said could have touched the hearts of the two older children or stirred their imagination more quickly, or so emphasized his loneliness. Unmarried, Roddy had reported, and, of course, no children – how silly of Roddy to ask – seventy-eight years old and living alone in a single flat and writing a book not about people or things or places or adventures or even a family that he wished to recall in his life, but just the birds that had come and gone in his one-time garden and those that had stayed.

Miranda spoke up as one who was not only Chief Witch and Diviner but whose House it actually was. 'Where did you say you live, Mr Fraser?'

'Flat E,' he replied. 'That is on the ground floor at the back. Not very spacious quarters, I must confess, but from a corner of my window I am able to see some branches of one of the trees in the garden space behind the block. Last week, a yellow finch stopped by there for a moment. It moved its head about as though it were looking for spring.' He reflected. 'Of course, I don't know the exact extent of your house . . .'

Miranda flashed a look and a signal to her older brother which meant that a private discussion was required.

'Michael and I will have a look,' she said. 'If you'll excuse us, Roddy will stay here and entertain you.

Mr Fraser bowed a smile of thanks, and Miranda and Michael hurried out of the drawing-room and back to the playroom, closing the door behind them – but not before they had heard Roddy enquire of their guest, 'Have you ever killed anyone?' Roddy was a great believer in the direct approach to get a conversation going.

In the playroom-bedroom Michael took out the plans of

the House that he had drawn and they both compared them with the original architect's floor plans of Hallam Hall.

'Here's where Flat E would be – at the back,' said Michael, pointing.

'Oh, dear,' Miranda said. 'There's nothing there. What are we going to do?'

'Tell him.'

'We can't.'

'Why not?'

'Don't you see? He wants to awfully – otherwise he wouldn't have come, would he?'

'Well, what *are* we going to do?'

'Well, something,' Miranda snapped with a curious kind of fierceness. 'Even if perhaps we ought not.'

Thereafter they fell to a brief discussion, then, shortly afterwards, re-entered the drawing-room just in time to hear Mr Fraser conclude what must have been a fairly exciting narrative, for Roddy was sitting on the edge of his chair round-eyed.

'Of course, I'm speaking about 1916, when aeroplanes were rather new and bombs weren't so accurate. I always tried to drop mine in a field or in a forest or even into the sea, where I hoped there wouldn't be anybody . . .'

Mr Fraser suddenly noticed that Miranda and Michael had returned. 'Well?' he queried, smiling, and they read more than anticipation in his eyes.

'We're awfully sorry,' said Miranda, 'but you're actually not in the House.'

The old gentleman was still smiling, but it was astonishing to see how a tinge of sadness could suddenly come to a smile.

'But if you don't mind,' Miranda continued, 'you're living – or at least I think your bedroom is – in the gardener's shed.'

'The gardener's shed?' repeated Mr Fraser, and his face became as beatific as if he had just been awarded a knighthood. 'Is this true?'

'Yes,' said Miranda, and looked to Michael for corroboration.

'How absolutely delightful,' exclaimed Mr Fraser. 'Of course, we had a potting-shed in our garden.' He folded his bony fingers around his bony knees and peered for a moment into the past before continuing. 'Yes, the potting-shed. A fascinating place to me when I was a boy . . .'

As he began to reflect again, the children heard the sound of a key rattling in the lock of the front door, and their mother entered, carrying parcels destined for the kitchen. The unfamiliar voice in the drawing-room, however, drew her in immediately. Mr Fraser at once arose and said, 'Mrs Maitland, of course. I do hope you will forgive me. Merriman Fraser. How do you do? The children have been so kind as to listen to an old man reminiscing. Had you been at home, as I told them, I should, naturally, have asked your permission before speaking to them. But this young man here,' he nodded in Roddy's direction, 'was so good as to –'

'I'm sorry,' Mrs Maitland broke in. 'I'm sure it is most kind of you to have been entertaining them, but I'm afraid I don't quite understand.'

Mr Fraser hastened to try to explain, but the circumstances did not permit making too good a job of it. 'I am in Flat E, on the ground floor in the back. I live in the gardener's shed – or at least that is to say that is where I seem to be. You see, I had heard about the house that used to be here – or rather the rumours that there had been one, and that your children had either discovered it or were the custodians of it. I wasn't quite sure, and it seemed to me such an amusing idea that quite a few of us in Melton Court are inhabiting not one but, in a sense, two sets of quarters, and my curiosity being aroused – well, I took the liberty of coming to enquire.'

Mrs Maitland could only make the obvious remark: 'I hope they were polite.'

All three children realized now that there were fires burning which would erupt upon the departure of their visitor.

'Oh, yes indeed,' said Mr Fraser. 'Most. Delightful and

extremely well-mannered – which is so unusual for today, isn't it? I must congratulate you. Well, if you'll excuse me, I'll be off now. I can't wait to examine my new quarters, to be perfectly frank. Thank you again.' And so he took his leave.

Mrs Maitland was so angry that she knew she must control herself and not let fly immediately, so she merely said, 'Wait here for a moment while I take these things through to the kitchen.'

As she went out, Roddy declared, 'Mummy's angry.'

'I don't see why,' said Michael. 'We didn't do anything we were told not to do.'

Miranda was chewing her lower lip. 'Well, I'm not sure about letting people in we don't know.'

When Mrs Maitland returned she had herself under control, and used an opening gambit she knew was far more effective than shouting at the three of them.

She said quite quietly, 'I thought that I could trust my children.'

'You can, Mummy,' Miranda rushed to reassure.

'I thought I made it quite clear that you were not to disturb anyone in the block –'

'But, Mummy,' Miranda interrupted, 'he came to see us – you heard him say so.'

'And so you let him in?' Mrs Maitland finished for her. 'I thought I told you to keep the chain on the door and never, never let anyone in we didn't know. I have told you how dangerous –'

'But, Mummy, we *did* know him,' Miranda protested. 'I mean, after Roddy interviewed him and he introduced himself. The chain was on all the time then.'

'Roddy?' exclaimed Mrs Maitland, now thoroughly confused.

'I'm Chief Contact Man,' Roddy proudly announced. 'Like in offices when you want to see someone and first someone else has to find out if you're important enough. I asked him his name, age, and to state his business, like Michael said.'

Mrs Maitland was beginning to feel slightly dizzy. It was all getting so out of hand.

Michael suddenly asked her, 'Anyway, what *are* we to do if people come to us like that? I don't suppose they'll always be ringing at the doorbell. They might meet us in the hall downstairs or in the garden – that's if the rain ever lets up. It wouldn't be polite if we just turned and walked away, would it? We thought Roddy could find out if they were really serious and wanted to know.' Then he added, 'If you'd been at home, you would have let him in.'

Mrs Maitland gave up. The direct thrust of the children's attacks often was too much for her to parry. She had never been able to get over the surprise of such attacks, and so she equivocated: 'Well, I'm glad you have told me the truth at least.'

Michael was in at once, as she knew he would be. 'Then it's all right if people do come and ask us and we tell them?'

Mrs Maitland sighed, 'I suppose so,' and then salvaged what she could with 'I'll have to speak to your father though.' Then, finally, she turned away, saying, 'Come along, Miranda, and help me unpack the shopping.'

CHAPTER X

A Protest and a Ban

Everything was back to normal after the visit of Mr Fraser that afternoon, until the doorbell rang again, at a tricky moment between Mrs Maitland and the oven and while Miranda was earnestly whisking a mousse for supper. Mrs Maitland called Michael, but knew that it was useless, for during kitchen operations, when she and Miranda were busy at women's work, Michael would be buried in a book and would hear nothing else than a supersonic bang. And so she called, 'Roddy, go and see who it is, will you, dear?' knowing that he would be hovering somewhere about.

There came the sound of running footsteps, followed by another which Mrs Maitland was in a sense relieved to hear: the rattle of the short chain being fastened to the entrance door. At least *that* she had been able to lead the children to remember. There was a brief murmur of voices, and then the struggle of inserting too large a dish into too small an oven occupied her attention. When she solved this, as she always did, by getting it in slightly tilted, and the whisk had been turned off, all was quiet in the flat again, and Roddy stood in the doorway to the kitchen looking reflective.

'Who was it, Roddy?' Mrs Maitland asked. Still flushed from her struggle with something inanimate, she hadn't had time yet to concentrate fully on her younger son or she would have seen in his expression and attitude certain danger signals long experience had taught her to recognize.

'A man,' Roddy said.

'Oh? What was it? What man?'

'I don't know.'

Mrs Maitland was now alerted. 'Come, Roddy, don't be silly. It must have been someone. What did he want?'

'He was angry.'

'Angry? What about? Who did he ask to see?'

'Us,' Roddy answered softly.

Mrs Maitland was beginning to experience that irritation Roddy was always able to arouse in her when he was obviously thinking one thing and saying another. 'Who do you mean, Roddy, "us"? Me? Your father? You? Who? Come on, don't just stand there. Where is he?'

'I didn't let him in.'

'Didn't let him in? You mean you shut the door on him? Roddy, how could you do such a thing?'

'I didn't like him.'

'Why, Roddy? What actually happened?' asked Miranda, with little doubt in her own mind now.

Roddy struck his narrative pose, which meant planting his feet firmly on the ground, legs spread wide apart, brow screwed up in concentration, as he tried to get things in a sequence that would satisfy his determined questioners. 'I put the chain on the door,' he began, 'like Mummy said' – looking to his mother for approbation, which in this instance was withheld – 'and then I opened it and he stuck his face in. It was all red.' Adding as an afterthought, 'His teeth were a horrible colour too.'

'Roddy,' said Mrs Maitland, 'what did he *say*?'

Roddy again screwed up his brow. 'He said, "Are you one of the kids who have cooked up this ab-, ab- something story –"'

'Absurd?' Miranda filled in the missing word.

'Yes – "absurd story about a house? I want to have a word with you. Open the door".'

Mrs Maitland was experiencing a sickening feeling at the pit of her stomach, and Miranda was not entirely comfortable either. Miranda, in fact, now took up the interrogation.

'What did you say, Roddy?' she queried.

Roddy now understood that he had better be somewhat

on the defensive with his narrative, and replied, 'What you told me to: "State your name, age and business".'

'Oh, dear!' said Mrs Maitland.

'Well, did he?' asked Miranda.

'He said, "My name is Murchison, my age is none of the business of a fresh young boy, and I am here to stop this . . ."'

'Well?' asked Mrs Maitland.

Roddy suddenly looked pious. 'He said a bad word. The one that begins with "b".' Then he continued his quotation as though there had been no break at all: ' "– nonsense about some house that was here on the grounds and the room we're supposed to be living in." '

Mrs Maitland mentally completed the outburst, and joined Roddy in an instant dislike of Mr Murchison.

'What happened then?' Miranda asked.

'I said, "Go away", and shut the door.'

Miranda, who could see a problem developing, said, 'Oh, Roddy, you shouldn't have. If he wanted to see us, he –'

'Well, you said I was Chief Contact Man,' Roddy protested, 'and they had to see me before they could see us. Anyway, he *swore*.' Then another of Roddy's afterthoughts struck him: 'His moustache wasn't nice either.'

Mrs Maitland found herself in her usual dilemma of being in agreement with Roddy's judgements but at the same time anxious to clarify to him the rules and regulations of manners and behaviour when the doorbell exploded into a series of short staccato bursts that were decidedly peremptory.

Mrs Maitland snapped the oven door shut with an 'Oh, Roddy,' and then said, 'Come along, Miranda. And get Michael.'

She marched down the hall, removed the chain and opened the door upon the by now wholly choleric Mr Murchison. Roddy's description had pinpointed all the most distinctive features of the man. What he had not yet got around to noting, however, had he had the experience, was that Mr Murchison also resembled a type of shark. His face was narrow and his lower jaw so undershot that it was obvious that, like any self-respecting specimen of the Class of Selachii, order of the Pleurotremata, he would have to turn on his side before he could bite one.

His eyes popped, due no doubt to the internal pressure of the explosion he was compelled to suppress at seeing the pleasant person of Mrs Maitland at the door in place of the child it had been his intention to annihilate.

Taken aback, he could only mutter, 'I beg your pardon.' And then, the purpose of his visit renewing his anger, he enquired, 'Are you the mother of these children?'

'I am Dorothy Maitland, and I am the mother of these children. I am sorry if one of them has been inexcusably impolite.'

Mrs Maitland's cool apology for her son's manners reminded Mr Murchison of his own possible lapse, and he said, 'That's all right, madam. Perhaps you are the one I ought to see.'

'Perhaps,' said Mrs Maitland, 'you ought to see us all. Won't you come in?' She was determined that she must not let her prejudice plus the first impression show in her attitude. One of the responsibilities of being a parent was coping as justly as one could with whatever one's children had been up to. 'I'm afraid we haven't met,' she continued. 'Somehow one doesn't seem to meet many people in a block like this. You are from –?'

'3D,' Mr Murchison completed for her, and crossed the threshold.

They foregathered in the drawing-room, where Mrs Maitland and Roddy occupied the sofa, Michael and Miranda a chair each, and Mr Murchison chose to remain standing, since it gave him a more commanding position, and enabled him to bristle more effectively.

'Now,' said Mrs Maitland, 'what is it exactly you're complaining of?'

With a direct question thrust at him, Mr Murchison found it difficult under the circumstances to give a direct and what might sound like a valid answer, and so was forced to take refuge by saying, 'They've been upsetting my wife.'

Mrs Maitland said severely, 'Roddy, if you've –'

But Miranda interrupted: 'Mummy, he didn't. He hasn't.' Then looked indignantly up at their visitor, her eyes fixed on him as she crossed her arms abruptly.

'I see,' said Mrs Maitland. 'Then in what way have they been upsetting Mrs Murchison?'

This was more like a question into which Mr Murchison could get his teeth, even though he had now to turn sideways to do so.

'All this nonsense about the house they say used to be here,' he began. 'It's got to be stopped. My wife is inclined to be rather superstit – I mean, Mrs Murchison is a highly nervous person, due to some unfortunate childhood experiences.'

The children sat up with interest at this statement, as though a story which belonged in their field might be forthcoming, and Mr Murchison saw that he was becoming involved.

He continued: 'We don't like the idea of being told that perhaps we are occupying an area where before someone might have been very ill, or died, or where some violence might even have taken place. My wife is psych – That is to say, she's terribly sensitive, and something like this is very bad for her. It must be stopped.'

He stood there glaring, and now wished that he had sat down, as he had been bade, for he felt that his position was suddenly not quite as clear as he had thought it to be – and this was immediately confirmed by Mrs Maitland's next question.

She asked courteously, 'Has anyone told you such a thing, Mr Murchison? Have the children?'

Mr Murchison was only a medium-sized shark – no twenty-foot monster. He was about five foot eight, thin, but the eyes set into his narrow face contained about the same amount of malevolence that one reads into the expressions in photographs of those man-eaters.

'No, but it's all over the block. Everyone's talking about

it. It's upsetting everyone. You ought to know better than to let children start rumours of that nature. Cellars where bodies have been buried . . .'

Mrs Maitland's glance went to her three children, who were all shaking their heads emphatically in the negative.

'There's a cellar,' said Miranda, 'but no bodies.' Her eyes turned upward for a moment as she concentrated hard to see whether she might have been wrong in not feeling any bodies in the cellar. It suddenly sounded like a splendid idea, but nothing came, and she was honest, and concluded, 'There aren't any bodies. There never were. And we never said so.'

'Well,' said Mr Murchison, 'I only know what the Milburns and the Osgoods have been saying – and I suspect you'll be hearing from the owners or the Superintendent shortly unless this is brought to an end immediately.'

Mrs Maitland's patience was beginning to wear thin. 'Come, come, Mr Murchison,' she said. 'I'm sorry if you've been put out. My children have simply been playing an imaginary game about a house that was here before this block went up. I'm afraid they have disturbed two or three of the tenants, but –'

'Disturbed!' Mr Murchison interrupted angrily, once more back on safer ground. 'Disrupted, more like. Why, these flats will never be the same again the way things are going.'

Mrs Maitland felt compelled to turn a reproachful frown upon her children, which caused Miranda to break out: 'But, Mummy, we can't *help* it. There *was* a house here, and people *did* live in it. I mean for ages there have always been people who lived somewhere before somebody else lived there.'

Mrs Maitland's mind suddenly turned to thoughts of vanished civilizations and ancient cities built layer upon layer, each upon the ruins of the last, and she had to veer sharply away from this concept which Miranda's words had brought to her and try to see what could be done, first of all to placate Mr Murchison and secondly to get rid of him.

'It seems to me, Mr Murchison,' she said, 'that you are making a good deal out of not very much, if you don't mind me saying so. And I might add that in our home children are not accustomed to being sworn at. They haven't bothered you. It is you who have come ringing our doorbell, and as far as the house that was here goes I am sure that there is no way it could possibly affect either you or your wife. This is a large enough block, and if it will be of any comfort to her, you might tell Mrs Murchison that your flat does not in any way touch upon it. Houses, you know, weren't all that big.'

'Oh, but it does, actually.' It had slipped out from Miranda. She hadn't meant to contradict her mother, but in her mind she carried not only the complete plan of the House but the layout of every floor or every portion of a flat that impinged upon its three stories. 3D was definitely a part.

And thereupon Roddy took his revenge. In addition to the child's instinctive recognition of a thoroughly unpleasant person from his mother's attitude and what she had said, he had now gathered that his *amour propre* had been violated. He was all ready for Mr Murchison.

'It was in your bedroom,' he said, 'where a little boy slept. A man came in – he had a big knife – he got the knife from the kitchen. He was going to kill the little boy in case he made any noise. The man put the knife into the little boy and there was blood all over. There was blood over everything, and the man too. That's how they caught him, because he had so much blood on him. And the little boy died. It was in all the papers.'

'My God!' said Mr Murchison. 'Now do you see what I mean? If my wife . . .'

Roddy had simply been borrowing from a somewhat grisly affair which had been in the newspapers quite recently, in which a demented father had killed his entire family, but Mr Murchison was quite taken in by it.

'My God!' he repeated.

'Roddy!' exclaimed Mrs Maitland. 'Michael! Miranda! Really!'

She looked to the unspeaking Michael to destroy this bit of arrant nonsense from Roddy, but he only regarded her with pained silence. Of course it was nonsense, and no such scene in a bedroom had ever been assigned by them to the House. But solidarity demanded that Roddy be supported.

Mr Murchison's eyes were popping again, and he was looking more like a shark than ever as he repeated yet again, 'My God!' Then he added, 'In cold blood? Where our bedroom is? My wife always said there was a strangeness about that room . . .'

Mrs Maitland felt herself caught up in something over which she felt she had suddenly lost control, and it made her angry. She said sharply, 'Children! I forbid this. You are to tell Mr Murchison at once that this whole thing is a make-up – that there is not a word of truth in it. Tell him it has nothing whatsoever to do with his bedroom or anything else.'

But they remained stubbornly silent, only exchanging quick glances.

Mrs Maitland had no way of knowing that Miranda was simply furious with Roddy, and when they were alone he was going to catch it for intruding upon Miranda's function as Chief Witch. If anybody was going to say what had or had not happened in any part of the House it was she.

Nevertheless, according to their own private code of living, which demanded that Roddy not be let down in front of such an obviously unpleasant character, Miranda relented to the point of saying, 'Well, actually not the entire bedroom. Only just one side.'

Mr Murchison pounced upon this. 'Oh, only one side, eh? Which side?'

'By the window,' said Miranda, and hoped for the best.

'Where my wife's bed is,' said Mr Murchison bitterly. 'She'll never close an eye.' He looked wildly about the room for a moment, searching for an exit line, and said, 'You'll be hearing from me again. This may be a matter for a solicitor.' Then he turned and stormed out of the front door so that the chain rattled as he shut it.

Although they were separated by the chairs on which they sat, and at some distance from one another, the three children drew together spiritually into a battle line of defence against what was obviously going to come. Either the storm when their mother really was angry and *almost* lost her temper, or the much more difficult one when she was hurt and sad with them.

It was to be the latter once again. 'Children,' she almost whispered, 'have you any idea of the harm you may be doing to innocent people? This poor woman . . .'

'But, Mummy,' Michael was the first to protest, 'how can we be blamed for something we haven't done? We've never even spoken to Mr and Mrs Murchison. Whoever's upset her or him or them both, it's not us – more likely others trying to home in on our game. Well, not *game* –' he quickly corrected himself, but was promptly interrupted by Miranda.

'Besides, it's Roddy who's really been upset,' she pleaded urgently. 'That man was *so* nasty to him. Roddy was just trying to get his own back, that's all – and the horrid creature asked for it.'

Roddy, silent for now, nodded in agreement and thanks.

Michael saw the opportunity for a swift divertive sally. 'Anyway, Mummy,' he said, 'Mr Murchison doesn't have to *tell* his wife about the room or the bed or anything that could have happened, does he?'

The combined offensive was more convincing than any of the children could have expected, for Mrs Maitland very well knew that Mr Murchison not only had to tell his wife, he could hardly wait. If she knew anything about this specimen, he was the type of man who, under the guise of sympathy and indignation, positively delighted in passing along bad news, upsetting and torturing people. And from all that she had been able to gather from what Mr Murchison had dropped, Mrs Murchison was not a much more agreeable character: an hysterical woman, who ruled her husband and made life miserable for everyone, getting her own way by claiming affinity with the supernatural.

Miranda said, 'He could move the bed.'

Roddy was experiencing just the faintest entering wedge of discomfort. He was still in the period of his life when fantasy far outweighed fact, but he was also at the age when he had encountered the lie and the penalties one could incur therewith, and so there were moments when he was not entirely certain about the dividing line between the two. With an older brother and sister to guide him, he knew that their principle, particularly in dealing with adults, was 'better be safe than sorry'. And so he tried to soften the blow.

'The man didn't really kill the little boy,' he said. 'He was only pretending. He had the blood in a bag, and when he went away the little boy wasn't dead any more.'

Mrs Maitland now knew that there had been no truth in Roddy's original statement, and had to remind herself that she was of course equally aware that there was none in any of this farrago.

She said gravely, 'I want you to listen carefully to me while I try to explain something very important. There are certain areas of life, or situations, where it is difficult for parents to meet their children, and this is one of them, because whenever we have forbidden you to do something we have always tried to tell you why, so that you would understand. But this is one of those instances where perhaps it is not possible because you are not yet old enough to understand the explanation – and perhaps there's not even one, except that, being older, we understand things that you don't – and so I'm afraid I must forbid you to play this game any longer. I think I know why you are playing it. We've had bad luck with this wretched weather, and Daddy and I too wish that we all might be living together in an old house somewhere, surrounded by acres and acres, and with a brook running through, or perhaps close to the sea. But we don't, and with Daddy's job we can't – not yet anyway. There we all have that much of a meeting ground. But you see I'm sure you are hurting people in ways you could never know and who do not deserve to be hurt. And so I am telling you that you must stop at once. Can you do this for me? Will you do this for me? And in return I'll not mention it any further to Daddy.'

The three children regarded one another for a moment, the two older ones in tune, but since it had been Miranda's project from the beginning Michael let her voice what was in their minds.

'Mummy, we would,' she began. 'We could. We'd stop it in an instant. I mean, right now. But . . .'

'But what, Miranda?' Mrs Maitland asked.

'The others.'

'I don't understand. What others?'

'Well, the people who are living in our House,' Miranda explained. 'You see, perhaps we could put it out of our heads – or try to. But grown-up people can't. Once something is put in their minds it stays there.'

Mrs Maitland felt utterly helpless, and hoped her husband would come home soon and the subject could be changed over a drink and a good dinner.

CHAPTER XI

Houses New and Old

Eleven o'clock in the morning was the quietest time in Melton Court. Everybody who was going out had gone and had not yet had time to come back.

Having promised their mother they would not go ringing any more doorbells, the Maitland children felt at liberty to combine their investigations if they didn't interfere with anyone else, so they went strolling through the lobby on the ground floor with a determined anonymity. Not altogether aimlessly though: Michael just happened to have the plan of the ground floor of the House in his pocket, and it was when he stopped to take it out that he said, 'As long as there's nobody around we might as well see where Daddy's study would be and what it is like.'

'Where would that be?' asked Miranda, peering over his shoulder at the plan as they both orientated themselves.

Michael turned the plan around so that the front door was behind them and the main entrance hall was where they were standing.

'Down the corridor there, I suppose,' he said, pointing left past the lift. 'And we know where that goes. It leads to the writing-room.'

'That's funny,' said Miranda. 'It matches. That's where Daddy would be writing. Let's go and look.'

They were, of course, familiar with every nook and corner of the lobby: Mr Thompson's office and the switch-board, the corridor leading to the ground-floor flats, the waiting-room, with its hotel-type furniture, on one side, and the writing-room on the other, with a single desk and chair, an ink-well that was always dry, a post office kind of pen, and for the rest there were the same chairs and sofas as in the waiting-room, with some dust-catching bric-a-brac and furniture.

The three were inside the room before they noticed that this time it was occupied. Probably for the first time since goodness knows when there was a man at the desk writing.

'Oh, dear,' exclaimed Miranda. 'We're bothering someone. We'd better go.'

In their lexicon of prohibitions 'bothering someone' now covered a wider field than ever. They didn't want to upset their mother any more, for she had stuck by them during the visit of that horrid Mr Murchison the evening before.

The person at the desk turned around at this, and said, 'No, no. Come in. This is a public room.'

He was a chunky, powerfully built individual, with a dark complexion, and a cowlick of hair that was almost black falling over a high and rather noble brow. He had a crooked nose, blue jowls, and the most bright and penetrating brown eyes. He was dressed in an old fashioned sack suit with waistcoat to match, and stiff collar and tie. His appearance was Semitic and bristling with a vitality that almost had a mystery about it. The children saw that he had three books on the desk, one of them opened, and that he had obviously been making notes from it.

He regarded them for a moment, and said, 'Did you wish to come here and write perhaps? I have almost finished.'

They liked him at once, not because of the aura of strength and wisdom that he radiated but because he was as polite to them as he would have been to any grown-ups.

Michael matched him in courtesy. 'No thank you, sir. We only came in to have a look.'

'Well then, by all means do so,' he gestured, adding, 'Do you live here?'

'Yes, we do,' Miranda replied. 'On the first floor – Flat 1A. We are the Maitlands.'

At this the man turned about as though fully prepared to abandon his work and looked at them with renewed interest.

'Ah, you are the Maitlands,' he said. 'I have heard so much about you these last few days, and in fact I am most pleased to meet you. I live here too. My name is Jacob Bettauer.'

Now that they thought of it they had seen him before, and no doubt at some time or other he had seen them as well, but when you lived in a block like Melton Court you could see all kinds of people and never know whether they were visitors or tenants unless you made enquiry.

In fact now Michael remembered noticing on the panel of glass-fronted letter boxes the name 'Dr and Mrs Jacob Bettauer' and the flat number, 6B. There was no clue, of course, as to what kind of a doctor he was, but he was also out of the range of their interest. Sixth-floor tenants in no way could be said to impinge upon the House, since they only hovered in the air space above it.

Nevertheless, Michael said, 'Oh, I know. It's *Doctor* Bettauer. I mean it says so on your –'

'That's right,' said the man.

'Is it for sick people?' Michael enquired.

'In a sense,' Dr Bettauer replied. 'Though not in the one in which you are thinking. The term today covers a multitude of mischiefs. I teach a great deal.'

Even after many years with a reputation he was still shy about the fact that he dealt mainly with the various aspects and vagaries of the human mind, which always seemed to upset people and put them instantly on their guard – in itself depressingly revelatory of most of the population's fear that any expert was bound to discover germs of lunacy in them.

Roddy, as usual, went directly to the point of whatever occurred to him. 'Why do you work here instead of in your flat?' he asked.

'Because,' replied Dr Bettauer, 'we have just had a new addition to our family – a baby boy – who has come equipped with a noise-maker for which the walls of these flats were never designed. There is no escape. So I come down here.'

'Oh, dear,' said Miranda. 'Then we really mustn't disturb you.'

'No, no,' Dr Bettauer shook his head. 'Not at all.' Then he asked, 'What exactly is it you were looking for?'

'Our House,' Roddy answered immediately. 'You're writing in my Daddy's study.'

The half-amused expression on Dr Bettauer's face gave way to the lighting up of intelligence. 'Ah,' he said. 'Of course, the house. That house. So you *are* the three who have turned this block upside down, as it were?'

It wasn't really spoken as an accusation, but Michael, as the eldest and in charge, felt that he ought to get in his defence at once. 'But we haven't done anything at all,' he said. 'We've just –'

'Frightened some people out of their wits,' Dr Bettauer took over. 'Made others laugh, made some sad, some angry, some unhappy, others uncertain and uncomfortable. The block is seething like an ant heap that has been stirred up with a stick. I am really most obliged to you. It has been most entertaining as well as instructive to observe. Now, since it is you who are responsible for all this, suppose you come in and tell me what you know about houses.'

'Do you mean about our House?' asked Miranda.

'If you like to begin there,' said Dr Bettauer. And he seemed so interested and natural that they trusted him. They trooped in, Miranda and Roddy seating themselves on a blue moire-covered sofa, while Michael took a chair.

'It's only about the House that was here before,' Miranda began. 'I mean, for instance, it stood where we are sitting now . . .' And then she launched into the telling, to which Dr Bettauer, his hands now folded, listened with whole-hearted attention and without interruption.

Of course, Miranda's story did not include their investigations into the area covered by the House, nor their divisions of activity – though Dr Bettauer would have been one of the few adults who would, or at least might, have understood these – but for the moment they were keeping their two worlds apart.

However, she did feel that some kind of an explanation was due for their general explorations, not to mention their particular concern with the dwelling which they had conjured into being, and so Miranda concluded with, 'And so in a way, you see, it's like *living* in a house almost. I mean, our part of it, for instance, on the first floor, is where all the main bedrooms are. Then on the floor above us is the nursery and Nanny's room and the playroom. Well, and for the other parts, if you know what a house is like, you can pretend that it's still there – and, of course, if you pretend hard enough . . .'

'It *is*,' concluded Dr Bettauer. 'Tell me, have you ever lived in a house?'

'No,' said Michael, 'but we've been in quite a few.'

Dr Bettauer nodded. 'I suppose you would all like to live in a house really, though, would you not?'

To this none of them replied, since they felt it was so self-evident from their fascination with the House and everything connected with it that it was more a statement than a query, which indeed it was – though the query followed.

Turning to Roddy, Dr Bettauer said, 'Well, young man, why do you want to live in a house?'

'His name is Roderick,' said Miranda. 'Roddy.'

'Well then, Roddy, why would you rather live in a house?'

Roddy gave some thought to his reply, as he had learned to do when asked a direct question. 'Because then nobody could ever find me if I didn't want them to. I could hide.'

'And you?'

'I'm Miranda . . .' as Dr Bettauer's look was now directed at her. 'And that's Michael.'

Now that it came down to something concrete, Miranda realized that she had never really thought of any specific reasons, because there were such a great number of them. Didn't everybody want to live in a house with a front door and a cellar and an attic, a garden, stairs and lots and lots of rooms? How could you pick one? Finally, to her surprise, she blurted out, 'Well, you can be cosy inside a house.'

'And you, sir?'

Whether the 'sir' was an acknowledgement of his seniority or simply meant that Dr Bettauer had not quite caught his name the first time, it gave Michael a wonderful feeling, and kept him from hurrying his reply. Finally he answered, 'Well, because it would be all ours. Nobody else could get in and bother us if we didn't want them to.'

Dr Bettauer nodded thoughtfully, then, leaning back in his chair, said, 'How very interesting. Between the three of you you have just about all the reasons why prehistoric man, when he came down out of the trees, provided himself with a shelter. In other words, began the slow evolution of the house – an evolution that continues even today.'

He turned to Roddy. 'Hide, you said. Yes, you are right. Quite right. Hide from danger, hide from prying eyes, hide from things bigger and stronger than you, who want to make a meal out of you – and, I suppose, when one was your age, Hide and Seek. Isn't that what you were thinking?'

'No,' Roddy replied simply. 'Just hiding.'

'Houses,' said Dr Bettauer half to himself. 'The desperate need at times not to be seen, not even to have anyone know one is there. To lock the door, pull down the blinds, put out the lights and be able to face only oneself. To know that nothing can suddenly come upon you. Do you know what the first house was?' he asked, addressing himself to Michael now.

'It was a cave, wasn't it, sir? Didn't they call the people cavemen?'

'Exactly,' Dr Bettauer nodded. 'When man started to walk erect and use that slowly developing brain and cleverly articulated thumb, he was terrified of the dark, for out of the dark things could jump on to his back. That is why a shudder takes place down the spine – that vulnerable spot on our bodies whence the attack cannot be seen.'

All three children twitched involuntarily as they remembered how at some time or other they had been in fear of exactly that: something jumping on to their back out of the dark.

'I'm not afraid of the dark,' Roddy protested.

Michael would not have this. 'Oh, yes you are,' he said. 'Why does Mummy let you have a night light by your bed?'

'So if I wake up I can see,' Roddy replied logically.

'One day,' Dr Bettauer continued, 'a member of a primitive tribe – perhaps his name was He-Who-Is-Frightened-Of-Things-In-The-Dark – found an empty cave in the rocks, some cleft or fissure abandoned by an animal. He went in there and felt good because three quarters of his fears had been removed. Since the cave narrowed to a point, nothing could jump from behind, and since it had two walls nor could anything leap upon him from either side. For the first time he spent a night in which he was not wholly afraid. The next day he brought his family.'

'And he had a house,' said Miranda excitedly.

'No, not yet. Almost, but not quite. For something of importance was missing.' He regarded them to see if they would guess, but they remained silent, watching him and waiting, each one of them totally at ease with this kindly man.

'The front door,' he said. 'They were safe from three sides, but not from that last important one, the fourth. So in time they made one.'

'How could they?' asked Michael. 'Since they'd never heard about a door, or really knew how to make anything.'

'Fire,' Dr Bettauer revealed. 'They built a fire in the opening of the cave. They had learned its power and the fear it inspired, and now those hungry, prying eyes of the night on the other side, and the snufflings and snarls and growls no longer worried them, because no creature would attempt to cross that burning threshold. And so they were enclosed on all four sides, and over their heads they had a roof.'

'Now it was a house, wasn't it?' cried a fascinated Miranda.

'By night, yes. But not yet by day. For still there were the prying eyes of others who were not afraid of the fire, having learned its ways.'

'People?' Miranda queried tentatively.

Dr Bettauer nodded and replied with a trace of sadness in his voice, 'People. For when man became man, in addition to all the enemies of savage beasts surrounding him he created yet another and more deadly one: himself. His house was not yet finished. And so he made a day-time door.'

'But how?' asked Michael. 'I thought that he couldn't . . .'

'True,' smiled Dr Bettauer. 'But he could at least begin to think and reason in sequence, which, as you probably know, along with our thumb, has been the secret of our development. He found himself secured on three sides by impregnable stone walls. He therefore made a fourth by rolling boulders and piling up rocks in the entrance to the cave. He roofed over the top and covered the narrow entrance with skins, and when he wanted to block it up he shut the door by moving the boulders into the space.'

He turned to Michael. 'And note that in essentials the design has not changed over hundreds of thousands of years. Four stone walls, a roof overhead, a front door that can be locked – everything else is just a refinement.'

'I'd like to live in a cave,' said Roddy.

'No, you wouldn't,' said Miranda. 'It couldn't have been very comfortable.'

'But what about in places where there weren't any caves,' Michael asked, 'like in the forests or the jungles? What happened there?'

'Man had to invent or make artificial caves. The need for shelter, a house, a third skin beyond his own and those of wild animals that he wore for warmth burned so fiercely within this new kind of specimen trying to make his way, beset with danger on all sides, that he achieved it.'

'But what did he have to copy? How did he learn?' Michael asked.

This fallow morning was turning out better than they had ever expected. Dr Bettauer not only took them seriously –

he knew things about houses that had happened a long time ago, and yet somehow, without their ever realizing it, managed to fit in the things they had thought or felt about their own House.

'Oh,' replied Dr Bettauer, 'not too difficult. A copse of bushes held together by vines or thorns into which they could retreat when pursued. A stand of bamboo as solid as the wall of a stockade. Why, some primitive men even built their houses in trees.'

Miranda could not contain herself. 'Children have tree houses, don't they? There's a tree walk and a tree house at the fun fair at Battersea Park. We went there. Oh,I wished I could have lived in it.'

'Naturally,' Dr Bettauer assented. 'And so would we all. But to find food, eventually man had to come down out of the trees. And therefore he built his huts on the ground in forest clearings so he could be aware of what might be approaching.'

Dr Bettauer suddenly spread his hands wide as he added, 'And do you know, in the main, over all those years, that basic materials really haven't changed *very* much. The hut is the parent form of all timber houses, built of wood and stuck up with plaster – while every house of brick or stone or masonry stems from the cave dwelling.'

There was a considerable silence as the children thought things over, and then Miranda began another question: 'When I said that I wanted a house because it would be cosy, you said –'

'Yes, it's really a wonderful word, because it covers so much and is so very right because of what it comes from – the Gaelic word *cosack*, meaning "abiding in hollows, full of holes or crevices, sheltered, a hollow, a crevice". Well, there you are, right back in your cave. It also means comfortable, easy, contented. And then the word has a friend, another which is different but really almost like it, except that it has even more to say – for "snug" means compact, close, secret, private, sheltered or protected. All things that one finds and feels inside the four walls of any kind of house. And then again it means neat, trim, comfortable. Where "snug" implies tremendous closeness or security, "cosy" suggests warmth, shelter and ease. "Snug" and "cosy" are words that you can put about your shoulders like a mantle and be warm and secure inside.'

Miranda gave a little wriggle of delight, as though she were fitting herself into a soft, fur-lined cloak, and said, 'Oh, yes. That's exactly it.'

'In one way or another everybody feels a need or a yearning for – a wish, a necessity, a hunger for – everything that a house can mean to a human being: shelter, safety, snugness, cosiness, the nest, the family home.'

Suddenly Miranda saw Dr Bettauer's eyes were watering. It made her want to put her arms around him and hug him. But she felt her brothers wouldn't approve – and, after all, they had only just met him. She realized, though, that at that moment he too was actually wishing he could be living in a house, with a study of his own where he could shut the door and no one could intrude upon his thoughts.

Even as she realized, the hall clock chimed and Dr Bettauer looked up red-eyed at it. 'My goodness,' he said, 'it will be lunch time. I must go. Well, perhaps some day you will all live in a house – a real one. I hope so, my children. Goodbye.' And he rose, then, with a passing bow, not looking at any one of them again, left the room.

'What a sad and fascinating man,' sighed Miranda.

'I could just listen to him for hours on end,' said Michael, still not moving.

'I think we just did,' said Roddy, as he shuffled off the sofa. 'I don't know about you, but I'm starving.'

CHAPTER XII

House of Many Colours

Sometimes when he wasn't busy, Michael, Miranda and Roddy would drop in upon Mr Thompson, the Superintendent of Melton Court, at his office on the ground floor.

The door was always open, and if Mr Thompson was seated at his desk anyone could call in at any time. In fact it was his boast, and he carried it out as well, that his door was open twenty-four hours night and day. This did not mean that he slept with the door of his private flat, one of those on the ground floor, also open, but if there was an emergency he could be called on the telephone no matter what the time.

Thus, when the three lingered outside his door that afternoon, he cried, 'Hello! Hello! Come in if you like. Now what have you all been up to? Not been going round upsetting any more of my tenants with this house story of yours, have you?'

Hesitantly for once, the children stood at the door, reluctant to enter what threatened to become the headmaster's study.

Rising and striding round his desk, hands plunged deep in his trouser pockets, and stopping just before them, legs astride, Mr Thompson boomed down, 'Well?' with an almost grin in his challenging eyes.

Cautiously, Miranda looked up then spoke up in protest, 'Certainly not, Mr Thompson. We don't go round like that any more. Really we don't. But it isn't a story – and it isn't our fault, is it – that there was a house here before?'

'*Before*, no,' Mr Thompson conceded. Then, after a pause, he lowered his head and his voice to ask half playfully, 'And so where do you reckon we all might be now then?'

Miranda and Michael exchanged that glance of suspicion that crosses between all young people when suddenly grown-ups start questioning them on what they choose to call their stories or their games. How far was Mr Thompson to be trusted? Yet they were after information, and so Mr Thompson had to be trusted. Anyway, he was nice really, he was kind, and he always had time for them.

Miranda signalled Michael that he could tell, and, knowing, as he did, every floor plan by heart now, he answered authoritatively, 'In the breakfast-room. It opened off the main dining-room – but that's where the waiting-room is in the lobby.'

Miranda added, 'It was – I mean, it is – a big house, you see, and the breakfast-room looks out over the garden. It was nice there in the morning – sometimes they called it the morning-room. The dining-room was too big just for breakfast, you see.'

Mr Thompson nodded but said nothing.

'*You* don't mind, do you?' Miranda asked.

Mr Thompson reflected, then, hastily at first, replied, 'Me? No. Not at all. But from what I've heard, as I told you, several of the tenants are considerably put out. You see, they don't like the idea of living in someone else's house – and I think that one or two don't like the notion of living in a house at all.'

'Is Mrs Potter upset?' Michael asked, in a voice slightly overloaded with innocence.

'Ah!' said Mr Thompson. 'Old Mrs Potter?'

Mrs Potter was known to one and all in Melton Court as The Witch, because old age had bent her back, dispatched her nose on an errand to meet her chin, ringed her eyes with red, added unsightly hairs to her face, whitened her locks, and enflamed her disposition. She bore the burden of too many years, suffered fools not only ungladly but not at all, and maintained her freedom of action with a fierceness that belied her actual strength. She walked with a cane, but wanted the arm of no one, nobody else, for the few steps to and from her door.

'She isn't really a witch, is she?' asked Miranda, already clear in her own mind about the difference between the kind of witch Mrs Potter was supposed to be when people referred to her as such and the kind of witch she herself was styled now: a Chief Witch, responsible for the affairs of the House.

'No, of course she isn't,' Mr Thompson replied. 'She's just a very lonely and aged woman who has outlived her time.'

'But why is she always so angry?' Michael asked. 'The other day, when Harry Martin was on the door, she came in loaded down with a shopping bag, he offered to take it for her and she threatened to hit him with her stick.'

'Did she?' said Mr Thompson. 'I suppose that was because Harry insulted her.'

'But he didn't,' cried Miranda. 'I was there. He didn't say anything. He just went to take her bag.'

'Yes,' said Mr Thompson. 'And that was the insult, of course, because it implied that she was old and infirm and couldn't look after herself. And when the spirit is still there that's greatly insulting, you know. Now Tim Ryan wouldn't have made that mistake . . .'

Tim Ryan, the children knew, was the Head Porter of Melton Court, while Harry Martin was his assistant as well as the daytime switchboard operator.

'Tim would merely have said, "Good morning, Mrs Potter. Well now, and I see you've had a good morning's shopping," then he'd have kept a sharp eye on her as she went down those three steps from the door. He's still a fast lad, is Tim, and if she'd tottered or anything he'd have been at her side like a flash to have her by the arm, saying, "Drat that loose tile. I've been after them now to have it fixed for over a week", and she'd have scolded him about the tile and gone off quite content, with her dignity undamaged. For you know that is really all that is left to a very old person: dignity.'

'How old is she?' Miranda asked.

'Well, I couldn't tell you to the day,' Mr Thompson scratched his head, 'but I believe it is ninety-six or perhaps even ninety-seven.'

'Golly!' said Roddy. 'That's almost a hundred.'

Miranda did some quick mental arithmetic. 'Goodness, if she is ninety-six then she must have been born when Victoria was still the Queen.'

Mr Thompson nodded and smiled. 'I understand she's had quite an exciting life – travelled a great deal in foreign countries, and seen about all there is to see.'

'Then hasn't she anybody at all?' asked Miranda.

'Nobody that I know of,' said Mr Thompson. 'Only a lawyer. Sometimes she phones me up in the middle of the night or early in the morning – three or four o'clock.'

'What does she say?' Michael asked. 'What does she want?'

'Well,' said Mr Thompson, 'I pick up the phone and for a time there's quite a long silence at the other end of it, and then I hear her voice saying, "Are you there, Mr Thompson?" And when I reply that I am she might ask, "Is everything all right, Mr Thompson?" and I say I believe it is – why, has anything disturbed her? She might say she heard a noise outside, and I might say, "It's probably just cats, Mrs Potter. It's nothing to worry about." "Oh, yes," she'll say, "those cats. I suppose it's because I'm not sleeping too well these nights." So naturally then I'd say, "Not sleeping too well? Sorry to hear that, Mrs Potter. What seems to be the trouble?" Well, the trouble could be anything. Too hot, too cold, the humidity, a storm brewing perhaps, and then she'd remember a similar time once in Bombay or it could be Hong Kong, Singapore, San Francisco or Melbourne, where she'd been affected by the weather. And, of course, my having been there too at some time or other, in my Navy days, I could say, "That's right, the barometer there could do some very funny things, couldn't it, Ma'am?" Then we'd have a bit of a chat about the place.'

'What, at three or four o'clock in the morning?' said Michael.

'Yes, of course,' Mr Thompson nodded. 'Exactly then, because that's when she needs it most – when she wakes up at that hour and she's lonely. A bit of a chat, and when she hangs up I'll know that she'll be off to sleep again.'

Then suddenly he asked, 'But what made you ask about Mrs Potter?'

Another swift glance was exchanged between Miranda and Michael at this example of the odd and sometimes threatening perspicacity of grown-ups, who seem not to have heard or paid very much attention to something and then suddenly, out of the blue, will come back to it. So Mr Thompson had been wondering all the time about what their interest was in Mrs Potter.

Roddy stood twisting and untwisting a piece of string from his pocket, and pretended he wasn't listening.

Because she saw that her elder brother was uncertain, Miranda took over, feeling that the truth was called for. 'Well,' she said, 'really it's about the House. We know what part of the House she lives in – I mean, what was there – but we were just wondering what it was like now, and what she was like and whether she might be pleased. It could even be kind of company, couldn't it, if she knew she was living in a house at the same time?'

Mr Thompson frowned ominously. Then, before he could answer, the telephone rang on the desk behind him, and as he turned and went over to pick it up Miranda said, 'Oh, dear, we're bothering you. We'd better go. Thank you so much. Come along, Roddy.' And the three walked back into the main lobby.

They stood there for a few moments. Miranda filled with a strange sadness at the story of the old lady who telephoned in the middle of the night for a chat, and who, in her long – so long it was almost impossible to imagine – lifetime had been in so many places and seen so many things. In her young breast was a sudden ache and a wish that somehow, as Mr Thompson was doing, she might comfort the old lady. That curious bond that exists so often between the very young and the very old was exercising its tug though she did not even know Mrs Potter.

'What shall we do now?' asked Roddy.

Michael's thoughts had been upon Mrs Potter too, but on a different wavelength from Miranda's, as the interpreter of the House who had transformed it into something physical on paper. His interests extended beyond the visionary.

'It wouldn't matter,' he said, 'if we went past her door, would it? And then we could go on down to the end of the corridor and see what else is there. That wouldn't hurt anybody, would it? Maybe that would be where the House ends, if it's where I think it is.'

'All right,' said Miranda. 'But we mustn't make any noise.'

It was not the thought of the possible boundary line of her House that interested her just now as much as passing by Mrs Potter's door, which could bring her for that moment closer to the old lady. And she wondered whether she was in or out in that pouring rain and lashing wind, refusing to yield to them any more than she would to a helping arm.

'Come on,' Michael urged. 'We mustn't let the old witch catch us.'

'Would she eat us?' Roddy asked.

'At one bite,' said Michael. 'You just hang on to me, Roddy, and tread softly.'

It was a pleasant, shivery game, trying soundlessly to pass by a door behind which something menacing might be imagined to lurk.

Suddenly the door opened a crack, they were peered at momentarily, and then it closed again.

They were petrified, not knowing whether to go on, stand still or run. They had been caught – but at what? Nothing really, and yet both the older children were aware that the door had been off the latch, as it were, so that it could be opened as silently as they were trying to stalk, otherwise they would have heard the click of the door handle. And then, before they could break out of the spell, the door opened again and Mrs Potter stood in the opening.

She had a black knitted shawl upon her shoulders, and a black bow on the top of her head, the white hair of which was so sparse it barely covered the pink of her skull. She was tiny – smaller than the children had imagined – and all bent over with her nose hooked like a beak and the black shawl like black wings. She reminded the children of a buzzard.

'What do you want?' she asked, her voice, so used up by the years, hardly more than a dry whisper.

Strangely enough, Miranda found that instead of giving way to panic she was wondering why the old lady's door had been just that tiny fraction ajar. Had she been standing behind it, sitting behind it, waiting or listening? And if so, for what? Even though they really hadn't been making a sound, was her hearing still so acute that she had detected them?

'We wondered whether we might have a chat,' Miranda said. And wherever that came from she would not know to her dying day – or the courage to say it, at which her older brother was to marvel later. The 'chat' part, of course, remained from their talk with Mr Thompson, but still Miranda was surprised herself at how calmly she had been able to reply.

'A chat?' said Mrs Potter. 'Why?'

'It's still raining,' Miranda replied. 'It's been raining for days. It's Easter hols, you know. There's nowhere to go and nothing to do.' And then she added, 'We're the Maitlands from upstairs. That's my brother, Michael – and then Roddy – and I'm Miranda.'

'I see,' said Mrs Potter, and her seeing took place out of those red-rimmed, ancient eyes which reminded Michael even more of a picture he'd seen of a vulture with its bald head settled between its shoulders. He was upset and ill at

ease, and not a little frightened, yet at the same time excited
by the feeling that they all might be on the threshold of
some kind of adventure.

'I see,' Mrs Potter repeated. 'Well then, come in. Come
in.' And she opened the door wide to let them into the
entrance hall.

Miranda, with no fear at all within her, entered first,
with Michael following, but Roddy hung back.

'Well, young man?' said Mrs Potter. 'What's the matter?
Are you frightened?'

The shock itself magnetized Roddy, who found himself
stepping in behind Michael before he was even ready.

The flat was like nothing very much that one could
describe or remember, except that by its simplicity and
neutrality one could come to the idea that perhaps Mrs
Potter was not anxious to remember too much.

In the minds of the two older children, Mr Thompson's
references to the far-off places discussed in his middle-of-
the-night chats with Mrs Potter suggested rooms full of
curios and souvenirs of world travels. There were none of
these here. The furnishings were neat, simple and tidy:
chairs, sofa, tables, matching curtains, but all in a neutral
shade of beige: comfortable but expressive of nothing.
And it was this nothingness, except for the photographs on
the tables and on the mantel over the usual fake fireplace,
that puzzled Miranda. An older and more experienced
person might have gathered that because of its colourless-
ness and neutrality it was almost like a hotel room. It was a
lived-in apartment, and yet somehow not yet wholly so, as
though the inhabitant was merely pausing there for a little
on the way to somewhere else and hence had surrounded
herself with only the minimum of keepsakes or personal
articles of value or memory.

In the midst of this stood Mrs Potter at home, an alien
figure, and yet, as Miranda regarded her with curiosity, and
that same stirring of affection she had experienced even
before seeing her, she saw in the tiny bent figure all the
dignity of which Mr Thompson had spoken – and some-

thing else as well. Miranda could find no words for it, since what it was that animated the old lady was the grace of courage, and of this Miranda had had no experience, though the perfume of it reached her.

'Sit down, all of you,' Mrs Potter gestured, and herself went to an armchair. In her own surroundings she seemed less bent over, more active and at ease. She lowered herself into the chair, drawing her shawl about her. The children obeyed, Michael choosing the sofa, Roddy a straight-backed chair with his legs not touching the ground, and his large eyes gravely taking in his surroundings, while Miranda settled herself in her favourite spot in any room, on the floor with her legs curled up underneath, her skirts neatly pulled down over her knees.

It was one thing to have said bravely that they had come for a chat, but quite another to break the silence that now enveloped them all, or to stop from looking.

Mrs Potter, managing even a slightly mischievious air as she looked from one to the other, said, 'I see you are looking at my photographs. No, please, don't be embarrassed. I've always been intrigued by other people's photographs myself. Now that one over there was my father.' The one she indicated was of a tall, handsome man in some strange kind of dress uniform that they had never seen before: a frock coat, much gold braid, and many medals, in breeches and white stockings, and shoes with buckles. 'He was an ambassador. When I was a young girl we travelled with him a great deal as he moved from post to post. It was a habit I was never able to break. I have travelled hence all my life.'

On the table next to her, silver-framed, was the picture of an equally tall young man, and the resemblance to his grandfather was unmistakable. He, too, was in uniform, but his was khaki puttees, a leather jacket, and a rakish officer's cap. On his left breast was a pair of wings.

'My son, Peter,' said Mrs Potter. 'Lieutenant Peter Potter. Was killed in World War One. Have you ever heard of Baron von Richthofen?' Mrs Potter gave a barely audible sigh, and added, 'I suppose not. I have a letter from him saying he was sorry that he had to kill my son.'

After this there was such a stillness in the room that the children hardly dared to breathe. Michael did remember something he'd heard or read somewhere. Of course, Baron von Richthofen was the Red Baron, the famous German flyer in the First World War.

'Those,' said Mrs Potter, indicating a group of a pleasant-looking man of about forty with a lovely woman some years younger and two handsome children of approximately Michael's and Miranda's ages, a boy and a girl, 'were my grandchildren, my daughter and her husband. My daughter was already widowed when she and the children were killed during the blitz in the last war.'

Close on hand, on a table beside her, was a small oval miniature, painted upon ivory, in a gold frame. It showed a fair-haired, blue-eyed young boy on the threshold of manhood. He had a fine, open, charming smile. 'This was my husband,' said Mrs Potter. 'Of course, I have many other pictures of him as well, but this is my favourite.'

'And now,' she said, 'that I have met your wonderings, supposing that you satisfy mine. What is it you wanted to chat about?'

There was another silence as none of them knew how or who was to begin, until Michael received the silent signal from Miranda.

He sat forward on the sofa and began, 'Well, you see, it was Miranda here who discovered about the House that was here before. I mean, the one that was where this block is now with people living in it, and . . .' Here he hesitated just a second or two. 'And which is still here.'

Mrs Potter cocked her head to one side and her bright eyes were fastened on the girl. 'The house that was here before,' she repeated, and the interest awakened in her quite seemed to transform her and bring even a curious echo of youth to her wrinkled features. 'And how did you discover this?'

'I didn't really discover it,' Miranda replied. 'I just knew.'

Mrs Potter nodded and said, 'Yes, of course.' And now she no longer reminded Michael of a vulture but rather a tiny sparrow almost disappearing into the armchair, but pert and interested.

'I just woke up one morning,' Miranda explained, 'and there it was – just as though I'd always known about it.'

Mrs Potter seemed lost in reflection for a moment, and then the strangest expression came over her face. It was almost as if for an instant another Miranda was looking out from behind her eyes, and, as one child speaking to another, she said, 'Do you mean it? Are we really? Where are we? What part of it? Tell me all about it.'

At a nod from Miranda, Michael said, 'Well, actually this room is the laundry, but next door, where your bedroom is, is the staff sitting-room.'

'You see, it was a very big house,' Roddy added. 'And we were just going past your flat to see where it ended.'

Then the whole story came out between the three of them, from the very beginning of the morning when Miranda first told them about the House, about their dividing up the work of exploring it, the things that had happened to them, how some people, when they found out, had seemed to be pleased and others less so. In short, everything the children knew about it, to all of which Mrs Potter listened in a manner of another child, fascinated by a fairy tale.

When they had done, she said, 'So, I too am living in your house. I am very pleased to do so. More than I can tell you.' And then, in a sudden switch from the trust of a young person to the suspicion of a very old one, she said, 'But how do you know really? How am I to know that what you say is true?'

'Oh,' Miranda replied, 'that's easy. We can show you. Michael has made a plan. Show Mrs Potter, Michael.'

Michael drew the plan of the ground floor of the House from his pocket, spread it open, and they all forgathered at the feet of Mrs Potter, where she looked down upon it. Her cane was beside her chair, and with it she traced and marked the various rooms: drawing-room, hall, the main staircase, the library, the master's study. Then, resting the tip of her staff where Michael had marked the laundry and servants' sitting quarters, she said, 'So here I am,' and seemed to fall into deep thought.

'Oh, dear,' said Miranda. 'Do you mind? You see, we can't help where . . .' And she trailed off, terrified that Mrs Potter might be upset at finding where she was living. Such a very old lady might not like to be told that her bedroom had been the place where the staff relaxed, continued their quarrels, or gossiped about the people upstairs, and her drawing-room where they laundered all the dirty linen of the House.

Her concerned enquiry had brought Mrs Potter out of her reverie, but with a strange reply, almost like one in pain. 'Mind? Living in a house again when I never thought to do so? Ah, no, no! I don't *mind*. I'm *pleased*! *Pleased*! I have always had a house until now . . . So I am all the more delighted to find myself in yours.' Then, quite suddenly and unexpectedly, she asked, 'What colour is it?'

Michael stared at his diagram. 'Colour?' he said. 'By golly. I forget now. You did say, Miranda. Do you remember?'

'Yes,' said Miranda. 'Grey and white, with a maroon-coloured door, and a roof of slate.'

As Miranda described it to her and Michael produced his drawing of the front elevation of the House, Mrs Potter nodded and said, 'Ah, yes. They built lovely houses in the old days. I was born in a Georgian house myself.' And then to Miranda: 'Have you ever been in or lived in a Georgian house?'

'I'm not sure,' said Miranda. 'I don't think so. Perhaps. Actually, we've never lived in any kind of house, ever. We've always lived in a flat, ever since I can remember.'

Mrs Potter nodded, murmuring, 'It doesn't matter.' And then said, 'I've lived in many houses of many colours.'

'Oh,' said Michael. 'Have you? Which? What colours?'

'Any colour?' queried Roddy.

Mrs Potter looked down upon him and said, 'Supposing

you name whatever colour you like and I'll tell you.' Then, taking them all in, she added, 'Each one of you, if you like.'

Roddy thought very hard, then looked up and said, 'Green.'

'Green,' echoed Mrs Potter, and still staring, her hands upon her staff, looked upwards and inwards then said, 'Yes. A green house where we lived in Nagasaki in Japan, with a roof like a pagoda. It was all green tiles on the outside, and it shone like an emerald in the sun. There was a Japanese garden in the back with tiny little foot bridges over lily ponds.'

'Pink,' said Miranda, tentatively. 'I mean really pink all over.'

'Oh, yes,' replied Mrs Potter. 'The Palazzo Necchoni in Venice was painted pink. Of course, there was also the colour of the stone scroll work, but pink was the predominant colour, and I remember how, in a certain light, it could turn the water of the canal in front of it pink too, so that when we arrived in our gondola it was like floating in a rose-coloured pool.'

Now that the game was on, the fun would be to see how difficult one might make it, and so Michael said, 'Purple.'

'Oh, now, purple,' Mrs Potter mused, then softly misquoted before continuing, ' "I never saw a purple house, I never hope to see one . . ." Well, I both saw and lived in one in Shiraz, not far from Tehran in Persia. It was actually of white stucco, but it was beautifully decorated – the walls and over the door and around the windows – in Persian designs, with purple tiles, and we always called it our Purple House. All the carpets had purple in them too.'

Was there no stumping her?

'Brown,' suggested Miranda. 'A real dark, leathery kind of brown.'

Mrs Potter was enjoying the contest now as much as they, and smiled with immediate triumph. 'Not only leathery coloured, but of leather,' she added. 'You would never guess.'

Michael had a go: 'Some kind of peasant hut.'

'Close,' replied Mrs Potter. 'An Indian tepee, near
Flagstaff, Arizona, when I was a very little girl and we were
the guests of the last of the great Indian Chiefs of the Far
West in America.' And then she added, 'But fortunately
only for a few days, because it smelled quite horribly.'

Roddy thought he had her when he said, 'Rainbow
colour.'

Mrs Potter smiled. 'Well, we had a house in Bavaria
once, and there were pictures painted on the outside, very
gay and bright, and in all the colours of the rainbow.
Pictures of peasants and lords and saints, and geraniums all
around the balcony in the bargain.'

'Oh, Roddy, that wasn't fair,' said Miranda. 'Only one
colour at a time.'

But Mrs Potter had indeed travelled the world, always
with her family, and wherever she had paused for any
length of time she had been in a house: blue, red, yellow,
grey or white. She had known the timber exterior and high
peaked roofs of the Normandy farmhouses, the forbidding
grey stone of a Scottish castle with moat and keep, the
friendly white and yellow clapboard of New England, the
Kentucky log cabin, the rambling western ranch, the half
timbers and thatched roofs of medieval England – and when
Michael, in a last attempt to win the game, said, 'Colour*less*,'
she named a house where she had once lived in Connecticut
which was almost all of glass.

'But perhaps,' she said, 'I ought not to call it colourless,
for it reflected the lovely woods in which it stood, and in
autumn, when the leaves turned, it would indeed have suited
you, for then it reflected every colour of the rainbow.'

With her family she had always dwelt within the shelter of
houses, not only of every colour but of every material,
which lent their natures to their tints: stone, brick, woods
of many kinds, concrete, paints, tiles, stucco, shingle.

After the game was over, there was a pause, and Michael
asked, 'Don't you like a house any more then?' But how
Miranda wished he hadn't asked it, for she was far ahead of
him in guessing the nature of the loneliness of Mrs Potter.

The old lady said, 'There is no pleasure to be found in travelling alone, and an empty house can be filled with echoes that are deafening.' She paused a moment, then added, 'Take care that none of you live too long. I, who have all my life lived in houses, thought that I would surely die in one, surrounded by my family.'

It was at the borderline of Miranda's lips to say, 'But you do live in a house now. You do,' but she kept it back, and was glad that Michael had seen fit to be silent as well.

'Would you like us for a family when we're not busy?' Roddy asked.

Mrs Potter replied with a hint of a smile in her whisper, 'That's a very kind offer, but I'm afraid it's too late – and I'm afraid it wouldn't be very rewarding. You see, I haven't even any cake or biscuits to offer you. My eating is very frugal these days.'

'Oh,' cried Miranda, 'but they wouldn't be cupboard visits.'

Michael looked at his sister in astonishment, not having understood in the least her meaning, and Roddy too, his offer refused, had tuned out. But Mrs Potter had understood very well the reference had to do with that older one about cupboard love, and that, in her own way, Miranda had sent her a message of affection.

'Thank you,' she said to her, 'but you have already done more for me than you will ever know.' And with that she struggled to arise from the depth of the armchair – and it was a struggle, but the three children, remembering what they had heard, made no move to assist her.

They too arose, and Michael said, 'Thank you, Mrs Potter, for letting us chat with you, and for telling us about all your houses.'

'Thank you,' said Mrs Potter, 'for telling me about ours.' And not until they were outside the door and halfway down the corridor did Miranda realize that she had used 'ours' instead of 'yours' when referring to the House.

As they left, Mrs Potter said to them, 'Don't close the door entirely. Just leave it on the latch.'

When they were alone, Michael asked, 'Do you suppose she leaves her door open that way all the time?'

'I think so,' said Miranda.

'But why?'

'Perhaps,' Miranda replied, 'with the door like that you're not quite so alone. A draught could blow it open, couldn't it?'

As they passed the office of Mr Thompson they saw that he was talking to Mr Diggs, and so they were unable to tell him of their wonderful visit and adventure with Mrs Potter.

Two mornings later, the three children, dressed in raincoats and Wellingtons, came down into the lobby with their mother, to go shopping, which they loved.

They found the lobby astir with several knots of people talking in hushed voices: Mr Thompson, the staff, and strangers in dark overcoats and bowler hats with briefcases under their arms.

'Oh,' said Mrs Maitland. 'Something must have happened. I wonder what it is.'

Harry Martin, the switchboard operator, and Tim Ryan, the hall porter, were standing around looking lugubrious.

Mr Thompson came out of his office and said to one of the two men with briefcases and bowler hats, 'Here are the keys, Mr Briscoe. You will see that nothing has been touched. And I gather you will be making all arrangements.'

The man, with his partner, went off across the lobby and down the corridor.

Mrs Maitland enquired of Mr Thompson, 'What is it? What is the matter?'

He stopped to reply to her, and for the moment was seemingly oblivious to the three children who were standing there – which was probably just as well, for Miranda, the Chief Witch, could have told her mother what had happened. She knew it so strongly.

'It's Mrs Potter,' Mr Thompson said. 'She died suddenly in the night – in her sleep, mercifully. Or rather in the morning since she spoke to me on the telephone shortly after three. She was a very old lady, you know. Ninety-seven, her lawyer tells me. That was him just went in there. Still, it's always a shock when it happens.'

'Spoke to you on the telephone?' said Mrs Maitland. 'How very odd. Was she ill? Did she require assistance?'

'Oh, no,' said Mr Thompson. 'It was quite usual.' And then for the first time he seemed to notice Michael, Miranda and Roddy, and, nodding his massive head in their direction, he said, 'I was telling them only the other day how she used to ring me up sometimes in the night just for a chat. She called me this morning to say she couldn't sleep, and, as I told you three here, she had a wonderful way of bringing in some place where it might seem that both of us had once been. This time we got to talking about the Golden Gate.' He paused a moment, as though something in this had struck him, and then continued: 'The Golden Gate. That's San Francisco, you know. We came in there for three months to refit during the war after we took a Kamikazi.'

Mr Thompson paused again in reflection, and, doing so, made the futile gesture of putting a non-existent pipe into his mouth, since he held none, having left it in his office, and so looked at his empty hands and said, 'Now that's odd, come to think of it.'

'About San Francisco?' asked Mrs Maitland. 'Or her calling you? The poor old soul must have been very lonely to do that – and how kind of you at that hour of the morning.'

Mr Thompson shook his head and said, 'No. I just remember her saying after she'd thanked me, "I think perhaps I shall sleep now, because I am in my house".' He scratched his head over that one for an instant, and then added, 'And she said, "Would you look in on me perhaps in the morning, Mr Thompson?" Now, come to think of it, she'd never said *that* before,'

'And did you?' Mrs Maitland asked.

'Of course,' he replied. 'And found her door was open. I hurried in, suspecting foul play, but of course there wasn't any. She was just there sleeping as she said she would – except that one could see she would not wake up.'

'I understand how you must feel, Mr Thompson,' said Mrs Maitland. 'I only hope I have an ending like that.' Then she moved off with her silent children following her.

They went out into the fresh morning, so thoroughly washed by the rain, to the smell of spring, and Mrs Maitland murmured, 'Ninety-seven. I hope I never live to be that old.'

The three children said nothing still, but trailed along with her. But Miranda's mind was as young and fresh as the blue sky showing at last where the clouds had consented to part for a moment, and she thought instead of that name which she did not quite understand but which had rung so beautifully: 'The Golden Gate'. And the terror and even the sadness left her.

Mrs Potter was gone, but Miranda knew very well that they had shown her that their House was her House too – the kind of house in which she had been born, to die in.

CHAPTER XIII

The Man Who Hated Houses

Mr Thompson was quite right: there were indeed some tenants of Melton Court who positively disliked the notion of living in a house at all. And none more so, surely, than Mr Brant, a bulky, white-haired, retired newspaper reporter, who lived just along the corridor from the Maitlands in Flat 1D.

He button-holed Michael, Miranda and Roddy as they were setting off to the lift the morning after their first and, as it was soon to prove, only meeting with Mrs Potter.

At first they thought he was hurrying to catch the lift with them, and so Michael smiled and called, 'It's just coming, Mr Brant.' But then he surprised them all by saying sharply, 'It's not the lift but you I want,' and so, just then as the lift arrived and the doors opened, the children stepped back, looking up at him uncertainly, and let the doors close again automatically and the lift descend empty still.

'All this rubbish about a house,' he chided. 'If only you knew how lucky you are to be living in a flat you'd very soon forget all that stuff. I wouldn't live in a house today even if you gave it to me. I've had houses.'

And thereupon, as the Maitland children exchanged warning frowns, he was off on what was obviously one of his pet hobby-horses, which, to anyone able to last the course, made it abundantly clear that somewhere, some time, a house had done him wrong.

'Do you know what a house is?' he asked rhetorically. 'A house is a money-eater. Why, a house is worse than a wife to support. You've never done paying out. There it sits, staring at you out of its windows, just waiting for things to be done to it. Own a house and you've never finished. You think you are, but it's always one ahead of you. Fix that leak in the roof, and a drain blocks up in the cellar. Do up the floors, and when you look up to heaven to say, "Well, thank God that's done", that's when you see the crack in the ceiling. Paint, paint, paint. Varnish and polish.

'Anything that can ever happen to a man in a house has happened to me. Chimney fires. Damned lucky if you can get one of those out without burning the whole place down with everything you've got. Came home one night after a rainstorm and cloudburst – cellar full of water. Cat floating around on a packing case. Had to call the fire engines to pump it out. That cost a pretty packet, I can tell you.'

Miranda tried to interject some words of sympathy, but Mr Brant was oblivious. He was well under way now – and the children began to feel this was more like being at Speakers' Corner in Hyde Park on a Sunday than the first floor of Melton Court on a Thursday, as they recognized they had no choice but to hear out his soapbox lecture.

'Don't talk to me about houses,' he went on – and Michael smiled to himself at the sheer impossibility. 'I know it all. What kind of heating do you go for? Coal? You might as well be a navvy in a stoke-hole. Every morning and every night shovelling coal, raking ashes, putting out ashes. Don't bank your fire properly and out she goes. Waste another hour getting her started in the morning. Oil heat? Great when you read the advertisements in the newspapers. "Clean heat never lets you down". That's a good one. If it's not the oil-suppliers that let you down it's when the electricity goes off at the pump and the damn lot packs up. Gas? It just takes one leak to asphyxiate you and your family or blow your head off if you don't go about lighting it the right way.

'If it's trouble you want, you've got three ways of finding it with the heating you put in. And that's not all. Pipes going all through the house. You know what happens to

pipes if you go away in the winter and leave them? They
freeze up, that's what happens. And when they freeze they
burst, and when they burst they flood the place, and when
the place is flooded it comes through the floor and the
ceiling below, and the ceiling comes down.'

Mr Brant was steadily gathering more momentum. 'Do
you know what a house is for? I'll tell you what. To support
plumbers, carpenters, masons, electricians, painters and
builders. And do you know what it starts with? It starts
with a little hole or crack in the wall up near the ceiling
that needs filling in. So you call the mason. Nothing to it.
Patch of cement, dab of paint, and, Bob's your uncle,
except Bob isn't your uncle and he's not your maiden aunt
either. The mason comes and looks at the hole, and the first
thing he does he takes out a hammer and chisel and makes it
a bigger hole to find out what made it a hole in the first
place. So he comes to you and says, "We've run into a bit of
trouble up there. There's a pipe just behind the hole. We'd
better have the plumber in." You better have, too, if you
know what's good for you. So while the mason is chipping
all around what was once an innocent little hole and now
looks like the cave of the winds, the plumber and his helper
are having a go at the pipes.'

Without drawing breath, he continued, 'Two days later
you get home from work only to hear from your wife,
"Darling, there's some trouble. The plumber said the pipe
runs around a beam. We've had to get the carpenter in – I
phoned him this morning." Well, now you're for it. The
mason has got a side of the wall down and is crawling
around. The plumber has got your water shut off and the
pipes unscrewed. Then the carpenter is sawing through the
beam, when he sends his helper to tell you that he's come
across some wiring that he doesn't want touch. Wiring's
not his business. Call in the electrician.'

The children felt totally trapped, standing, as they were,
like dummies against the wall. Mr Brant's expression
reminded them of those grinning carnival figures as his
narrative took him back to all that he was no longer involved

with since his escape from houses. 'Mason, plumber, carpenter, electrician,' he reiterated. 'But the fun is only just beginning. You come home at night and the electrician is waiting for you. He says, "About the wiring. I've had a look at it. That's about twenty years old, you know. It's not safe. That could go any minute, and no telling how it might end up – short circuit, fire in the walls. No inspector would pass that. I'd say if ever there was a bit of re-wiring needed it was there."

'Well, the plumber's already told you that you want copper piping unless you want the corrosion that has set in to continue. And the carpenter has informed you that the woodworm's been at that old beam. "Here, sir, just take a look 'ow it's crumbling", and he crumbles some of it for you. "You've got a lot of weight on this floor, sir. I'd say a steel support across there is what's wanted, but I wouldn't like to touch it without the word of an architect or a building engineer. I certainly wouldn't want to put my trust in a beam like that."

'Now who haven't we on the premises here at Melton Court?' continued Mr Brant, his eyes lighting up with the job of what he was escaping by living in his flat. 'Well, the glazier for one. And what's the glazier doing? Fixing anything from one to three broken window panes which the mason, the plumber, the carpenter or the electrician manage to smash, bringing their gear into the place. They've got your wall down now, and, if you're lucky, they haven't discovered that your bricks have gone, or that the cement binding the stories of your house is crumbling, or the shingle's rotting, so that before you know it you've got a scaffolding outside the house and lorry loads of sand, cement and building materials blocking your entrance. From what? All from one little hole.'

Mr Brant's face, the children noticed, was becoming flushed now, and his moustache was bristling with delight and excitement. 'Oho!' he cried. 'So, a month or six weeks later, when that crew of pirates have left and it's cost you a packet to clean up the mess, not to mention the furniture they've ruined by forgetting to cover it, you think you're done, don't you? Well, you've forgotten the painters. The painters or the paperers. You can't leave the whole side of a room like that, so you get the painter chappy in. He says he'll do the one side, but he can't guarantee to match the rest of the room. "Those walls are pretty dirty – and look over there, sir. You can see where the paint's beginning to come away. Better do the whole room." That'll teach you to want a house.'

Somewhat exhausted by this effort, Mr Brant rested a moment by enjoying a brief outing amongst the clichés of apartment living.

'Here I shut the door and walk away. Come back when I please. No trouble. No worries. Something goes wrong, not my responsibility. Old Mr Briggs comes up and fixes it. Heat, light, water – somebody else's job. When they go bust you pick up the phone and give 'em hell. No trouble to clean. Woman comes in. In an hour she's gone.'

And then back on the track again. 'Your damn house you're cleaning all day long, and then it's never done. Start at the bottom, dusting, and by the time you've worked your way to the top and done all the bedrooms the bottom's dusty again. And those blasted stairs! Polish, polish, polish! All the time, until they're so slippery you could break your neck. When you've got a house you've got to keep the stairs polished – and don't ask me why. Unless you have stair-carpeting, and then the brackets or the cross pieces are always working loose. One house I owned I fell down a whole flight of stairs and was in bed for a week. The old woman wouldn't polish the piano or the furniture, but she just loved to polish those stairs.'

This then gave Mr Brant the notion to depart on yet another tack. 'And what about the maid with her mop and dust rag and polishing cloth? What about privacy in a house? Do you think you have it? Do you think you own it? Do you think you can live for yourself in it? Not on your life! You know what a house means if it's going to be run properly? Servants. You know what servants mean?

"Hush, John, don't talk so loud, the servants will be sleeping." "Turn the telly down, John. You'll wake the servants." "Cold supper tonight, John. It's cook's night off." "Oh, dear, I don't know what to do. Annie's broken my favourite bit of china – the one the Dingles gave us for a wedding present. You know, the piece with the shepherdesses on it. It can't be mended."

'No use having them in for just a couple of hours when you own a house. It's a full-time living-in job – a man and his wife, and then what? Eat you out of your larder, cheat you out of your grocery bills. Never there when you want them, always around when you don't, putting their troubles on you, having babies they oughtn't to be having. So what do you say? Have a small house? One of those bungle things all on one floor? Then you might as well have a flat. Shut the door and walk away – that's what I say.

'Because, I'll tell you another thing,' Mr Brant went on unbidden, now veering to another wind blowing out of his house-checkered past. 'You live in a house long enough and it eats into your soul. Ancestors hanging about that you can't get rid of, even when you take down their portraits and stow 'em in the attic. Houses get atmospheres that ride your shoulders like The Old Man Of The Sea. Tragedies stick to 'em, and you can't get away from 'em. That's the room where little Emily lay ill for two months and almost died. Upstairs is the room where Grandma and Grandpa and God knows who else did die – and if you live long enough and the house doesn't fall down, the bed where you're sleeping and the room where you're living is the one where you'll die.

'Good times too, as well as bad, leave their echoes in a house, but the bad ones are those you seem to remember. That's the chair where you were sitting when the doctor came downstairs with a long face and told you he didn't think the Missus was going to pull through. Or when they handed you the telegram with the bad news from the office. Things on the table, pictures on the wall – everything that's been around too long reminds you of something you would prefer to forget.

'What you want to do to stay happy is cut out the past and get on with the future. When you get fed up with a flat you move off and find another. Different set-up, different neighbourhood. Leave all the old memories behind. Fresh start.

'Your parents ever tried selling a house when they wanted to?' Mr Brant took a quick look within himself at that part of the game, and was off downfield again. 'Strangers tramping in and out of your premises, looking into your closets and cupboards, whispering in corners or sneering at your possessions or taste with their eyes, or shamelessly doing over your place right in front of you. "We could take that wall out, dear, and make this into one room, with the bath over there, and that would make it so much lighter, wouldn't it? Isn't it strange how people seem to live in darkness?" Or "What an odd place to put the dining-room. I suppose one could convert the small drawing-room, but then one would have to make changes in the kitchen as well." And the estate agent johnnies calling you up every hour of the day for appointments for people they know aren't going to buy, but by showing them around it makes the boss think they're keeping busy. Half the people don't want to buy anyway. All they're after is a day out snooping into other people's houses to see what they've got or whether they can get any ideas for themselves. The other half can't make up their minds, and keep you hanging in the air or back out from signing at the very last minute, leaving you to start all over again.

'And what about all the rates?' Mr Brant suddenly shouted, as something which he had totally forgotten suddenly smote him. 'What about what you have to hand over to the Government or the local council in blackmail for the privilege of occupying a house that you've built or paid for on land which the deed says that you or your heirs own in perpetuity? "Own" did I say? You own nothing, and what you think you own owns you. No. Don't talk to me about houses.'

The last warning was, of course, quite unnecessary. None of the children had had a chance to get a word in edgeways from the start. And it was clear that they would have none now, for Mr Brant, his eyes glazed in a kind of furious satisfaction, pressed the 'down' button hard and held his finger on it until the lift arrived and the doors opened. He then stomped in alone and, as he prepared to press 'ground floor' from inside, called out sternly, 'So let's have no more of your nonsense'. Then the doors closed and he was gone.

Stunned and incredulous still, the children looked at each other and up and down the empty, carpeted corridor, so very quiet now.

It was Michael who finally broke the silence and the mood as he smiled and said, 'He's really *mad* about houses, isn't he?' They all laughed while he then pressed the lift button for them – and laughed even more when Miranda tilted her head and mused, 'But I wonder why.'

CHAPTER XIV

A Palace on Wheels

The steady downpour which for so long had held Michael, Miranda and Roddy prisoner had at last yielded to that meteorologist's dodge known as 'showers and bright periods', and it was during one such bright period, when the pale April sun had momentarily broken through the cloud cover and was adorning an encouraging patch of blue, that, at their mother's suggestion, they had gone down to the garden square at the back of Melton Court, and there found Mr and Mrs Tosello sitting on a newspaper which they had placed upon one of the benches to protect them from the damp.

The Tosellos were very much on the 'wanted' list of the three because, occupying as the couple did Flat 2F, they were actually, without, of course, being aware of it, living, at least partly, in the nursery of the House. And since the nursery had been established as the principal domain of the children, they naturally wished to know all about the couple. The prohibition against visiting the Tosellos' quarters certainly couldn't extend to talking to them, should they come across them by accident, and here in the square, against the gloomy fortress of the flats, only mildly relieved by the bed of pansies, primulas and daffodils – the Easter floral dressing furnished by the Truciman Estates – the Tosellos might be said to be 'a fair cop'.

It was Chief Contact Man Roddy, of course, who went immediately to the heart of the matter, with 'Hello. You're living in our nursery. Is it nice?'

Mr Tosello came back from wherever his thoughts had been and turned his eyes upon the three young people. They were strange eyes, not so much in colour as in shape, being almost buried at the corners by folds of flesh that came down around them. If Miranda had been asked to describe them she would not have done so in terms of colour either: the thought that came to her was that they were eyes that seemed to be full of remembering.

'Your nursery?' repeated Mr Tosello. 'Are we indeed? Well, well. And how would you account for that?'

'You're in our House, and there is a secret room in it where there is something awful,' warned Roddy.

'Oh,' said Mrs Tosello, in mild and puzzled alarm. 'Is there really?'

'Oh, Roddy,' said Miranda. 'There really isn't anything awful at all, Mrs Tosello. He's only talking about our House – the one that was here before.' And she stopped, not quite knowing just then how to go on.

Mr Tosello seemed to have departed again, and Miranda had the feeling that he was looking at something that was far away. He also gave her the impression that he was hearing things as well that they did not.

Mrs Tosello, not yet with it, but indulgent of children, said nothing, and so Miranda, perforce, had to go on.

'The House that was here before they built –' and she waved a hand up at the block. 'There really was a house here once, you see, and so my brothers and I are pretending we're all living in it instead of where we do. I mean –'

Mrs Tosello now revealed the tolerant smile of one who for years has not only looked after a family but a husband who was as much a child as a man. She was a handsome, statuesque woman, taller than her husband – that was clear, even though they were both seated – with a corona of white hair atop the remnants of a fine Roman face which once must have been compellingly beautiful.

'Oh, I see now,' she said. 'Of course, there must have been. How clever of you to think of it. Was it a nice house, dears?'

Both husband and wife spoke with the faintest of Cockney accents, for in spite of their Italian name the Tosellos were Londoners.

'Oh, yes,' Miranda replied. 'It was – is – beautiful. It has gables, with little windows, a great big attic and a cellar. Mr Biggs lives in the cellar, and doesn't mind at all.'

'Where your flat is,' Michael followed, 'means that you and Mr Tosello are living mostly in the nursery part.'

'Are we now?' said Mr Tosello. And then repeated, 'The nursery, eh?' He turned his drooping beagle's eyes upon his wife and added, 'We never, ever had a nursery, did we, mother?'

'No, that's true,' said Mrs Tosello. 'We never did.' And Miranda's sensitive spirit detected a trace of sadness in her voice, and wondered. It was strange how everyone seemed to have some kind of secret sadness that appeared to be connected with their House when the subject came up.

Yes, and talk about the House had stirred something in Mr Tosello too, for with two huge hands folded over the stick upon which he had been leaning he turned now to them and said, 'I'll wager you would be surprised if you knew the kind of houses we've lived in for nearly all our lives. And fair bona they were too, every one of them. I wouldn't have had any others.'

'What does "fair bona" mean?' Miranda asked.

'Ah, yes, of course. You wouldn't understand,' said Mr Tosello. 'It's from another language.'

'What kind of language?'

'Well,' Mr Tosello replied, 'the kind of language spoken in the house we lived in. "Fair bona" means right, good, wonderful, splendid, things the way they ought to be. Fair bona it was. Everything tickedy-boo.'

Roddy immediately adopted these fascinating new words: 'Our House is bona tickery-boot, too,' he said.

'Ah, yes,' Mr Tosello agreed, nodding gravely and turning his powerful body still further towards the three children. 'I wouldn't doubt it. But not like ours.' And here his voice sank to an intimate confidential whisper, as though he were confiding, which indeed he was. 'Our house was on wheels. Guess!'

'On wheels?' exclaimed Miranda, and failed to complete the immediate picture. Once, on television, they had seen an entire house, but not a very large one, being moved from one place to another, but it had been on rollers that only inched it along.

'Say!' put in Michael, who was groping too.

It was Roddy's devastatingly speedy mind that came closest. 'A bus?' he asked.

Mr Tosello laughed and said, 'Well, son, you've come near to hitting the nail on the head. *Caravans*. Wagons like gypsies live in.'

'With a crooked chimney sticking up? asked Roddy, delighted.

'With a crooked chimney sticking up,' nodded Mr Tosello.

'Oh, but you aren't –', Michael hesitated, 'gypsies.'

'No,' Mr Tosello smiled. 'Guess again.'

'Oh, aren't we stupid?' said Miranda. 'The circus, of course.'

'Circus? Oh, goodie gumdrops!' cried Roddy, jumping up and down.

Mr Tosello's hound's eyes turned bright with approval. 'Bang on,' he said. Then he added, 'Have you ever heard of Bimbo? Or Lilianne?'

For a moment the smile left the face of Mrs Tosello, and there was an admonitory flick of the hand as she said, '*Nunti parlari*.' The language, a return to circus argot for 'don't talk', was obscure to Roddy, but not the look or the gesture. 'She doesn't want him to tell!' he burst out.

'Oh, but why not?' said Mr Tosello. 'Bimbo was a clown, and Lilianne, in her day, was one of the greatest flyers ever.'

'And they were you,' said Miranda.

'Did she fly aeroplanes?' Roddy asked.

'No, no,' Mr Tosello smiled. 'Not that kind of flying. She was an aerialist.' And here, looking at his wife with great love and pride, he explained, 'She was the only woman ever to do a triple somersault from trapeze bar to catcher. No woman ever did it before.'

He reached out and put a hand upon his wife's arm. 'Each time before she attempted it I was terrified. Of course, then when the children came she had to give it up. Proud as I was of her, I wasn't sorry. You would never have seen, of course, her other act with trained white dogs and doves and white ponies. When she entered the ring driving her carriage with the doves flying about her head the children used to stand up and cheer. But, as I say, all that would have been before your time.'

'And Bimbo?' Michael asked. 'I think Mummy and Daddy have talked about him.'

It was the turn of Mrs Tosello now, and she said with the same quiet pride that had been her husband's, 'He was one of the most famous clowns ever. There was nothing he could not do.'

Mr Tosello folded his features into an expression of modesty and self-deprecation. 'Come now, mother.'

'Ah, but it is true,' Mrs Tosello insisted. 'Riding, trampoline, slack wire, perch, bar and flying trapeze – and a dozen musical instruments as well.'

The three children stood regarding the Tosellos silently, for they were of the new generation to whom the circus was no more than a series of variety acts – colourful indeed, but taking place behind the glass window of the television set. It had been a number of years since there had been a performance under canvas or in the big arena at Olympia. These were children who had never breathed the exciting mingled smell of horses, elephants, sawdust and candy floss, or ever had delicious shudders spilled down their spines at the first entrance of the grotesque clowns.

'We were "The Riding Tosellos" also,' said the old man.

'They're all scattered or gone now. Times change. Perhaps it is just as well. We had our day.'

Mrs Tosello glanced at her husband, and said, 'He was even Ringmaster once. I can tell you, he cut a fine figure in top hat, red coat, doeskins and boots. Everyone admired him.'

But Mr Tosello was not to be cheered. He said, 'Well, when the joints and muscles grow stiff, then you no longer do a back somersault from one horse to another. You teach it to your kids, and then they pick up and leave it.'

'Not all of them, Alfredo,' said Mrs Tosello. Then they fell silent too.

Their sadness fell heaviest upon Roddy, who was sometimes capable of the most infinite tact.

'Were you always with the circus?' he asked.

'Oh, yes,' replied Mr Tosello. 'Always. Or at least that's how it seemed. My grandfather was "The Great Tosello". Have you ever heard of Blondin? No, you wouldn't have. He was a high-wire walker who once walked across Niagara Falls in America. Grandfather Tosello was even greater. They stretched a wire from the top of the cathedral spire in Milano to a building a hundred yards on the other side of the square, and my grandfather walked it blindfold. He was born in Mantua. We were of Italian origin. His son, my father, came to England and founded the British branch of the family. There were eight of us – "The Riding Tosellos" – but there was nothing we couldn't do if we had to. Even pulling up and taking down the canvas. The Riding Tosellos were famous. We once even went to America and toured with Barnum and Bailey. We were in the centre ring. It isn't just Barnum and Bailey any more, is it mother? Everything changes so.'

Mrs Tosello said, 'They're called Ringling Brothers as well now.' And then to the children: 'But best known of all was Bimbo the clown – my Alfredo. He was the star. When he came into the ring, they stopped everything – all the other acts. Oh, but he would have made you laugh.'

Mr Tosello, at that moment, did not look as though he could make anyone laugh. He seemed to have shrunk and lost some of his bulk. He sat with his shoulders hunched and the corners of his hound's eyes drawn down to match the droop of his lips.

Miranda wished that she could have said, yes, she knew the two names very well. Bimbo was a funny one, and so he must have been a funny man. Lilianne had a ring and a glint to it, and into her mind came thoughts of a lovely girl in tights with sequins and coloured spangles flashing. Sometimes, when there was a circus on television, something on the costumes of the performers would throw back a blinding stab of light at the camera and thence into the eye of the beholder.

She found herself staring at Mrs Tosello trying to penetrate her exterior to see within the once lithe and exquisite body, clad in pink, soaring like a jewelled butterfly through the air. She saw instead only a grandmotherly woman trying to protect her husband against the sadness that had come to him. It seemed she had not wished him to talk from the very beginning because she had known that this sadness would come. Somehow the conversation had wandered off from what Miranda was really longing to know about – namely, those houses on wheels. But possibly that would make Mr Tosello even sadder, and so she thought that perhaps she ought not to ask.

Roddy had no such inhibitions. 'Tell us about your house,' he said. 'What was it like? How did it go? Did it have an engine?'

To the surprise of all three children, and certainly the relief of Miranda, these questions seemed to dispel the sadness from Mr Tosello. The folds of his jowls relaxed, and as he turned his face towards Roddy the melancholy departed from his eyes and was replaced by a slight glint of mischief.

'First, one,' he said, answering Roddy's last question, 'and then, two. But they had to have hay to make them go.'

'That's not so,' said Roddy. 'Engines have to go on petrol.'

Michael gave his younger brother a push and said, 'Oh, stupid. They were horses, weren't they?'

Mr Tosello's head began to nod up and down back into

the days that had been. 'That's right. We had horses,' he said. 'But first there was only one. Then, when the children came – Carlo, Maria, Tony and Lucia, to begin with – one would no longer do, and so we had to have a pair. He turned to his wife and said, 'Do you remember, mother, Castor and Pollux and the beer barrel?'

Michael, eager to show that he recognized some names at last, said, 'Oh, weren't Castor and Pollux the Heavenly Twins? So the horses must have looked alike. But what was the beer barrel?'

'Well, the caravan, of course,' explained Mr Tosello. 'It was shaped like a cut down beer barrel, so what else could we call it? We didn't travel by rail in those days. Everyone had to have his own wagon. We bought ours from the gypsies. The side of it was carved and filigreed, and we had a striped awning over the driver's seat. She was painted bright yellow, with "Billy Barnett's Circus" in fancy lettering in red on the sides, and Roddy's crooked chimney stuck up out of the roof.'

The subject was now open, and Miranda was bubbling over with questions. 'But there were six of you.' she said. 'How did you get everybody in? Were they all still tiny babies that you could put into carry cots?'

'Ho! Ho!' laughed Mr Tosello. 'Tiny babies, did you say? Well, they were once, but not then. They were just about your age – nine, eleven, thirteen and fourteen. You had to know how to stow things, I'll tell you: children, costumes, food, coal . . . The beer barrel wagon,' he continued, 'was what gave us the extra space. The gypsies had learned that. You'd be surprised what you could get into that bulge. Well, for one thing, a bunk on either side into which you could pack two kids each – especially if they were limber like us. Why, you could fold Carlo and Tony up into a suitcase if you wanted to.

'Do you know what else we had in there? A bunk big enough for mother here and myself, a folding table, a chest of drawers, and a cooking range. There were drawers and lockers underneath the bunks and behind the doors, and two brass oil lamps hanging from the ceiling with plenty of hooks for clothing, with every other inch of space occupied by shelves for dishes and cups and saucers, tinned fruits and vegetables, eggs and tea and sugar and things, and nails to hang pots and pans from. Also, I can't remember now just where, we had room for a big tin wash tub, which was used for make-up boxes and brushes and shaving gear – and there was still room for two mirrors and a strip of red carpeting and two folding chairs. Then besides all this there were the steps and things like wash cloths and towels and lines which we hung outside.

'And, do you know, when everything was in its place – and anyone who didn't remember to put things where they belonged soon found out – there was still plenty of room to move about and lie up and have a read, or for two of the kids to fight though mother here wasn't any midget, and the kids took after her rather than me. A tight squeeze, you might say, but we got so used to it we never noticed.'

'Gosh,' said Michael. 'I'll bet it was fun.'

There was one part of the narrative at which Roddy sniffed as eagerly as a dog on a scent, but he chose to tackle it in reverse. 'We have to have a bath *every* night,' he said.

Almost in disbelief, Miranda frowned, 'And you could cook in there for everyone?'

Mrs Tosello, the former Lilianne, had now been swept up in her husband's reminiscences. 'Oh, yes, my dear,' she said. 'Three meals a day. And couldn't they eat! Bacon, eggs, ham, kippers for breakfast, with lashings of coffee.'

All three children, without realizing it, had undergone a sudden change of heart. Where previously their longing, out of which the House had been born, had been for space to expand the walls of their rooms to where they could play and jump about and move freely, now, suddenly, as their minds turned the Tosello's words into pictures, they longed for no space, and the cramped quarters of a beer barrel with an entire family of six crammed into one weird shape loomed as even more attractive.

What an infinity of houses there seemed to be when one

thought about it, or heard about them. And how much more thrilling to *carry* one's house upon one's back like a turtle, or have wind and waves waft it over seas to far countries whose people were brown, black or yellow, and everything was different and more exciting than it was at home.

Mr Tosello, now fairly launched, was adding fuel to the fire. It was not often he got to talk about it and to an audience of large-eyed wonder of the kind to whom, in the days gone by, he used to play.

'Over hill and dale, as you might say, we went, never mind what the weather was. Sometimes in rain, with thunder and lightning ' And here he digressed for a moment. 'No, the children weren't frightened. We were only frightened of lightning when the Big Top was up.' Then he resumed: 'Sometimes there was sleet and snow, and, in the spring, fields of meadow flowers, or passing through little villages where the children ran out to cheer and begged us to stop. We saw lakes and streams and rivers and mountains. Easy going at a steady walk. We never pushed the horses, because whenever we arrived where we were going we knew they had to perform.

'The kids could handle the reins, as the horses understood that all they had to do was follow the road that wound through down and moors and sometimes, when we went north, over high passes. It seemed like they knew every twist and turn, and sometimes when we reached a signpost and another road branched off for us to take they seemed to remember that too. Oh, they were clever, those prads.'

'Prads?' queried Michael.

'Horses,' Mr Tosello explained. 'I see we shall have to teach you circus lingo. They were the first ones who were looked after when we reached the tober. That was the pitch where we were going to show that afternoon and evening and put up the big tent just outside some town. They were unhitched, watered, fed and rubbed down and got ready for the performance. Animals first, humans after. That was the rule of our circus, because our rum cul – that is to say, our boss – was a good bloke and knew that we were only as good as our cattle.

'But in the meantime,' he continued, now thoroughly warm to his narration, 'mother here wasn't idle. Idle? That was a word none of us knew. All the children had their own special jobs. In a jiffy the steps were down at the back of the wagon, water in the tub, fire in the stove, something frying in the skillet, clothes line up, and, no matter where we might be finding ourselves – north, south, east or west – we were home. The back of the wagon was our porch, where between shows we could sit on the steps for a natter or ask a neighbour over for a bite and a beer. You'd be surprised how many of us could get around, once our tables were unfolded. Smoke came out of the chimney just like from any other house in the town. We were warm and dry in the bad weather, and cool in the summer, with the windows opened and the breeze blowing through, shifting mother's curtains till they waved like the flags on the Big Top.

'Then, after the show was over, just before midnight, we would pull down and pack up. It was two or three o'clock often before we were on the road again, but we didn't mind, because we were still at home. We were taking it with us, and if the road was a straight one we could let the prads have the reins and have a kip ourselves. And if it came on to rain then it would drum on the roof and the sound would make sleep all the better. Now, isn't that the kind of house to have?'

'Where did you go to the loo?' Roddy asked suddenly.

'Roddy!' Miranda reproved, and Michael gave him another push, saying, 'Must you always ask private questions?'

Mr Tosello boomed a delighted laugh, and said, 'Ah, well, we had arrangements for the kids when they were small, and then there was always a field with a big tree or some woods or a ditch at the side of the road. When you're young and get used to it, nature is never a worry. But, of course, in the *Palazzo* we had the finest WC a king could want for a throne, with a knitted seat cover made by mother, wash basin, soap, towel and all.'

But now he had opened a new mystery to his three listeners – a new word, a new concept certainly, that did not belong with the beer barrel wagon, where every inch of space was occupied. And now, too polite, and Roddy too intimidated to ask, the three simply exchanged those swift glances of bewilderment that children can throw out like radio messages – but not too swift for the eyes of Mr Tosello.

He laughed again, and roared, 'Aha! The *Palazzo* – also known as the Palace. Now you're puzzled, eh? That's what we called her, and a palace she was. You know, we weren't always a company of poor performers trekking down dusty roads to put on a show for two or three hundred jossers in little towns and villages, or wherever we could gather a crowd. Oh, no. Not when Bimbo and Lilianne were the stars of Billy Barnett's Circus. Then we had the finest motorized caravan that money could buy – finer even than that of Billy the boss, and bigger too.

'Why, mother and I had our own bedroom, and there were two more for the kids, with three bunks each – for by that time we had Angelo and Rosina as well as Carlo, Maria, Tony and Lucia, and we were a big, important family – kitchen and dining-room, and the way every inch of space would pull down or open up or pop out was a fair surprise after the old beer barrel and some of the other vardos we had after that. Bigger and better there may be, but nothing to compare with the Palace, where everything was in formica, stainless steel and silver chrome. A roustabout to drive it through the night, and mother and me living like a King and Queen, except wherever we went the Palace went with us. We even lived in it when we went into winter quarters, because there was no finer house anyone could wish for. And if you'd once had wheels under you, well then, you never want anything else, even if you weren't going anywhere, because the best thing in the world is to feel that you could if you chose to. Pull in the steps, shut the doors, see that all the kids are aboard and where they ought to be, start the engine and away you go. Where you've been doesn't matter any more.

'Why, folks in Pullman trains hadn't it no better. Look out the windows and see the world passing by, and a new place and new people and another way of living and thinking may be just ahead of you. With the horses it would take all through the night and often half the next day to reach the next town. The Palace would roll there in three hours. Fair spoiled, it made one, but when you're a star you've got to live like a star. Oh, you'd have loved the Palace, you three, I'll wager. Take a shower after your act, sleep in a proper bed, roll the highways of France and Italy, Norway and Sweden, Spain and across to Yugoslavia, or through the Black Forest and down the Danube. And always at home, living like royalty.'

The three children were away. The vistas opened to them now surpassed anything they had ever imagined – far better even than those of Mrs Potter. Every day a new place to explore, to learn, to compel to give up its secrets to them, and, no matter where they might find themselves, what kind of country – hostile or friendly – or what menaces they might dream up as lurking in the woods or dark glens, the safety of home was just at their backs.

Michael had a sudden moment of thoughtlessness, which was not like him, since he was at the age, unlike Roddy when he was careful as to what he said to grown-ups. They were so inexplicably touchy, and there was no telling how they might react. But he had been completely carried away by the pictures painted by the Tosellos. 'Why did you stop?' he asked. 'Why don't you still live in the Palace? You could put it anywhere, couldn't you? And when you were tired of anywhere, go somewhere else? I wish we could.'

'Ah, well,' was all that Mr Tosello said for a moment, and his wife remained quite silent.

Miranda wished that Michael hadn't asked, but then that was something one learned early: that when any words slipped out that you wished you hadn't said, it was too late.

You couldn't get them back. There could very well be a private reason why the Tosellos were living alone now in a flat in Melton Court, and whatever it was, after the wonderful life they had led, it could not be very pleasing to Bimbo and Lilianne.

But the one-time circus performer recovered his smile very quickly as he said, 'Times change, and the roads aren't the same any more. There'd be hardly any room for the Palace – and besides, you want a few kids underfoot when you live like that.'

'Especially when it's somebody else has to look after them,' Mrs Tosello concluded. And then added, 'But it's true. Like Alfredo says, it's the children that make a home and make whatever you have to do to keep it up worth doing.'

Having committed the original error of tact, and unable to backtrack, Michael felt compelled to compound it. 'What did you do with the Palace?' he asked. 'Where is it? Could we see it some time?'

'Not unless you go abroad,' Mr Tosello replied. 'Carlo, our eldest son, has it. Children will grow up, you know. He and his wife and *their* kids are living in it now, travelling with Circus Knie.'

'And Maria and Tony and Lucia and the others?' Michael persisted.

'All married with children – except Tony,' Mr Tosello bowed his head and paused a while. 'He was killed in an accident. He fell from the high-wire.' Then, clenching his hands and looking up again, he jerked his shoulders and added, 'The others, they were wiser than any of us. They left the circus before the circus left them.'

Michael completed the job with 'And don't you mind not travelling any more and being stuck here in a . . .'

Miranda was measuring the distance, but it was too far for her foot to reach to kick him, though Michael in fact, now aware of his entanglement, had broken off his own sentence before completing it.

There was no self-pity in the Tosellos, or grief or

regret, and the ex-clown merely smiled affably and said, 'Not at all. No, no. Not at all. It's very comfortable and easy on us both. What you haven't got, you don't see, and what you've had, it's better to remember.'

'Anyway,' put in Roddy, to whom the drift of the conversation, if not the unvoiced emotions evoked, had penetrated, 'you're living in a house now, even if it doesn't move. Our House.'

To Miranda's intense relief, Mr Tosello picked it up immediately, and the subject was safely changed.

'So we are, young fellow. So we are, I'm to understand. And living in two places at once, I'd say, was almost as good as going from one place to another. It keeps you sort of betwixt and between, doesn't it?'

'Yes, and the nursery where you live is *very* big,' said Roddy, 'with a slide and a rocking horse and everything. I bet you could do all sorts of tricks on them. Just imagine,' he added to Miranda and Michael, his eyes glazing at the possibilities for a real circus clown in their nursery.

Mr Tosello laughed and said, 'Oh, you bet we could. And what else would we find in this House of yours?'

Since it had been Miranda's discovery, Michael and Roddy looked to her to reply – although it was obvious that Roddy was bursting to tell – and so Miranda obliged.

She felt no need to be restricted, since she was not boasting of personal possessions but simply telling about a House which had once been there and in which a family had lived, and, in their leaving, had left behind their memories and even shapes and sizes which Miranda, like a delicate receiver, had picked out of the air or fashioned from her own yearnings until they had become almost tangible again.

The nursery, which thus far had lain dormant in Miranda's mind, now came brilliantly to life, aided by more than occasional interjections from Roddy and Michael who added their favourite items.

The bathroom turned into a marble tessellated splasher's paradise, containing a tub only slightly smaller than an Olympic swimming pool, special lockers, for floating toys, huge bath towels in which one could wrap oneself completely, and a coloured lavatory seat.

Miranda was not aware that she was furnishing what must have been a grim, dark, Victorian house with items and decor from the Age of Aquarius. Here were quarters suitable not only for them but fit for the Tosellos, who used to ride around the country in a palace on wheels.

'And there's room enough in it for all our flat?' Mrs Tosello asked.

'Oh, yes. All of it,' said Miranda. And then she added, 'And we're very happy to have you.'

'I can show you some time,' added Michael. 'You just fit.'

'Now isn't that nice, mother?' Mr Tosello said to his wife. 'And aren't we lucky?'

To which, however, Mrs Tosello did not reply, but only rested her gaze upon Miranda, Michael and Roddy, and if there was anything in her look one might have thought it to be akin to hunger.

Mrs Maitland suddenly appeared in the doorway leading from the block to the garden, and called, 'Children'.

'Oh, dear,' said Miranda, 'Mummy wants us. We shall have to go. Thank you for a lovely talk, We enjoyed it so much.'

With that the children ran off to join their mother and disappeared inside again.

Left to themselves, the Tosellos remained sitting on their bench, silent now, the man unaware that his hand had somehow managed to steal across and cover one of his wife's. He had a left-over smile that had been on his face, and he said, half to himself, 'Children! Why must they ever grow up and become like us?'

No reply came from his wife. Only a slow, far-gazing nodding as she rested her other hand on his, and patted it.

CHAPTER XV

In the Dark

'What do you think we ought to do?' asked Michael, that evening.

'I just don't know,' Miranda had to admit. 'Mummy would be livid if we went.'

Theirs were voices in the dark, in the boys' room, where Miranda was visiting for an important after-goodnights-and-light-out conference.

'Well, why do we have to tell her?' dared Michael. 'It's all Roddy's fault anyway for all that twaddle about a child being killed in the room and blood all over the place. That's really what got him started.'

They wanted to see whether there would be any protest from the corner where Roddy had his bed, but there was only a momentary turning on and off of his precious torch, which had been bestowed upon him by an uncle as a gift and which for an instant threw a circle of yellow light upon the ceiling and then vanished as he clicked it off. If Roddy had heard the accusation, he wasn't having any part of the conversation at the moment.

The brief flash of light had shown Miranda sitting cross-legged on Michael's bed.

'In a way, it *is* cheating, isn't it?' she said. 'I mean, if you know someone is going to say no and so you don't ask them and go ahead and do it, it's just as though they had said it, isn't it?'

'Well,' equivocated Michael, 'she might say yes – especially since they have asked us to help them. Aren't we supposed to help people whenever we can, particularly if they ask us?'

Miranda did not reply to this directly, but set it aside in that compartment of her mind where she parked problems until she could determine whether they would reconcile with her conscience.

'What do you suppose a seance is like anyway?' she asked instead.

'I don't know,' Michael shrugged. 'I think people sit around in the dark, and then the spirits come and tell them things.'

'What's a spirit?' Roddy asked.

'Well, a kind of ghost,' Michael explained.

'If I turned my torch on the ghost, would I be able to see him?'

'Of course not,' Michael scoffed. 'You can only see *through* ghosts. Anyway, you're not supposed to have any kind of a light, otherwise the ghosts don't come.'

'Would they be ghosts of our House?'

'I don't know,' said Michael. 'Ask Miranda.'

Roddy spotlighted Miranda's head with his torch, aureoling her hair in the dark.

She closed her eyes and shook her head and said, 'Don't Roddy. You'll just wear it out, and then you won't have it any more.' Turning back to Michael, she said, 'I suppose perhaps we ought to find out – for everybody's sake. Then we'd know for certain.'

'Yes, and what harm could it do, after all?' Michael persuaded himself as much as Miranda. 'Especially if we were all back in bed before anybody knew. And they did say that *you* had to be there, Miranda, because you're a sensitive.'

'What's a sensitive?' Roddy asked again.

'A Chief Witch, I suppose,' Miranda replied. 'It is my House, after all.' She hugged her knees. Her conscience was beginning to get itself sorted out, partly via the sophistries of her older brother as well as her own burning curiosity. 'But I don't like *him* at all. I think he's horrid the way he came the other day and Mummy had to put him in his place. I don't see why we should have to bother to help him.'

'Oh, I don't think it would be helping *him*,' Michael sat forward on his bed. 'He doesn't believe any of it at all. At least he says he doesn't. But it's his wife who's been frightened. If we can help to unfrighten her I think we ought to do it, even if it isn't our fault that they are so up in arms about our investigations generally.'

'Why is she frightened?' Roddy asked, 'I'm not.'

'You with your man with the knife,' said Michael, 'and the child, and blood all over. Grown-ups don't understand things like that – that they're just for fun. Now if Miranda could turn up some nice ghosts then they wouldn't be afraid any more, and everybody would calm down, including Mummy and Daddy.'

'How do I know they would be nice ghosts?' Miranda asked. 'I can *think* about nice ghosts, but supposing some of them really weren't – some I didn't know about?'

'Well,' said Michael, 'that would be their problem, wouldn't it? I mean, they're asking for it, aren't they, not we? All they're really wanting is for us to be there – or Miranda rather – but they know we wouldn't let her go without us.'

'But when *could* we go?' Miranda asked.

'It would have to be on a night when Mummy and Daddy were out,' Michael replied. 'It would only be for an hour or so, the wife said.'

Miranda's voice, out of the darkness, had lost its tentative and questioning note. Conscience had about been put to sleep. 'That would be the day after tomorrow,' she said. 'Mummy told me they're going to the Baldwins' for dinner, and we're to be allowed to cook our own for a treat.'

'Well, that's even better,' said Michael. 'The wife said that afterwards they'll have a kind of party – sandwiches and cake or maybe ice cream, I don't know.'

To put a final quietus to her conscience Miranda said virtuously, 'We wouldn't have to stay for that.'

'Oh, why not?' Roddy asked indignantly – and the other two had no answer to this practical query.

Finally, Michael said, 'Well, do we tell them yes, then?'

Miranda's virtue was still upon her. '*If* they speak to us again about it – I mean, ask us. Remember, we can't go there. We promised Mummy.'

The conference had been occasioned by the waylaying of the three children in the lobby by Mrs Murchison, as a part of the tactical manoeuvre to ensnare them into attending a seance that she was planning.

Mrs Murchison was an ardent spiritualist, with a tame medium, a Miss Paradone, to whose support she made regular contributions in exchange for snatches of conversation with such as the late Conan Doyle, Camille Flammarion, and occasionally Lloyd George, as well as Mary Baker Eddy and a number of other departed greats, some of whom were materialized physically along with an assortment of Indian Chiefs and a Turkish harem girl slaughtered by her Sultan, who acted as Miss Paradone's controls.

Mr Murchison was emphatically not a spiritualist, and if the children were puzzled as to how Mrs Murchison could prevail over such a disagreeable character as her husband in this field, it was because they did not know the simple fact that it was Mrs Murchison who had the money. Hence Mr Murchison's panic at the first rumours to reach his ears about the House. He knew this was exactly the kind of thing to set Mrs Murchison off, and the next moment their flat would be crowded with the sort of people he characterized as weirdos – holding hands and singing hymns in the dark, while, from a curtained-off and put-together cabinet enclosing Miss Paradone, would emerge noises and manifestations and half-luminous apparitions which were, to say the least, upsetting. And of course it had. The phantom House and a strange girl to whom it had come as though in a dream was too good to miss. Here was virgin territory of the occult to be explored, and Miss Paradone, when apprised of it, had been enthusiastic and both excited and prepared to deliver.

Spirits of people departed, whom no one attending the seance had ever known before, would be a piece of cake, with the possibility of expansion into who could say what lucrative sidelines. The presence of the three children who had dreamed all this up would lend verisimilitude. Miss Paradone felt that with twenty-four hours for preparation she would really be able to turn out something worthwhile, and increase her hold over Mrs Murchison and her generous treasury.

Miss Paradone was unusual in the medium business in that she was, of course, unmarried. Most of the professional spiritualist harpies who preyed upon the gullible had 'Mrs' for a prefix, which lent them more dignity and solidarity, or rather 'Madam', as they prefer to be known. Miss Paradone, however, used her taut, tight spinsterhood of some sixty-five years to enhance her credibility, claiming that as a virgin, unsullied, the spirits could pass through her without danger of contamination of any kind. She was that rarity in these modern days of increasing scepticism, a physical medium, but a good one. Once her father had been a famous conjurer, long forgotten, and his daughter had inherited his library of illusions. Since conjuring had gone out of fashion and there was no market anyway for lady magicians, Miss Paradone, with the cynical contempt of the spinster who felt that the world had let her down, had simply adapted her father's mechanics and become an old pro who could produce whatever was wanted in the way of departed friends or relatives floating disembodied about one's head, or any shape of spirit photos, slate writing, voices and oracular messages from beyond.

At the request of Mrs Murchison, she held herself ready to people the ghost house of Melton Court with whatever might be conveniently going.

Mr Murchison loved his wife with the hatred born of living a greater part of his life with a semi-hysterical woman, whose concern with and fear of the occult was such that no contracting floorboard could crack or curtain blow from some vagrant draught without it being a visitation from the other side, or, at the very least, portent of some kind of disaster in the offing.

Her husband, in the manner of husbands put upon, had often entertained fantasies of getting rid of her by rigging up some kind of manifestation which would scare her to death, but never put it into operation, since he was too unfamiliar with the mechanics of such an affair. Besides which, when not involved in spiritualist research or the pursuit of messages from the hereafter, Mrs Murchison was a nice enough woman who looked after his creature comforts in a satisfactory manner.

Mr Murchison had a vague suspicion that the seances he was compelled to attend from time to time had something definitely fishy about them, but he had neither the mentality nor the courage to explore the matter. He was a vacuum-cleaner salesman, and a successful one, whose intellectual accomplishments were limited to those gambits of salesmanship needed to persuade the customer to sign the contract and agree to the full load of unnecessary accessories. Knowing nothing about the subject of the life hereafter, except that he didn't believe in it, he was not inclined to tamper with it – particularly since clients of seances and visitors were always warned of the most dire consequences should they break the circle or attempt any contact with the medium during the course of one of her trances.

As Mrs Maitland had surmised, Mr Murchison, after his visit, had indeed hardly been able to wait to reveal to his wife the ghastly details of the infanticide which was supposed to have taken place in the area they now occupied in their flat in Melton Court. In pursuit of that subconscious desire to have his wife cured of her obsession, even if necessary permanently by means of a heart attack, upon his return from the Maitland apartment, full of wrath at the manner in which he knew he had been politely savaged by Mrs Maitland, he let go at his wife.

If Mr Murchison resembled a shark, which indeed he did – one of those big threshers with undershot jaw, made more prominent by his half-walrus moustache and staring eye, an eye he used to transfix potential customers as he went from door to door with his vacuum cleaners – Mrs Murchison was his pilot fish. She was as tiny as he was huge. Meek, un-aggressive, spineless, with soft, haunted or slightly injured eyes, and the corners of her mouth turned down with the piety of her addiction to the religious aspects of spiritualism. Thus, a mere wisp of a woman, and apparently helpless, her strength was as the strength of a hundred, since there was no way of defeating her or her will. Not for nothing were the children to agree very quickly between themselves that she would be referred to as 'Mrs Mouse'.

'Hacked the child to pieces with a blunt kitchen knife,' narrated Mr Murchison, determined to make a thorough job of it while he was at it. 'Right here in this room – that is to say, the room where it happened used to be where we are now. Those people below seem to have latched on to the story somehow. Blood all over, they said – that's how they caught the monster. Had hanging in those days, and a damn good thing. Too much softness today. Over there by the window, they said.' And he indicated the spot occupied by one of the twin beds to which Mrs Murchison retired each night.

To his intense surprise Mrs Murchison did not react with the immediate hysterics he had anticipated. In fact there were no hysterics at all, but a strange icy cold, in which her haunted eyes took on a kind of luminous understanding.

'I've always known it,' she said.

'Wha – what? Always known what?'

'That there was something, someone there wanting to get through to me. I've felt it on, oh, so many nights.'

'What? What are you talking about? What wants to get through to you?'

'That poor little boy. He wants to come back and tell us about it. I must 'phone Miss Paradone at once.'

This was not at all according to plan. Instead of scaring his wife out of her wits he seemed to have initiated another one of those abominable gropings around in the dark with that dreadful woman who looked like a wrestler.

'Here now, Louisa. I say, wait a minute. How do you know? It's only those three children. They might have made up the whole –'

'They're sensitives. We must have them present. They all are. I have seen them about, I have always felt it. The murdered child has got through to the younger boy. Miss Paradone will help him to get through to us, and perhaps we can ease his poor little life in the hereafter.'

'Supposing the fellow they hung for it gets through too?' put in her husband almost viciously, in increasing panic as the matter grew out of hand.

'He would be on a much lower plane, of course, but we would be able to help him too, perhaps, to reach a higher one. He must be suffering terribly. We'll move the bed and Miss Paradone can have her cabinet right here – or we can do it with a curtain and have our chain in the drawing-room. We'll ask our group with the Reverend Smealey to lead the singing. But I know Miss Paradone will want the children there for her controls. We've never really had such an opportunity before. I mean, actually so close to something. One almost feels as though the poor fellow were here now. Victor, you must arrange that those children are able to be here on whatever night Miss Paradone feels her fluids are the strongest. Oh, I do hope her fluids will have been piling up.'

'What?' cried Mr Murchison, now in complete panic. 'Me get them here?' The prospect of bearding that tigress mother in her den in Flat 1A again and requesting that she lend her three offspring to such a performance seemed not only completely terrifying but likewise insuperable.

'But of course,' said his wife, now in the grip of that immovability he had come to know so well. 'You've met the mother. You could invite her too. I'm sure she'd be most interested, and we might even make another convert. You know how persuasive Reverend Smealey can be – particularly if there has been a manifestation.'

'Look here, Louisa, that's impossible. I'll have you understand –'

'I am sure you'll be able to arrange it, Victor. Use your best selling voice. I'd better call Miss Paradone at once, before she is too booked up. *Everyone* seems to be after her these days. We oughtn't to leave it too long. It was only last night I woke up and had that feeling come over me.'

Cold at the pit of his stomach, Mr Murchison knew from experience that nothing would move or change his wife from her project, and that somehow, in the very near future, another one of those abominable rituals would be taking place. And, what's more, those three blasted children from 1A would be there.

CHAPTER XVI

Seance

When it came to it, Mr Murchison's task turned out to be not as insuperable as he had feared it would be. The invitation once extended to Miranda, Michael and Roddy evoked such obvious enthusiasm in all three that he even felt he could leave the problem of parental permission or parental handling to them. In a moment of inspiration he added the cake and ice cream party afterwards, being perfectly willing to provide this himself if it would get him off the hook – quite unnecessarily. He did not realize that the very prospect of encountering a real live ghost under the proper auspices in the protection of adults would prove irresistible to young people who, less than a fortnight before, had faced the prospect of the most boring Easter holiday ever. The rain, after all, as the Meteorological Office guiltily kept pointing out, was not going to let up properly for any length of time owing to an unusual mix-up in fronts somewhere over Iceland – and was again now at practically monsoon strength.

Ever since Miranda had envisioned the House, though, the experience had been producing the most unexpected dividends of novelty, excitement and new acquaintances. And now here was the greatest prospect of all: Roddy's blatant lie was to result in a ghost gymkhana to which they had all been invited.

The fact that Roddy had lied to irritate Mr Murchison and had been properly set upon for it by his brother and sister, and the fact that Miranda had never envisioned any such

kind of occurrence in that particular part of the House
where now the Murchisons had their flat, had nothing
whatsoever to do with the anticipation with which the
three looked forward to the affair. If the adults actually
believed that such a thing had taken place, and acted in
good faith upon such a belief, one never could tell what
might develop. And maybe Roddy hadn't, after all, told a
complete lie, but, without knowing it, had fallen victim to
an inspiration similar to the one which had seized Miranda
and led her to produce an entire dwelling.

Thus it was that, having salved their consciences and not
burdened their parents with the worry that their brood might
be wanting to do something silly or even dangerous on the
night Mr and Mrs Maitland kept their dinner date with the
Baldwins, Michael, Miranda and Roddy, clad in slippers,
pyjamas and dressing-gowns, with Michael as the leader,
shuffled along at half past eight to Flat 3D.

Michael bravely pushed the buzzer, and within seconds
they were admitted to an utter confusion and babble of an
assortment of strange adults.

Since they were to be such an important part of the show,
the three were treated with a deference which went a long
way to dispelling any fears they might have had.

The names of the guests, or, as Mrs Murchison referred
to them, the congregation, were impossible for the children
to remember: Mrs Breadle, Mr Whitehouse, Miss Auger,
Mr and Mrs Purtle, Miss Winbastle, Dr Handbow, and so
on, to the number of fourteen, and so for the purpose of
rapid reference the three assigned substitute names for all.

This they were able to do since after the first perfunctory
introductions nobody paid any attention to the children,
who were allowed to collect in a corner while the grown-ups
circulated buzzing, chatting and speculating upon the forthcoming demonstration and what it might be expected to
reveal.

Having naturally begun with Mr Murchison as Mr Shark,
and his wife as Mrs Mouse, the temptation to continue
zoologically – if only for identification purposes – was in-

escapable. Thus a husband and wife were broken down into
Mr Goat and Mrs Camel. There was a Mr Parrot, Mrs Cow,
Mr Hippopotamus, Mr Beagle, Miss Ostrich, Mr and Mrs
Monkey, Mrs Crocodile, Mrs Pelican, Miss Giraffe and
Mr Bear.

So rapidly had hosts and guests fallen into their proper
classification by the quick minds of Miranda and Michael
that Roddy had no opportunity to bestow even one of his
own, and protested. There was only one fussy little man
with a semi-bald head and sharply hooked nose and round
eyes behind large spectacles remaining, and who seemed to
have some sort of special status as an officer of the group,
and so he was awarded to Roddy in the expectation that he
would, of course, name him Mr Owl. But he didn't.
Instead he declared, 'That's Mr Tiddlypom.'

'Oh, come on, Roddy,' said Michael. 'Don't be silly.
What's a tiddlypom?'

'*He's* a tiddlypom,' said Roddy, ending the argument.

A disinterested observer looking upon the scene in the
drawing-room of the Murchisons would have noticed that
this semi-isolation of the three children was more than just
the normal manner in which adults and the very young
naturally separated at any gathering. He would have seen
that actually all the glances and conversation rather centred
on the corner where the three were collected, that they were
the subject of discussion, and that some of the glances
thrown in their direction even contained some awe and trepi-
dation. They had already been touched, in the minds of the
gathering, by the finger of the unknown and the mysterious.

It was really building up to a fine evening, the suspense
being heightened when Miss Paradone kept them waiting a
half hour before she swept into the flat. With the power and
violence of her six-foot presence, she had the musculature
of an all-in wrestler, topped by a handsome, compelling face.
She was clad in a voluminous kaftan of some dark material.
Everything about her, naturally, was a part of the equipment. Her muscles had been developed, as had her father's
to further her profession – and the kaftan, of course, was a

storehouse. She nullified every other person in the room, with the possible exception of Mr Shark, who, two inches or so taller than she, looked upon her with an unenthusiastic and unimpressed eye.

Miss Paradone apologized for her lateness. She had, for all her size and strength, a soft, beguiling speaking voice, almost with a lisp, which thoroughly disguised the fact that she had a range from high soprano to *basso profundo*, so that whenever she produced alien voices listeners were able to swear that they could not possibly have been her own.

'You must forgive me,' she began. 'I was preparing to come away when I was overtaken. A trance, you know. It has only happened to me once or twice before when there has been great power. Oh, there's great power stirring tonight. We shall see. We shall see. Now, where are my little helpers?'

It was Mr Tiddlypom, whatever his capacity was, who escorted her over to where the children were collected, and she towered over them so monstrously that she became in the minds of all three, almost simultaneously, Mrs Monster.

Her height was augmented purposely by coils of thick black hair piled up on top of her head – useful not only for the impression it conveyed but also to contain what magicians refer to as a 'load': that is, anything concealed about the person which is later to be produced.

She stood gazing down upon them with wide-spaced, slightly prominent eyes. She had quite strong teeth, backed by a powerful jaw that gave the impression that anything she might bite would come away.

'Yes, yes,' she said. 'You are quite right. The power is there. They are adepts. I feel it. I feel it.'

Miranda, Michael and Roddy took an instant and thorough dislike to her. She smelled of mothballs – or perhaps it was only the kaftan. She laid a hand that was surprisingly shapely and delicate for one so large and seemingly gross upon the smouldering flame of Roddy's head, and said, 'Yes, my little man. You and I shall go far tonight.'

Michael and Miranda experienced mutually a moment of

desperate anxiety waiting for the explosion from Roddy. Past experience indicated that anyone who 'little-manned' Roddy got what he or she was asking for.

Oddly enough there was no immediate retaliation. Roddy was either too shocked or surprised or perhaps intimidated by the gathering. He merely looked up once balefully from under his fox-coloured eyebrows, then dropped his eyes and shook his head loose from under the patronizing hand.

Michael merely said to himself, 'Oh, boy!'

Miranda felt a moment's qualm of jealousy. After all, it was she herself who was Chief Witch and not Roddy, she who had conjured up the House, and but for her none of these funny people would have been there. But she was not actually a jealous child, and the emotion was soon replaced by one of scorn. The monster couldn't be much of a witch to make a mistake like that.

In fact, in predicting that she and Roddy would go far that night together, Miss Paradone had come closer than ever before in her life to attaining the role of a genuine seeress, and parting the curtains of the future.

'Has everything been prepared?' she asked.

'Yes, yes,' replied Mr Tiddlypom, and steering her by the elbow like a tug pushing a liner he showed her the arrangements.

Since the crime originally testified to by Roddy had taken place in the bedroom opening off from the drawing-room, and from which entrance could be effected from the corridor side as well as two decorative glass double doors from the drawing-room itself, the medium was to operate from there. Two three-sided screens set opposite one another with an aperture left in the centre made a practical makeshift cabinet, and, with a curtain hung across the aperture, effectively concealed the person of the medium.

A chair was provided for her inside the cabinet, the double glass doors thrown open, and the sitters arranged in a semi-circle from the drawing-room facing the doings. Before they were ushered into the bedroom where Miss Paradone had decreed they were to join her, the three children noticed that, in addition to blinds and curtains being drawn over the windows, heavy black drapes had been hung over them and over the doors as well, so that not so much as a crack or a chink was left through which light might show. Lights were extinguished once or twice experimentally, with the result that there was a total blackness so thick that one felt one could almost grope it away from its envelopment of one's face and body.

'Sit there in that corner,' Miss Paradone ordered the children. 'And hold one another by the hand. You can sit on the floor and, whatever happens, you mustn't be frightened.' She wanted them close not only for the value of the suggestion of their psychic powers but also not to have them blundering about in the dark.

The company seated itself in the semi-circle, and Mr Tiddlypom made his little speech. 'I believe all of you have been here before and are familiar with our methods. You are to hold each other by the hand and under no circumstances, no matter what might transpire, move or leave your places, for to do so might endanger the health or even the life of Miss Paradone, who, when in trance, is in an extremely delicate situation, balanced, as you know, between our two worlds.' He turned to the three children sitting cross-legged on the floor and said, 'Is that understood? You hold each other by the hand.'

'Yes, sir,' said Michael. He and Roddy were each sitting on the outside, with Miranda in the middle, and they obediently did as they were told. Michael, the scientist-cum-engineer-to-be, wished he had four eyes, the better to observe everything going on. Miranda, the creator, was thinking that no matter what dire punishment might be visited upon her if their escapade was to result in discovery she wouldn't have missed this for anything. If you were going to be a real Chief Witch you really wanted to know everything about one. Roddy was finding himself simply conscious of the place on his head where Miss Paradone's hand had rested momentarily, and he kept brushing it with his free hand to make it go away.

The curtain over the aperture of the cabinet had been drawn aside briefly. Miss Paradone sat down upon the chair placed therein, and held out her hands in a curiously submissive gesture. 'I am ready,' she said.

And now, to the astonishment of the children, Mr Tiddlypom, accompanied by the bearded gentleman nominated as Mr Goat, appeared holding coils of rope with which they proceeded to bind Miss Paradone's wrists, feet, legs and body until she was trussed like a fowl for the spit.

'What are they doing that for?' Michael asked in a whisper. 'Is she being punished?' Roddy wondered. To him any kind of restraint constituted correction of some kind.

Miranda, who was beginning to germinate what would eventually grow into a woman's practical cynicism, said, 'I suppose it's so she can't cheat.'

The word 'cheat' did not fall too sweetly about Miss Paradone's ears, and for a moment she questioned her wisdom in having placed the children in such proximity and whether it might not have been better to have located them in the other room with the sitters, or perhaps even behind them. However, it was too late for any changes now, and she could further, she felt, count upon the fact that when she began operations, and manifestations commenced, the three would be so gripped by terror that they could not possibly be of any danger to her.

'Lights,' ordered Mr Tiddlypom. Mr Goat at one door, he at the other, flicked the switches and plunged the flat into a darkness more thickly and solidly black because of the loss of the light that had just been extinguished. This was followed by the noise of the two taking their seats in the dark and the rustling of the sitters settling themselves and reaching for their neighbours' hands.

Out of the darkness came the bleat of Mr Goat, who apparently functioned as choir master. He said, 'We will begin with *Rock of Ages*, after that *Abide With Me*, and then *Praise to the Lord, the Almighty*.' He must then have produced a pitch pipe from his pocket, for a reedy note pierced the darkness, after which the sitters let go with not too much discord in rendering the well-known hymns.

The three children really enjoyed this. The Maitlands, being Church of England, managed to attend one or two Sundays out of four *en famille*, and so Michael, Miranda and Roddy knew the hymns by heart, and, beating time with their clasped hands in the dark, raised their young voices lustily, to the great satisfaction of Miss Paradone, who now was certain she had done the right thing in keeping them close.

The racket that they and the other sitters were producing adequately drowned out any noise she might have made as she busily freed herself from the clumsy and amateur rope ties with which she had been bound, and prepared to provide the evening's entertainment.

She gave them ten minutes of complete silence to warm them up and intensify their mood of apprehension, then from the cabinet came first a series of low moans followed by rustles and thumps and the sudden metallic rattle of a tambourine, followed in turn by two slaps on the skin of the instrument.

Something faintly luminous appeared at the top of the screens, floating out through the doorway and across the ceiling into the drawing-room, where it dipped and bobbed in a kind of antic ghostly dance which brought forth a little squeal from one of the women guests: 'Oh! Something touched me! I felt it! It was cold!'

'Shsh,' warned someone else.

The blob disappeared, and now there were voices – a man's, a woman's, a baby's – cries, ejaculations, snatches of sentences, gibberish, a bit of a sea shanty.

A trumpet suddenly appeared in the air, glowing, floated once around the room and returned from whence it had come. The noises in the cabinet increased. From the babble of voices it might have been a meeting of the Security Council of the United Nations.

All this was more or less familiar territory to the sitters, who were being warmed up for the physical production in which spirits no longer disembodied would appear before them. While Miss Paradone was a practised and adept magician and illusionist, she was far from being an original one. Like her brethren on the open stage or in night clubs, she seldom departed from standard routine. True, on information dredged up from the prior chat with Mrs Murchison, some special preparations had been made for this particular evening – a main event in keeping with what was expected in the light of the crime supposed to have been committed – but the prelims were strictly standard.

Strangely enough, it was the tough, shark-like and irascible Mr Murchison who was the only one to give a thought to the children, and he was worried. True or false, the things that were taking place in the dark might well be calculated to frighten the wits out of anyone who had never attended such an affair before, and, in particular, impressionable young minds. After all, it was he who was responsible for their presence there, and if one or more of them should be made ill through fright, or suffer a siege of hysterics, he did not like to consider the repercussions. There could even be law suits from the Maitlands.

He need not have worried. Fascinated the children were, entertained beyond their wildest hopes – but frightend, no. For their incontrovertible logic was working for them.

Had the cabinet been seen to be originally empty, they might reasonably have been terrified. But as it wasn't, since they had seen and knew the woman to be inside it, the knowledge fortified by their sense of smell, the musty mothball odour being still perceptible, it provided them with a simple point of reference and sense of security. All the grunts, groans, rattles, thumps and bangs, as well as the objects sailing about the premises, could only be coming from her. For whatever reason or purpose it was going on, it was *her* game, and therefore *her* business, and hence of no menace to them. Miss Paradone, as a professional performer, might have been flattered, and, as a medium, irritated, if she realized that the children were accepting her performance purely as entertainment.

The repertory continued through the usual floating objects, ghostly touches on the shoulder, chill winds and cheery messages from the departed, containing no novelty but without which the sitters would have been disappointed in the manner of children who, listening to an oft-read fairy tale, want no word or comma left out in its repetition. This finally trailed away to a series of mumblings and mutterings from an assortment of voices, as though the spirits were assembled informally at a cocktail party, nattering as they awaited the arrival of the guest of honour.

This momentous event finally was heralded by the violent ringing of the dinner bell, which had already made several clangorous voyages around the drawing-room but now tolled from the region of the cabinet. This was followed by the manifestation in voice only of Lala Prad.

Lala was a little Hindustani girl who, at the age of fourteen, had been ravished and cruelly murdered by a wicked Rajah some time in the eighteenth century, and whose travail in the other world was apparently eased by occasional visits to this one. She had been both seen and heard on other occasions by clients of Miss Paradone. A dusky face trailing a white garment like smoke behind her, jingling her bracelets and piping her messages in broken English in a childish voice containing just a hint of Miss Paradone's own lisp, if one thought about it.

The voice said, 'Salaam, effendi', Miss Paradone having ascertained beforehand that there were no old India hands in the audience. When there might be such she was careful not to trot out this particular control for questioning.

'Lala Prad glad to see you. She come here tonight, bring little friend from other side with her. He like to see you. Little friend, he live here one time many years ago. He maybe say you how he feel come back for hello from trouble he have in older time. Poor Tommy.'

Michael whispered to Miranda, 'Did Roddy say the boy's name was Tommy?'

Miranda whispered back, 'Shsh!' and then added, 'He didn't say at all.'

Then there ensued a colloquy between Lala Prad and her developing friend, first faint and then clear.

'Are you there, Tommy?'

A faint boy's voice replied, 'Yes, I'm here,' and a rustle passed through the sitters.

'Can you come through, Tommy? Everyone here, they like see you.'

'I fink so. It isn't easy. Is my bed still there?'

The reply came startlingly from Mrs Murchison: 'Oh, yes, it is. It's right over there in the corner. Just where it . . .' The rest of her sentence was drowned out by a chorus of shushes.

'Hello,' said Tommy. 'I haven't been here since the man came with the knife . . .' And forthwith he began to material-ize to the sound of rustles and murmurs from the sitters.

At first he was no more than a faint glow at the entrance to the cabinet, a phosphorescence through which emerged suddenly the face of a boy about seven or eight years old, never wholly distinct in the gloom as it waved here and there, but sufficient to catch a glimpse of brown hair slicked back and a handsome childish face which, with the piping voice that accompanied it, and in particular after the build up, gave a startling illusion of reality and of another presence.

He seemed to be having a struggle, and explained, 'I can't get all of me through yet on my first visit, but I will come again and see you, because I'm not unhappy or frightened any more.'

This indicated to the veteran sitters that Tommy would not materialize wholly and walk amongst them in the dark to be touched and fondled as had other physical manifesta-tions upon different occasions, but for the return of the victim to the scene of the tragedy it was not too dis-appointing.

'Is the man with the knife here?' asked Tommy, his head floating from one side to another as if in search.

'No, Tommy,' Lala Prad answered him. 'He's not here. He in bad place. All here are friends.'

'That's good,' said Tommy. The glow in his vicinity increased somewhat as, apparently having gained confidence, more of him began to materialize. Not any shape of a human body but in the traditional guise of an acceptable ghost: something long, white, trailing and undulating so that Tommy seemed to grow above the entrance to the cabinet and cross the threshold into the drawing-room.

'I can't see,' said Roddy. And this was true, since squatting on the end and furthest inside the bedroom he was at an angle where Tommy, having passed the threshold, had disappeared – that is to say, his face was no longer visible to him: only the disembodied whatever it was he was trailing after him.

'Shsh!' cautioned Miranda. 'Be quiet, Roddy.'

'Why did the man with the knife come?' Tommy enquired.

'It was over there.'

Roddy registered a second protest. 'But I can't see. I want to see.'

This time it was Michael who hissed, 'Shut up!' And, reaching around behind Miranda, gave Roddy a hard pinch on the arm – a not unusual thing for an older brother to do to a younger brother, but this happened to be the wrong moment for correction.

While Roddy could not grasp entirely what was going on, the affair of a boy, a man and a knife rang a bell in his mind as something that he had initiated a little while back which was having fascinating results, but his sense of justice told him that, whatever the consequences, they stemmed from his story and, but for him, they wouldn't be. Hence he was perfectly entitled to see.

He therefore reached into the pocket of his dressing-gown and produced his beloved torch, which was likewise his moon-radar-laser-beam-cum-death-ray, and clicked it on so that the yellow circle, like a theatrical spotlight from the balcony, revealed Miss Paradone in the act of holding up a stick to which had been fastened the near life-sized head of a boy cut out from a magazine advertisement and pasted on

cardboard, while at the same time she was regurgitating an
ever-increasing trail of white cheesecloth.

'Oh, look!' cried Roddy. 'The lady is being sick. Everything is coming out of her mouth.'

'Put that light out, you little brat!' came in muffled tones
from Miss Paradone, since she was still engaged in bringing
up the spirit remains of little Tommy.

'Roddy, you mustn't!' Michael shouted.

'But she's being sick,' protested Roddy. 'Look at all that
white stuff coming out of her mouth. Ugh!'

From the circle of sitters came a yell from Mr Murchison:
'What the hell is going on here?'

From Miss Paradone, whose rage was causing her to
begin to choke on the swallowed cheesecloth she was
regurgitating, 'Poof 'ow the li'.'

Another voice called, 'Put on the light! If the woman's
ill . . .'

The switch clicked and the drawing-room was brightly
illuminated to the tune of a wail from Mr Tiddlypom:
'No! No! No! You mustn't! You'll do her an injury!'

But at that moment the only injury was being done to
Mr Murchison, who had rushed over and was wrestling
violently with Miss Paradone, who had been revealed as
free of all her ties, her cabinet exposed as full of all the junk
which had been floating about the enclosure, and the last of
the cheesecloth emerging to give her freedom of speech,
which included a string of curses well outside her repertoire
of incantations.

The tableau developed as Mr Murchison endeavoured to
hold the struggling medium and was getting the worst of it
until Mr Hippopotamus took a hand. As the name bestowed
upon him would indicate, he was a fat man, but he was also
extraordinarily strong, and, with Mr Murchison, was on the
verge of subduing the angry medium, who was fighting like
a wildcat until, reaching into her hair to get a better grip,
he cut himself on a small pair of scissors she had concealed
there. Blood appeared as he let out a bellow of pain, and
the seance suddenly turned into a general punch-up as

sceptic and believer joined battle in a wild *mêlée* of uncontrolled hysteria and released tension. A zoo gone mad, in which Mrs Cow had already pulled off Miss Ostrich's wig, Mr and Mrs Monkey were assaulting Mrs Pelican and had torn her dress, Mr Beagle and Mr Bear were exchanging wild swings, Mr Goat, Mrs Camel and Miss Giraffe were on the floor in a furious tangle of thrashing arms and legs, with only Mr Tiddlypom and Mr Murchison disengaged, the latter screaming like a circus calliope, the former wringing his hands and wailing, 'No! No! You mustn't! Stop it! She's in a trance!'

'Trance, my foot!' yelled Mr Murchison. 'Look at my cheek.' It too was bleeding from lacerations caused by the fangs of Miss Paradone, now enveloped in the clutches of Mr Hippopotamus.

Footsteps were heard in the hall, as doors in the corridor opened and other tenants came out to investigate the extraordinary sounds emerging from behind Flat 3D.

'Call the police!' quivered Mr Tiddlypom.

'Oh, no! Not the police!' shouted Mr Murchison. 'We'll handle this trickster ourselves.'

The wild battle in the drawing-room rose in crescendo – for there is no creature so aroused as the dyed-in-the-wool spiritualist in the face of exposure of his or her medium. Under no circumstances will they give up their belief, no matter how blatant the trickery is shown to be. And at this instance the shock of the revelation coming upon the tension of the seance had abolished all restraint, with the sceptic and the credulous, the agnostic and the faithful having it out once and for all.

The startled listeners in the hall heard the thumps and knocks from within, and muffled cries of 'Oh, you will, will you?' 'Take this! And this!' 'Leggo my hair!' 'I'll scratch your eyes out!' Cries of pain, cries of aggressive jubilation.

Mr Thompson suddenly appeared, a bunch of keys in his fist. Somebody had had the sense to summon him. He inserted the proper pass key into the lock and threw the door open, so that now the sounds of battle were no longer muffled.

But his entrance upon the scene and the sudden egress it provided brought a change in the situation. The open door, as seen from the bedroom through the drawing-room and via the entrance corridor, suddenly gave Miss Paradone the strength of ten. With a mighty thrust she threw off both Mr Murchison and Mr Hippopotamus, gathered up her kaftan above her knees so that she would not be impeded, and fled out of the door, down the hall, down the stairs adjoining the lift, and out of the front door of Melton Court into the night. That part of the seance which called for her participation was obviously over.

Michael said to his brother and sister, in his capacity of head of the expedition, 'I suppose we had better go now. Hang on to me.'

Nobody saw them or so much as noticed them thread their way out of the flat, in which, the battle over, the protagonists plus the visitors from outside and Mr Thompson were milling about trying to explain all that had happened. Thus the children gained their own premises and let themselves in.

There was so much to be chewed over, discussed, queried, cleared up and reviewed, once they had regained the safety of the boys' bedroom, that there really was at the moment nothing that would have sufficed, and they knew it. And again Miranda's sensitive instincts warned her that this was not the time, and that the thing to do was to go to bed and sort it all out the next day.

And that they did. As they settled down in their own respective rooms, with lights out, the church clock down the road hammered eleven times. Five minutes later a key rattled in the door, and Mr and Mrs Maitland returned from the slightly dull dinner with people who fortunately liked to retire early and had signalled as much.

Mrs Maitland paid her motherly visit to her children before even removing her coat.

Miranda said sleepily, 'Was it a nice dinner, Mummy?'

'Very nice, darling,' Mrs Maitland replied. 'Go to sleep now. We're back.' And she kissed her daughter softly on the forehead.

She went next into the boys' room, where sounds of sobs came from Roddy's bed.

'Why, Roddy,' she gasped, and went over to him. 'Whatever's the matter?'

'I've lost my torch,' sobbed Roddy.

'Never mind, darling. We'll find it in the morning.'

Michael then thought he had better quickly contribute. 'I think perhaps he's been having a bad dream. He does quite often have them, Mummy.'

'Of course,' Mrs Maitland agreed. 'Come on, now, Roddy. You're a big boy. You know all about dreams. They're not real, and they go away very quickly.' She kissed him, then Michael, and blew another kiss as she left the room.

'Are they all right?' asked Mr Maitland.

'Oh, yes. Fine,' Mrs Maitland assured him, and then began the routine of getting ready for bed.

The next morning, rumours and snatches of what in Melton Court had become known as 'the battle of the third floor' reached the ears of the Maitlands, but nothing to connect their children with it, though there was one touchy moment for all three of them that afternoon which might have opened up the entire can of peas, but, fortunately, was misunderstood.

It was the delivery of a parcel addressed to Mr Roderick Maitland, Flat 1A, Melton Court, which, when opened, revealed a pocket torch and, most resplendent, a boy's cowboy suit, with sombrero, chaps, high-heeled boots and spurs, checked shirt, yellow kerchief, gun-belt with dummy cartridges, and a replica of a Colt .45. The card read, 'For Roddy – Compliments of Victor Murchison'.

The torch might have been a give-away if Mrs Maitland, present at the opening of the parcel, hadn't quite forgotten the episode of Roddy weeping on her return the night before because he had lost it. On point of dire torture,

Roddy had been cautioned by Michael and Miranda never to mention the subject again.

'Why, how very kind of Mr Murchison,' said Mrs Maitland. 'You really are favoured, Roddy. You must write a thank-you note.' While to herself she mused, 'Well, who would have thought it? That old shark has a conscience, and realized how frightfully rude he's been – to Roddy especially – and has sent a peace offering. I suppose nobody is ever quite as bad as one sometimes thinks they are.'

The children, however, knew better – or at least they suspected better, since they would probably never know for certain. But from the way Mr Murchison had behaved, and the light of joy that had illuminated his face at what Roddy's torch had revealed, it seemed fairly obvious that some kind of service had been rendered to him through the affair. In some way, of which they could not be quite sure, they had helped, and since helping people was what they had been urged and taught to do, they could look upon the entire episode, including their own narrow escape, with a reasonable feeling of virtue.

CHAPTER XVII

A Slight Problem

Mr Henry Thompson, ex-Commander of forty years experience in Her Majesty's Navy, was basically a cheery person, who came to his office along from the lift on the ground floor of Melton Court each morning in the best of humour, having consumed a bang-up breakfast. His wife, Joanna, looked after him capitally.

He enjoyed his superintendency over the inmates of Melton Court as he had flourished as watchdog over his shipmates in the Senior Service. He was a well-adjusted, equable man, whom it was hard to jar out of his kind of soothing, pondering placidity. His bulk was as rock, his eyes still appeared to be reflecting the colours of the sea, and seemed freighted with innocence and filled with apparent sympathy for any complainant. The busy beard served to conceal any occasional distaste about the lines of his mouth. He was the ideal man to serve not only as Superintendent and director of the mechanics of a complex of flats but also as a buffer between management and tenants.

He liked to keep his house neat, taut and shipshape like a vessel prepared at any moment to up anchor and set forth on a trouble-free voyage, coaled, watered, victualled and mechanically impeccable. He was its captain and purser – and Melton Court itself was indeed something like a ship, filled with complaining passengers, who, for the most part, avoided one another: a ship that never sailed, but still had to be kept trim, up-to-the-mark, fully filled and staffed.

A man of such antecedents, background and temperament

is not easily thrown. It took some doing to move him out of his phlegmatic calm and control over any situation that might arise in connection with Melton Court. But he was thrown further than he had ever been at ten o'clock on the morning after the seance fiasco.

The affair was initiated with the presentation by Tim Ryan, the doorman, of a card announcing the arrival of one G. Harper Shepperton, and within the lower left-hand corner, 'Special Adviser, Foreign Office', followed, upon Mr Thompson's nod, by Mr Shepperton himself.

No one would have guessed from the blank and friendly welcome reflected in Mr Thompson's eyes and his manner that the occasion had not begun entirely auspiciously. While not a snob, the Superintendent had never been enamoured of those handles which indicated that the owner, for some reason, was ashamed of his first name, concealing under the initial the fact that it might be plebeian, and offering something fancy in its place.

The visitor himself was a young man in his thirties in a dark jacket and bowler hat, carrying a briefcase. He had tight-stretched sunken eyes and thin lips that appeared to stick together.

No searcher after trouble before it was upon him, Mr Thompson motioned G. Harper Shepperton into a chair in his office, and conjectured no more than that he was either in search of a flat for himself or someone connected. The sealed mouth, he gathered, was one of the occupational hazards or by-products of the diplomatic service, and he waited for it to come unstuck.

The young man, his briefcase resting on his knee, let him wait while he observed the simple effects of Mr Thompson's office: filing cabinet, desk, framed floor plans of the building, also under glass his Warrant and a photograph of the crew of the HMS *Royal Sceptre*, as well as photographs of members of Mr Thompson's family, two telephones, a wastepaper basket, an ash tray, and a desk lighter in the shape of a cannon, which, when one pulled a knob, produced a gas flame at the muzzle.

Mr Thompson's equanimity was not shaken by this scrutiny. He was not too busy at the moment, and could wait to find out what brought this specimen sailing into his ken.

But then at last the visitor began to speak. 'You are Henry Thompson?'

'Aye.'

'And you are the Superintendent of Melton Court?'

'That's right.'

'And you have been here since this block opened in August 1974?'

'Indeed I have,' nodded Mr Thompson.

'And thus would be familiar with all the tenants of Melton Court.'

'More or less,' said Mr Thompson, and wished his visitor would abandon what was obvious and get on to what had brought him there.

'Hmmm.' And here Shepperton opend his briefcase, took out a dossier, opened it, consulted the sheet of paper at the top, and, looking directly at Mr Thompson in a manner which his suspicious eyes made almost accusing, said, 'You have a Mr and Mrs Sen Sinsavang on your list of tenants.'

'That's correct.'

Sharpening the look with which he was transfixing Mr Thompson, Mr Shepperton then asked abruptly, 'Do you know them?'

'Naturally.' Mr Thompson was beginning to be aware of a faint irritation which, being something of a diplomat himself, he realized he must suppress until there might appear some particular cause for it.

'I mean, do you know *who* they are?'

Mr Thompson very much wanted to say, 'Chinamen', just to see what the effect would be on this immaculate young inquisitor, but refrained. Instead he said, 'I'm sure you've got all that there,' indicating the dossier.

Mr Shepperton nodded. 'Mr Sen Sinsavang, Cultural Attaché of the Lao Nam Embassy in London, was born in 1936 in the village of Bao Gho in the state of Lao Nam, which at that time, of course, was a province of French Indonesia. Educated in Hanoi and Paris, he became an ardent revolutionist and fighter for the freedom of Lao Nam, and took part in the campaigns against the French. In April 1974 he married Mei Dai, niece of the Prime Minister of Lao Nam, His Excellency Bin-Luang, and came to London to take up his appointment as Cultural Attaché to the Lao Nam Embassy in August 1974, which date coincides with the opening of the Melton Court block of flats. There is as yet no issue.'

'Well,' commented Mr Thompson, 'they seem to be a very pleasant couple.'

Shepperton's lips glued themselves together again as he silently ruffled through the file, and when once more they were, with difficulty, parted, he enquired in the manner of one who is convinced he is going to get 'no' for an answer, 'Have you a copy of their lease?'

'Naturally,' replied the Superintendent. He arose, went to his filing cabinet, and held it up.

This disappointment did not crack Mr Shepperton's façade. He merely remarked, 'Oh, I see you have.' Took a duplicate from his dossier and said, 'May we compare them?'

'But of course.'

Since in modern times landlords neither trust tenants nor do tenants evince any confidence in the honesty of landlords, the lease compiled by lawyers on both sides to deal with any eventuality covered a large number of pages of both bold and fine print, with extra paragraphs added marginally in ink, clauses numbered, clauses lettered – and Shepperton took his own sweet time with the cross-checking.

For Mr Thompson the visit was no longer a mystery. When the tenant or a tenant's representative demanded to see a copy of the lease there was usually a complaint of some kind involved, or the evaluation of some technicality. This in no way ruffled the Superintendent, for an important part of his job was dealing with complaints and settling them before they ever reached the rarefied strata of the

Truciman offices, and he had no doubt that he would be able to settle this one, whatever it might be.

After some few minutes of reading, Shepperton finally turned upon the duplicate pages, one being the Sinsavang's copy and the other that of the Truciman Estates: identical paragraphs of Clause K, Section 9, Paragraph 3, which was an addendum, typed and initialled by both parties on a separate but stapled sheet.

'Ah, I thought so. Here it is.' Mr Shepperton pushed the documents over to Mr Thompson across his desk, and pointed to the paragraph with an impeccable fingernail.

Superintendent Thompson's mild and friendly blue eyes focused on the paragraph. It read:

Tenant demands and Landlord agrees that the Apartment 3 A in Melton Court, herein referred to as the Premises and located on plan 4 of the aforementioned Melton Court, sold under the Truciman Mutual Benefit Co-operative Scheme to the party of the second part, herein referred to as the Tenant, is new as completed on the fifteenth August nineteen seventy-four and has never before been occupied. Landlord further guarantees that the Edifice of Melton Court as per plans filed in the offices of Wilmore and Putnam Architects is new from the ground up and before its completion and until it was made open to the public has never in any way been rented sold or occupied. If circumstances past present or future should prove Landlord in breach thereof Landlord guarantees indemnification in accordance with the nature and seriousness of said breach unto the satisfaction of Tenant.

Mr Thompson nodded and said, 'That's right. I remember that. What is the problem?

At the time he had first come across this lease he recalled having wondered both why the tenant had demanded this clause and why the landlord had granted it – and, what was more, signed. But upon re-reading and reflection it seemed to Mr Thompson that all it really amounted to was a lot of lawyers' words and obfuscation. Obviously in the case of a brand new block arising from a hole in the ground and the flat from which practically the plumbers, carpenters, electricians and painters had withdrawn only a few days before the tenants or purchasers began to move in there could not be any kind of such breach mentioned, and so the whole affair was academic.

Mr Shepperton gave the Superintendent a long hard stare, pulled his lips apart just wide enough to let issue therefrom the words, 'Mr and Mrs Sinsavang are complaining that the landlord is in breach.'

Having just read what he had dismissed as a silly and innocuous paragraph, Mr Shepperton's last three words, 'is in breach', set off alarm bells inside Mr Thompson's skull. However, he gave no sign of this. Long experience with incipient and unexpected trouble had taught him to reflect whenever such a moment presented itself. He, as well as Mr Shepperton, could play the silent game and not give anything away until it became absolutely necessary.

He therefore let Mr Shepperton's sentence lie on the desk between them in silence for a few seconds before he pulled open the bottom drawer, produced a stubby blackened pipe and a tin of tobacco, said, 'Mind?' and without waiting for a reply busied himself with loading it, tamping it, examining his handiwork, and, ignoring the cannon lighter on the desk, produced a box of matches and fired it up. Following upon the first clouds of slightly rank smoke he remarked, 'In breach, you say?'

This pantomime, however, had not shaken Mr Shepperton, who found himself rather pleased at the prospect of encountering a possible foeman worthy of his own routines. It wasn't any fun to prepare a sudden shock attack only to see the enemy flee in panic before him.

'Exactly,' he replied.

'In breach whereof?' queried Mr Thompson, to show that when it came to anything connected with Melton Court he had done his legal homework.

'In breach of Clause K, Section 9, Paragraph 3, attached to page 15, initialled and signed by both parties.'

Not by so much as a quiver of his bushy eyebrows or rattle of pipe stem against his teeth did Mr Thompson show his relief upon hearing the basis of whatever complaint it might be that the Sinsavangs were preparing to put forward via this young man whose connection with the affair was still not at all clear to him. Patent, however, was the fact that if it was indeed connected with that ridiculous clause there was nothing to worry about. So far the game was all Mr Thompson's, and he could afford to take it seriously.

'You have proof of this?' he queried.

'To the extent necessary to support the complaint of Mr and Mrs Sinsavang, we have.'

This quiet assertion and the complete composure verging on arrogance of Mr Shepperton would have shaken anyone but Mr Thompson, who remembered that he had been there to offer his services the very day the Sinsavangs had moved in, and that his wife herself had piloted Madam Sinsavang through the intricacies of the modern kitchen, with its push-buttons and complicated eye-level oven-timing devices. It was, of course, impossible that any such complaint should ever come to trial, but he knew that he and his wife would make impeccable witnesses for the company, since only a half hour before the Sinsavangs arrived the electricians had just finished putting the brass fittings over the electric light switches by the doors. In breach indeed!

'I see,' said Mr Thompson, which was always the best thing to say when one didn't. 'And in what way do the Sinsavangs contend that the company is in breach?'

Mr Shepperton now went into *his* act. He produced a leather cigarette case with three gold initials in the corner, opened it, extracted a gold-tipped filter cigarette, made a small hole in the thin line of his lips, into which he inserted it, eschewed using his own lighter, leaning over instead to pull the knob of the cannon, igniting the cigarette skilfully from the flame belching from the muzzle, and, after issuing the first cloud of smoke, replied: 'The Sinsavangs do not contend, they maintain.'

The use of his cannon lighter by the opposition had been so unexpected that Mr Thompson incautiously asked, 'Maintain what?' when there could have been considerable preliminary fencing over the difference between 'contend' and 'maintain'.

'That there had been prior occupancy in Flat 3A as herein described.' And Shepperton tapped the lease with that same well-groomed fingernail.

Well, there it was. Out now and on the table. Still, nothing to worry about, since it was absurd, and, Mr Thompson knew, wholly demolishable. Nevertheless, if the Sinsavangs and this smooth young man thought they had a case, it might be a good idea if they could be led to show their hands or at least gain a peep over the edge of their cards.

'I see,' Mr Thompson groped again. 'Hmmm . . . Previously occupied, you say?' He studied his copy of the lease for a moment, to make certain that there was no unexpected word inserted between the lines that might weaken his position. But there was none. 'Might I ask by whom and when?'

'By the members of the family occupying the premises prior to the time when they were taken over by the Sinsavangs.'

Mr Thompson enjoyed two more puffs of his pipe, lulled more and more into a sense of security. 'Family occupying the premises prior to the time when they were taken over by the Sinsavangs.' That was a good one. He already saw himself and his wife on the witness stand, utterly destroying cross-examining counsel with his irritable 'I-put-it-to-you's'.

'I see,' he said for the third time. 'And when and in what manner did this family occupy the premises or any part of the premises sold to the Sinsavangs under the guarantee of the Truciman Estates?'

'Why,' replied Mr Shepperton, tapping his cigarette ash into the bronze ashtray decorated with a large anchor made for Mr Thompson one year by the ship's artificer as a Christmas present. 'When they lived in the house located where Melton Court now stands.'

Throughout his service during the War, Commander Henry Thompson was recognized as a man of unshakeable nerves and coolness under fire. The story went that when splinters from an exploding shell had killed two ratings on either side of him he had not so much as turned a hair or raised his voice beyond what was necessary to be heard above the din of battle as he ordered two others, 'Parks and Daniels, come along lads. Step in here.' And he had carried on. But the word 'house' sent a veritable tremor through him as though a shell had actually exploded beneath his feet. Even so, he controlled himself mightily, and Shepperton would never see the fresh strong teeth marks indented into the stem of his briar.

House, house, house! Not that damnable house again! Not possible! Utterly absurd! Absolutely ridiculous! True, he had been discussing it with Mrs Thompson only the day before. Then it was a problem in the abstract which somehow had arisen from nowhere to be considered perhaps as a possible complication at some time. But that this could ever be put forward as something concrete and, as this popinjay was more than subtly hinting, actionable, had not so much as crossed his mind. For the first time he felt himself edged on to the defensive.

'You are serious, I gather?' he said.

'Absolutely.'

'The Sinsavangs are claiming that?'

'The Sinsavangs do not claim, they declare quite unequivocally that the premises they purchased are not as stated in this contract.'

'In what sense "not as stated"!' countered Mr Thompson, and felt he had Mr Shepperton there.

But he hadn't, for the diplomat replied coolly, 'Why, in the sense of the Sinsavangs, of course. The space they occupy was occupied by others as late as . . .' And here Mr Shepperton consulted yet another sheet from his sheaf. 'As late as 1968. But I am given to understand that there has been a dwelling or some kind of human habitation on this particular site or its immediate area since before the Great

Fire of London, when the original building burned down. And the last of several since then stood on this same spot until its removal to make way for Melton Court.'

On the verge of exploding into 'But, man . . .', yet controlling himself once more since one did not address such a person as his visitor in that manner, Mr Thompson let his eyes examine Mr Shepperton's card, and wondered, not for the first time, why the Foreign Office should be involved. He then said, 'Do I understand you to say that because a house once stood –' He then quickly corrected himself from this damaging admission. 'Might have stood – you are contending that it stood –'

'*Stating* that it stood,' Mr Shepperton interjected.

'Never mind which – that this constitutes a prior occupancy in breach of contract?'

Mr Shepperton replied coolly, 'To the Sinsavangs, yes. Actually, far more reprehensibly, since they may have unwittingly, and for the time they have been living here, suffered irreparable spiritual damage.'

This shattering allegation drove Mr Thompson to his second error: sarcasm – always a dicey weapon. 'And how, might I ask, was this irreparable damage inflicted and by whom?'

Mr Shepperton eyed the Superintendent as coldly as he deserved to be eyed, for he was disappointed in him. One ought not to give openings like that. He consulted his dossier again briefly and replied, 'Well, the last one known to have lived in part of the area of the Sinsavang flat, an unstable personage, a maid by the name of Daisy Daisy.'

'I beg your pardon?' said Mr Thompson. 'I didn't quite catch that' – because he actually had. 'What did you say her name was?'

'Daisy Daisy'.

'You mean her last name was Daisy too?'

'Exactly.'

'*Daisy* Daisy?'

'Just so.'

'And who might this Daisy Daisy person be?'

'A maid living in an attic bedroom, which same impinges upon a portion of the dining-room, kitchen and cloakroom of the Sinsavang premises.'

For the first time Mr Thompson began to distrust his ears, and wondered whether the heavy portions of nicotine sucked from the stem of his pipe might be affecting him, for the tense had somehow shifted from the past to the present, so that he felt compelled to enquire, 'Did you say "impinges"?'

'I did.'

It was so fantastically nonsensical and ludicrous that nothing but sarcasm once more would suffice. 'I suppose,' said Mr Thompson, 'that you have a dossier on this Daisy Daisy, and can describe her for me.'

'As a matter of fact, I have,' Mr Shepperton acknowledged, and leafed through his sheets for the pertinent documents. 'According to our informants, Daisy Daisy is or was a parlour maid. Eighteen years old, and an orphan of unstable character – no father or mother, you know.'

Mr Thompson resisted the temptation to annotate that lack of parents was usually the case with orphans.

'Her mob cap was always awry, and she was given to exclaiming, "lawks amassey, I must've forgot again" – this referring to instructions given her – and was always dropping trays and chipping china. She had red hands and a red face, prominent eyeballs, and a permanently terrified expression, though kind to children and animals.'

Here he interrupted, not in his reading but in his speaking voice, to murmur, 'One can almost see Daisy Daisy, can one not?' And then resumed reading.

'One of her bootlaces was always coming untied, and she had to bend over very frequently to tie it, so that when she stood up again her face was even more red. Daisy Daisy sang all day long at her work, but not in tune. She was frightened of cook, and sometimes, when she went up to bed, she would cry all night long. Then, next morning, her eyes were red too. Daisy Daisy was really the daughter of an Earl, but nobody ever found this out. She drove the family around the bend, but they could not get rid of her, because she had nowhere to go. She died at the age of twenty-one, of consumption, and is buried in the family plot.'

Mr Thompson's ears had not been so affected by nicotine that he had failed to catch the cadence and construction of this description, and had noted to himself that the Maitland children, who were apparently behind all this ridiculous rumpus, had been letting themselves go. Now he smiled to himself inwardly again with relief, and enquired, 'And who might be your informants as to this?'

'Why, the Sinsavangs, of course. It was incorporated in their complaint.'

'Yes, yes, of course. But who informed them?'

Mr Thompson knew exactly what the answer was to be, and it was.

Without a quiver of skin or muscle on his bland countenance, Mr Shepperton said, 'Three young people: Michael, Miranda and Roderick Maitland.'

Mr Thompson's inward smile now spread outwards, and even turned into a chuckle. On safe ground now, he said, 'Come, come, Mr Shepperton, can you possibly not be aware that the whole thing is a fabrication? A make-believe, invented by some children who . . .'

The cold look of the Foreign Office man choked off Mr Thompson's flow. 'Not to the Sinsavangs,' he said. 'Children in Lao Nam do not lie. This is axiomatic and incontrovertible. In that country the words spoken by children up to the age of fourteen, when puberty is recognized, are accepted as truth, since up to then they are considered closer to and under the influence of the infinite, from which they sprung.'

'Jesus Christ,' was wrung from Mr Thompson.

'No,' said Mr Shepperton 'They are Buddhists mostly.'

'I wasn't referring to that,' the Superintendent said with slight asperity. 'We will say, for the sake of argument, that a number of tenants of this block have permitted themselves to become upset because three bored children have invented a story about a house that was supposed once to have stood where Melton Court is now located, and people it with Lord knows what extraordinary figments of their imagination – ringing doorbells of other tenants, and generally making nuisances of themselves. I have already spoken to them about it, but I intend to have a word with their parents now that –'

Mr Shepperton halted him by aiming his still glowing cigarette at his head like a pistol.

'My dear Superintendent, I am not in the least interested in your other tenants. No matter what the facts may be, the Sinsavangs have been made to believe and feel that their premises not only have had former tenants but that these are still present. And they feel themselves seriously menaced by all this.'

Mr Thompson removed his pipe from his mouth, leaned back stiffly in his chair, and enquired, 'Exactly what is it that the Sinsavangs want then?' The question must bring forth a direct answer – money, compensation, revocation of contract, penalties, personal apologies from Lord Truciman himself, or Melton Court torn down and rebuilt to avoid the space where Daisy Daisy was supposed to have toiled and expired.

Mr Shepperton's face began to split into just a shadow of a tolerant smile. 'Oh, nothing to be upset about,' he said soothingly. 'Merely a purification of the premises in accordance with the ceremony as practised by the Buddhist monks of Lao Nam.'

In his relief at this seemingly reasonable attitude Mr Thompson could not be blamed for having missed the fact that Mr Shepperton had referred to 'the' not 'their' premises.

'I see,' he said – and this time really thought he did. 'Sort of hocus-pocus?'

'Hmmm, well, yes. As I remember it, the ritual technology of house blessing, purification, propitiation, placation and exorcising, is divided into two phases: *Suad Mon Yen*, which is an evening chant and very beautiful, and *Suad Mon Chaw*. In the evening phase the monks chant *Suad Mongkhon* and make lustral water. A cord is tied about the house. It begins at a window, around which it is wound and knotted; it is then attached to the Buddha image, and the next length is held by the abbot; then it is wound around a bowl of water, and the final length is held by other monks. The technique is clearly one of 'charging' or sacralizing the house, or, negatively, of driving away or keeping at bay evil forces. The power of the sacred word travels through the cord and charges the water and the house. The water is consecrated as follows: at a certain point in the chanting, the abbot picks up a lighted candle standing on the bowl, drops some wax into the water, and then at the concluding words of the chant completely immerses it.'

All this seemed to have taken Mr Shepperton back to the days of his tenure in Lao Nam, for he lit a fresh cigarette quite absentmindedly and said, 'After the evening phase they throw one heck of a party, I can tell you. Exquisite food and drink. I remember I got quite sozzled once . . .' But then he snapped back into formality and continued, 'At any rate, the next morning the monks return. They are given breakfast, which act is rewarded with the *Anumodana* blessing. They now chant *Suad Chaya Mongkhon*, the victory blessing, and finally sprinkle lustral water.'

Mr Thompson again leaned back, smoking carefully and with some dramatic implication as he reflected, 'So what was all the fuss? What the tenants did behind their own closed doors was their own business.' Then, leaning forward, he picked up a blank notepad and ballpoint, saying, 'Well, now. Let me get this straight. The Sinsavangs are prepared to subscribe themselves as satisfied – they to acknowledge the company as not in breach of contract – providing the said company grants permission for the aforementioned Sinsavangs to invite – was it monks, you said? –'

'Monks, yes.'

'– to come round one evening and perform their whatever-you-call-it, the Sinsavangs to be responsible for any damage to company property ensuing from sprinkling around all that water and candle grease, and returning the next morning, after which they invite some friends in for a feed – or was that the night before? Well, anyway, if that's all it is, as I say, and you are willing to put your signature to it, I can't see any harm in that. Presumably the Sinsavangs would be present when all this was going on?'

'Part of the time, yes. At other times, since some of the ritual is secret, the bonzes work alone.'

Considerably relieved now, Mr Thompson volunteered, 'Well, I imagine we could make the Sinsavangs comfortable during that time – either here in my office, or I could let them in to a furnished flat we have to rent on the second floor. The party, of course, would be held on their own premises. I suppose there'll be some beatings of gongs and that sort of thing inside the Sinsavangs' flat, but I can't see that this would constitute a disturbance to the other occupants of the Court. So if this is agreeable to your –' He had been about to say 'clients' until he realized that actually Mr Shepperton was not a lawyer, and changed it to 'friends'. 'I am prepared, without further recourse to the company, to give permission for this affair to take place in the manner described, relying, of course on your discretion that the matter will be kept strictly between the Sinsavangs and ourselves.'

Mr Shepperton had listened carefully, and seemed to want to interject at various stages, but by now he was both nodding and shaking his head with confusing impatience. 'Up to a point,' he got in at last. 'But, if I may say so, I don't think you have quite grasped the whole picture. The Sinsavangs are demanding the purification not only of their own premises but of the entire block – and if you will look upon it their way . . .'

The sentence remained unfinished because of the anguished cry of 'What?' torn from Mr Thompson, who, in one flash of comprehension, saw the abyss yawning at his feet and knew now that, as he had rather suspected all along, the affair was not to be resolved so easily.

'My dear sir,' Mr Shepperton followed up, 'surely you must see from what I have told you that it is not just a single set of rooms that needs to be exorcised by the Lao Namians. It is the entire building – and not only that, but the grounds on which the former premises stood: the earth, the trees, the lot – until the house and all that once was here have been rendered harmless.'

Now Mr Thompson groped for the worst. 'Are you trying to tell me that the whole of Melton Court –'

'Precisely,' Mr Shepperton rapped on his desk.

Mr Thompson needed a breather – a good long one – to recognize the picture and be quite certain this time that he had it straight. He knocked out the dottle from his pipe, opened the desk drawer and produced a pipe cleaner, ran it through the stem, studying the guck that came forth with it, chucked it in the waste basket, reloaded the bowl, and lit up.

'Let me understand this,' he then tried again. 'As I get it, you are proposing to evacuate the entire population of Melton Court, consisting of –' and here he consulted a number of sheets on his desk '– some thirty-eight families, amongst which are Protestants, Catholics, Jews, Episcopalians, I believe some Baptists as well, and goodness knows what others, while a collection of shaven-headed baboons perform heathen rites all over the show?'

Mr Shepperton hastened to interrupt here again, as the colour suffusing Mr Thompson's face had already passed what must be boiling point. 'Don't forget the party,' he said. 'The Sinsavangs will, of course, prepare a number of *phakuans*, as they call their repasts for the soul . . .'

That did it for Mr Thompson. He had heard more than enough talk of rituals by now. He cut Mr Shepperton short with a sharp snap.

'What you ask, sir, is utterly impossible. The company would never consent to such a preposterous . . .' Even as he groped for words to complete his denunciation Mr Shepperton leaned an elbow arrogantly upon the desk and pointed his cigarette aggressively at him once more.

'Now look here, Superintendent. Why do you imagine I am spending my valuable time with you here this morning?

Why do you suppose the Foreign Office and not some mere solicitor or the Sinsavangs themselves have taken up this matter?'

Mr Thompson spread his arms and replied rather lamely, 'I simply cannot imagine.'

'Well, I will tell you,' said Mr Shepperton, dropping his aggressive pose now. 'Madam Sinsavang is the daughter of His Excellency Cho Yuan, the Prime Minister of Lao Nam. The manoeuvring of the Chinese, the Americans, the Russians and the Cambodians since the phasing out of the Vietnam war has made Lao Nam the key country to the situation. The British Government is involved in the most delicate negotiations with Cho Yuan, which, if successful, will put Britain on top politically and commercially in that area for the next, shall we say, fifty years. Anything that might arise to disturb these, at the moment, tenuous negotiations – *anything* – would be disastrous. So you can see now, my friend, why what the Sinsavangs are demanding must be made possible and why the Foreign Office have been brought in. There is no alternative.'

CHAPTER XVIII

The Fire-Raiser

Throughout that day Mr Thompson pondered his problem alone. Determined not to involve Lord Truciman or any director of Truciman Estates – or, indeed, anyone else on the staff at Melton Court itself – he turned over in his troubled mind a whole series of slender pretexts and possibilities for evacuating the entire block in accordance with the demands of both the Sinsavangs and the Foreign Office. But as the afternoon blurred, with his thoughts, into early evening, a still more urgent problem rumbled and grumbled in the basement beneath him.

There Mr Biggs stood contemplating a carefully piled-up heap of rubbish, crumpled newspapers, oil-soaked rags, scraps of wood and torn cardboard, as well as some carpenter's shavings, with more horror and trembling than he had ever experienced in all his years of action in the War.

It was the two-gallon can of petrol standing nearby that froze him into immobility – and consideration of a malevolence almost too great for his imagination to encompass.

It was six o'clock in the evening. The pile of potential terror, misery, panic and death was just in the shadow out of range of one of the naked light bulbs, each encased in a wired cage against breakage, strung out along the corridors of his subterranean domain. It had not been there an hour before when, after closing down his workshop some hundred feet away, Mr Biggs had made, as was his custom, his evening round of inspection of the underground premises. This tour he made both in the evening and first thing in the morning, to check up on all the storage space, machinery, pipes, conduits and equipment upon which the safety and the comfort of all those variegated human lives above depended. Under his control were oil, water, gas, electricity – the ingredients for a cocktail of total catastrophe if they were ever allowed to mix.

There could be no guardian against the dangers of such elements more dependable than Mr Biggs. But at this moment the ex-naval artificer was motionless with incredulity as through his mind whirled a jumble of pictures past, present and future, the last of which were not even to be considered. He was trying desperately, none the less, to remember where he had been, what he had been doing, who had been there, who he had seen, who he might not have seen – everything, in fact, that had preceded his march down the corridor and his dreadful discovery.

Eventually his legs ceased their involuntary trembling, the apprehensions that had held him prisoner on the spot relaxed, and he moved slowly, as though wearing the iron boots of a dream, plodding some fifty feet to where there was a house 'phone attached to the wall. He plucked off the receiver and dialled his Superintendent.

'Mr Thomson, sir? Biggs,' he said, unaware of the dilemma he was himself compounding. 'Would you come down here a moment? I'm sorry, sir, but I'm afraid it *is* urgent. Thank you.'

A few minutes later an even more distracted Mr Thompson was standing by his side regarding the piled-up heap in silent gloom and horror.

The two men spoke only in snatches, in low tones at first, their voices dampened by the implications of what was there before them.

'God,' breathed Mr Thompson.

'Terrible,' said Mr Biggs.

The Superintendent's gaze took in the two-gallon can. 'Lord,' he murmured, 'if he'd set it off . . .'

'Him?' checked Mr Biggs.

'Him or her – whoever – we don't know, do we? But they knew their business all right, didn't they just?'

'Right by the shaft,' put in Mr Biggs. 'And the oil storage. One hell of a volcano, that's what it would have been.'

Mr Thompson shuddered. The mound had been so placed that once the blaze had penetrated to the oil storage space the up-draught through the shaft that rose through the centre of the building would have turned Melton Court into an inferno.

'When?' Mr Thompson snapped.

'Between five minutes past five, when I did my last round, and, well . . .' Mr Biggs looked doubtfully at his watch. 'Well, I wouldn't know exactly, sir, but roughly just before six. I didn't like the sound of the pump, and came out to have a look. Nobody there then. Probably frightened off whoever it was.'

Mr Thompson nodded. 'And who had been down here that you know of?'

Mr Biggs rubbed his chin and said, 'No one – except the children.'

'What children?' growled Mr Thompson.

'The three young Maitlands from 1A.'

Mr Thompson drew breath slowly, and repeated as controlledly as his morning encounter with Mr Shepperton would allow, 'The three young Maitlands, eh?'

'Oh, yes, sir. But there's no harm in them,' Mr Biggs hastened in.

'You think not, do you?' challenged Mr Thompson, privately unconvinced and almost vengeful after the morning's troubles.

'Yes,' Mr Biggs seemed virtually enthused. 'They just like to come down here when there's nothing better to do.'

'Or worse,' thought Mr Thompson.

'And there's been all this rotten weather, of course, sir. I don't mind them around. The oldest boy's got a mechanical bent, and he likes to watch. In fact he was with me most of the afternoon. Mrs Biggs was showing the girl how to make biscuits. And the little fellow – he can only be seven or so – was playing "Blast Off".'

' "Blast Off"?' Mr Thompson looked more intolerant than puzzled.

Mr Biggs, however, smiled calmly. 'When the lift goes up he pretends it's a space rocket. That's all, sir. It's a favourite game of his. Astronaut's helmet, the lot.'

It was more their wretched House game that concerned Mr Thompson again now, but he set all enquiries about that aside to quiz Mr Biggs about their most recent movements instead. 'Were they still around after your inspection?' he asked.

Mr Biggs reflected again, but couldn't quite remember exactly. 'I wouldn't rightly know, sir. I expect they went up shortly after I closed shop. They usually do.'

Mr Thompson nodded, and studied the obscene pile before them once more long and closely: the layers of combustibles arranged to ensure instantaneous heat and flare up. He shook his head slowly, and more realistically than reluctantly gave his verdict: 'Not children.'

Mr Biggs agreed readily, 'That's right, sir. Not children. Not them anywise. They're a clean lot.'

'Have you touched anything?' asked Mr Thompson, all his attention on the incendiary heap now.

'No, sir. Not me. That's for the police.'

Mr Thompson looked thoughtful, and merely grunted. Then he asked abruptly, 'Where did those wood shavings come from?'

'Carpenter's shop, sir. They've been planing the last two days. But they're fairly neat. They usually pack all that sort of stuff into bags and take it home for kindling.'

'Nobody could have got to them?'

'Possible, sir. Possible, I suppose.'

'And the petrol can?'

Mr Biggs shook his head. 'We don't keep anything like that down here, sir. No. I've never seen that before.'

Mr Thompson began a check-off now. 'And so outside of

the children, who could have gone upstairs any time after five o'clock, what about the carpenters?'

'They only worked half a day today, sir.'

'And deliveries?' Mr Thompson queried.

'Never nothing regular after five o'clock. I'd locked the outside door. Anybody comes after five o'clock I want to have a look at.'

'So where did you go after your last inspection?'

'To my quarters, sir – until, like I said, I didn't care for the sound the pump was making, and came out to look. It was just a valve needed adjusting. Then I found all this.' Mr Biggs looked down and shook his head in appalled disbelief still.

'Hmmm,' Mr Thompson muttered. 'Not children. Everybody out by five or shortly after. Not you or Mrs Biggs, that goes without saying. Outside delivery door locked. So someone must have slipped down from upstairs, wouldn't you say?'

'I suppose so. But it's a case for the police really, isn't it, sir? Do you think you'd better call them?'

'No,' said Mr Thompson. 'We don't want the police tramping around with notebooks, knocking on doors and making what they call routine enquiries, do we? They'd fair put the wind up everybody in the Court. Within an hour everybody would know there was a firebug on the premises. Lord Truciman wouldn't like that. No, this wants a bit of quiet work and nobody to know until we're on to something. I've got a better idea. Friend of mine at the Yard will know what to do and who to send. Here, Bill, you stick by this rotten mess while I give him a ring. Oh, and by the way, there's no point in alarming Mrs Biggs. Let's just keep this under our hats until we find out what's what, or rather who.' With that Mr Thompson walked briskly upstairs to his office, closed the door for once, and rang his friend Jock at Scotland Yard. Jock had been the then Commander Thompson's First Lieutenant aboard the destroyer which they had managed to bring through the four years of war and escort service in the North Sea fairly in one piece.

'So you think you've got a firebug then, do you, skipper?' said Jock when he'd heard the details. 'Very nasty. Very nasty indeed. Have you notified the Amory Street station? I think that's our nearest one to you.'

'No, I haven't,' said Mr Thompson. 'The last thing I want is a lot of heavy-footed constables nosing around here frightening the tenants.'

'Glad to hear it. I hoped you hadn't. Fire-raising is something of a speciality, and you'd best go about it quietly and not put the wind up anybody – particularly whoever's doing it. Tell you what. I'll rout out St Elmo for you and send him over at the double.'

'Who the devil is St Elmo?' Mr Thompson asked. 'I thought St Elmo *was* a kind of fire. St Elmo's fire, isn't it?'

Jock sniggered and said, 'Yes, skip, I know, and he's had to take a lot of kidding on account of it. That's his name though: Roger St Elmo. And this is right up his street. Knows all about the psychological and psychiatrical factors – talked with analysts, the lot. Well-read chap, too. You'll like him. Doesn't look like a copper, either. He'll probably bring someone along for dabs, just in case, but mostly the stuff these villains deal with doesn't lend itself to finger-printing. Anyway, you can count on his being discreet. He'll keep me in touch on how things are going. Good luck, skipper, and I'm really sorry you've had this bother. Still, sooner or later they give themselves away – like that engine-room saboteur we caught on the voyage off the Skagerrak in '43, remember?'

Roger St Elmo, in fact, looked something like an inquisitive stork, or perhaps even more, Mr Thompson thought at first sight, like an absent-minded professor getting about on stilts. He was so tall and thin that he had to bend over double from the waist to get down close enough for a good look at anything below knee level. He wore eye-glasses attached to a cord so that they wouldn't break when they fell off his nose, which was really too fine and narrow-bridged to support them. For the rest he had sand-coloured hair, interested eyes, which were grey-green with curious golden flecks in them, and he was soft-spoken, positive and knowledgeable.

'Oh, dear, yes,' he said, when, with Mr Thompson, he had joined Mr Biggs on guard over the horrid evidence in the basement, and had given it a first cursory examination without touching anything. 'Yes, indeed. It's professional all right. That is to say, as we look at things in this field.'

He turned to the man from the fingerprint laboratory who had accompanied him. 'Joe, you might see if you can pick up anything out of that mess – though I doubt it. The petrol can perhaps. But with all that oil on it there'll be nothing but smears.'

He sighed and said to Mr Thompson, 'It's a good thing you got Jock to call me instead of the boys on the beat. At least we're getting a clear start.'

After he too had heard from Mr Biggs the details and time schedule of the discovery, and whilst the fingerprint man was at his delicate job, which, as St Elmo had predicted, was yielding nothing, he lectured on his subject.

'Oh, anybody and everybody,' he said, with all the weary confidence of experience. 'Fire. One of man's oldest hang-ups. Destroys, purifies – you name it. And, of course, the trouble is that even careful examination into backgrounds, for the most part, can lead to nothing but vague suspicion, unsupported by any evidence whatsoever.'

'How is that?' Mr Thompson asked. 'I should think when you looked into the record of someone setting fires you would find –'

'That's the trouble,' sighed St Elmo. 'Unlike the burglar, the thug, or the psychopathic killer, the firebug rarely gets caught. He might have set two or three or even four fires in his youth, and never once been suspected, then outgrown it. Well, we shall have to try. From the looks of the care with which this one has been assembled they wouldn't be satisfied until they've had another go. But discretion, discretion. What kind of maintenance men or people would be about here, or staff who would not be noticed?'

'Maintenance men?' Mr Thompson queried.

'Chaps of ours we can put into overalls or fit out with credentials from the gas or electrical companies, who can call around the various flats and check on plumbing or utilities, you know.'

Mr Thompson looked doubtful for a moment, and said, 'Well, Bill here normally does that sort of thing, but only when there are complaints – and some of the tenants often call in their own electricians or whatever.'

St Elmo bent his quizzical gaze upon Mr Biggs for a moment, liked what he saw, and said, 'Ah, yes. Now, Bill here will want an assistant, won't he? Overworked. Too much to do. Nobody will think anything of it if you have another man to give him a hand, particularly on the night watch.' Then, speaking to Mr Biggs, he said, 'You'll find this chap very capable, and a good sort too. We recruited him from the fire department, but before that he used to be in your line of work. I should think for the time being, at least in the beginning, you'll have to divide up into watches, four hours on, four hours off. On calls from the tenants send him up as much as possible rather than going yourself. He has eyes for things you might never notice.'

Mr Biggs nodded and said, 'Yes, sir. I see, sir. I was wondering how I was going to be able to handle it if someone had another go down here, during the night, say.'

St Elmo nodded and said, 'Mr Thompson can send a note round to the tenants about his engaging a new assistant, and you can take him with you at the beginning on any calls, and introduce and identify him until they get used to seeing him. That should take care of the security belowstairs. That and calls from various inspector blokes should see us reasonably peaceful for the moment.'

The fingerprint man got up off his knees and said, 'I'm afraid we aren't going to get anything much, sir.'

St Elmo nodded again. 'I didn't think we would,' he said. 'One of the more unfortunate characteristics of arsonists is their cunning.'

'What about the upstairs staff?' asked Mr Thompson.

'The doorman, the switchboard operator, the porters, the housekeeper and the cleaning women?'

St Elmo shook his head. 'I wouldn't say anything. We usually find they can't keep their mouths shut or resist the temptation to play amateur detective. Before forty-eight hours were up every tenant in the block would know there was something in the wind, and, what's more, probably exactly what. Once you've tipped a firebug that you're looking for him you've lost him.'

He turned to Mr Biggs again. 'Can you collect some empty boxes for me, and Joe here will put all this stuff inside so we can take it back to the Yard with us.' Then, noting the half-puzzled, half-doubtful expression on Mr Thompson's face, said almost apologetically, 'Well, you know, all the stuff had to come from somewhere or something, didn't it? What newspapers do you read? There are bits of both *The Times* and the *Mirror* here, I see. Quite a gap. Ought to tell us something. Then what were these rags before they were demoted to this unhappy state, I wonder. And the cardboard – that was a container of some sort. One would eventually learn what it contained and even who sold it. That sort of thing. Long way round, but worth a go. Same with the petrol can, of course.'

'I see,' said Mr Thompson. 'Certainly. But what about motive? We've got a decent, ordinary crowd in this building. No one unusual in any way, I'd say. As for a grudge, real or fancied slights, I can't think of a single solitary occasion or any tenants who we are not on good terms with. Complaints are immediately looked into, and the building is sufficiently new that we aren't worried with too many of those. As for anyone nursing a grudge against Lord Truciman, or, for that matter, me, not one member of the staff has been dismissed since we opened.'

'Yes, indeed,' interjected St Elmo, who had been watching his assistant carefully dismantling the pile of inflammables and placing them in the boxes provided by Mr Biggs. 'Motive is always a problem, particularly because it's quite possible in cases of arson for there to be no motive – at least none that you can put your finger on. Or perhaps one so deeply buried within the subconscious of the fire-raiser that it would take a psychiatrist years to dredge it up. And then, of course, there are all the people who, when they hear that there is a fire in the neighbourhood, walk, run or get in their cars and go there just to stand and watch it. So perhaps we could take a look at your list of occupants next.'

Half an hour later, St Elmo sat with Mr Thompson in his office, smoking and fingering the list. 'That's fine,' he said. 'Just the ordinary mix, as you say. Now unless there's some unusual emergency you won't be seeing much of me here during the investigations. I am,' he smiled, 'as one might say, slightly conspicuous. But, of course, I've given you the numbers where I can be reached at any time.'

Mr Thompson fully expected St Elmo to take his leave there and then, but the Detective Inspector made no move. He sat on the straight-backed chair re-checking the list once more.

Suddenly, teetering back, he placed his long arms akimbo, with his hands clasped behind his head, and with raised voice uttered, 'Children.'

Mr Thompson looked up at him.

'Children,' repeated St Elmo. 'They are always a particular complication with us in any fire investigation. A baby of eighteen months can upset a lamp and destroy an entire family. Three boys stealing a smoke set a shack alight close to the amusement arcade at Southbay – d'you remember the case? – and killed sixty people and put another hundred or so in hospital. What goes on in their little heads? Too much or nothing? Nothing in the sense that they simply are unable to imagine or look ahead to the terrible damage and misery that fire can cause. Or too much in the way of imagination. They see the smoke pouring through the rooftop, the tongues of fire licking at the window frames, sparks thrown a hundred feet in the air, and the streams of water turning into clouds of steam as they are directed into the heart of the blaze. Exciting. Either way, they are insufficiently mature to understand they constitute a danger to the community. If you could only teach that to their parents.'

St Elmo crossed one long leg over the other. 'It is the imaginative ones I think I'm most wary of. I suppose you wouldn't have too much opportunity to observe the ones in your block to form any very firm opinions. But those Maitland children you mentioned, for instance, who were down with Biggs only this afternoon again. The oldest is technically-minded, the girl takes cooking lessons from Mrs Biggs, and the youngest sees the rising lift as a space rocket. I'd call them highly imaginative, wouldn't you?'

'I'd call them more than that,' said Mr Thompson, setting one arm down firmly on his desk. 'They've been a downright nuisance this Easter holiday of theirs, going round bothering and upsetting people with stories about their House. Why, only this morning I had a –'

'House? What house?' queried St Elmo, who suddenly removed his hands and long arms from behind his head, uncrossed his legs, and lunged forward on his chair.

'Oh, the house that was here before,' Mr Thompson replied, feeling rather embarrassed that he had not mentioned the matter earlier. 'I'm sorry. I've had a lot of problems lately, and this arson business put it right out of my head. When you asked me whether I had been aware of anything out of the ordinary recently and I said no, I just didn't tie the two together. But this block, or at least part of it, has been fairly set on its ear by those three children and their imaginary house where everybody is living. I mean, where everybody who lives where it used to be is living in it now. Oh, hell! They make you sound as though you were bereft of your senses when you try to explain it. Here, let me show you.'

Mr Thompson bent down to a drawer and produced his copy of the architects' original blueprint of the front elevation of the House, and said, 'This is the house that used to be here. Hallam Hall, it was called. Lord Truciman bought it and tore it down to put up Melton Court.'

St Elmo studied the sheet for a moment, and then returned his questioning gaze to Mr Thompson, who pointed to the drawing with the stem of his pipe and said, 'It turned up a week or two ago, when Bill Biggs was having a sort of clear out of a lot of junk that had been accumulating in his cupboards and drawers. The Maitland children were down there helping him. He turned out three copies, as a matter of fact. Kept one for me, one for himself, and was going to throw out the third when the children asked if they could have it. Bill saw no harm in that, so he let them. I wish now, though . . .'

'Which one was it that asked for a copy?' St Elmo asked urgently.

'Bill would be able to tell you. I've no idea myself. But I do know they all went off with it happy as sandboys – and that was the day their game started.'

St Elmo nodded, and his glasses fell from the bridge of his nose until they were brought up by the ribbon to which they were attached about his neck. He replaced them upon his nose, examined the drawing again, and said, 'This game. What is it like?'

Mr Thompson told him from the very beginning all that he had seen and heard, including a full account of Mr Shepperton's extraordinary visit that morning. He told the fascinated St Elmo of how the three children had imagined what the house was like inside, and how the eldest, Michael Maitland, had made tolerable drawings of the interior of the three-storeyed dwelling, superimposing it upon their own suite of rooms so that they could visualize themselves actually living in a house instead of a block of flats.

'How very clever,' St Elmo said. 'And what an exceptional realization of what must have been a most powerful sublimation. Every child wishes to live in a house, after all.'

'Well, that would have been all right,' said Mr Thompson, 'and no harm to anyone, until they made a spread of it.' He then went on to tell of how, since the interior of the house the children had imagined or constructed exceeded in space the actual territory of their own three-bedroom flat, they had set about finding out which of the other tenants on the same floor or above and below were living in the house with them. He told of Roddy's incursions and such other episodes as had come to his attention – though, of course, there were many of which he did not know – and how Mr and Mrs Maitland had eventually forbidden the children to continue their game, adding, 'But, as the middle Maitland child, the girl, pointed out, now that the house is in people's minds you can't just stop it from being there, can you?'

'No,' murmured St Elmo, half to himself. 'You can't.'

'I am sure you can see, though,' Mr Thompson pressed home, 'how the horror that Biggs fortunately came across in the basement drove that whole essentially trivial business from my mind, as I asked myself what kind of a mentality or a creature would want to set fire to an entire block of flats filled with innocent people – men, women and children.'

St Elmo took the great leap forward for which his speeding mind had prepared him. His eyes glittered behind the lenses of his precariously balanced spectacles, and he said, 'Yes, but, my dear fellow, don't you understand? It isn't the block at all that was meant to be burned. It was the house that has grown up inside it – the house that was here before. Thank you for telling me. You see, it considerably narrows our investigations.'

CHAPTER XIX

An Open and Shut Door

The following morning, Detective Inspector St Elmo laid nearly all of his cards on the table with Mr and Mrs Maitland, and was surprised when Mrs Maitland objected to having the same hand dealt to her three children. She agreed to allow St Elmo to question them but refused to let him reveal the true reason for the interrogation.

St Elmo had mentioned nothing of his speculation as to what might have lain behind the attempt at arson but had merely reported what Mr Biggs had found and the fact that the three children had been in the basement shortly before, and so might perhaps have caught sight of the intruder, or even identified him, but were too frightened to reveal what they had seen. Dorothy Maitland objected to having the spectre of fire raised before her children – particularly Roddy, who was still at the age when his dreams so often merged with reality.

St Elmo was astonished, since it was his impression that, considering what children of all ages were exposed to nightly on television, there was not too much that could either impress or frighten them any more. But John Maitland backed his wife. He was, in fact, like all Englishmen, against any kind of invasion of his privacy, particularly by the police, and tried to persuade the Detective Inspector to let him ask the children whether they had seen anything, and report what they had to say.

'For two reasons, no,' said St Elmo, firmly. 'If you are not used to dealing with the methods and behaviour of arsonists you might misinterpret or miss entirely an observation which might seem quite irrelevant but isn't. You see –'

'And the other reason?' Mr Maitland interrupted.

'Oh,' replied St Elmo quite seriously. 'I was just thinking that you would be denying them the pleasure of taking part in a police investigation.'

John Maitland had to laugh, but his wife said, 'These are *children*. I think it's horrid.'

'So is arson, Mrs Maitland,' said St Elmo gravely. He did not remark, as he thought, however, that these children had been involved in a weird kind of arson that was all their own. They had set fire to the minds of some dozen or more of the inhabitants of Melton Court, and that fire could not be extinguished now. Instead, he asked mildly, 'Then what would you have me say?'

'Anything provided it will not upset them,' snapped Mrs Maitland. 'I will not have my children badgered.'

Her husband came to the rescue. 'Would pilfering do?' he asked. 'Somebody after Mr Biggs's tools? Perhaps a delivery boy or something?'

St Elmo agreed. 'If they'll swallow that. Your boy Michael by the sound of him, is probably almost as familiar with police methods as I am.'

Michael it was, in fact, who announced to his sister and brother that there was going to be a conference with a real police detective from Scotland Yard. 'Daddy didn't mean to let on,' he said, 'but I think he's an Inspector.'

'Oh, dear,' said Miranda. 'Have we done something awful?'

'No, it's not anything we've done,' Michael assured her. 'But somebody's been after Mr Biggs's tools down in the basement.'

'What's an Inspector?' Roddy asked.

Michael found it a surprisingly difficult question to answer in a manner to satisfy his younger brother, or, for that matter, in a way to satisfy anyone. It was such a curious title to give to a high police official. An Inspector ought to be someone who literally inspects. But inspects what? Whether the policemen's rooms were tidy? Or walked down rows of bobbies standing to attention to see whether their uniforms were brushed and their helmets poised at the proper angle? He wiped that picture from the slate of his mind and said to Roddy, 'It's someone who asks a lot of questions to try to find out what people have done.'

'Bad people?' queried Roddy.

'Of course,' Michael replied. 'What would he be asking questions about good people for?'

Miranda was looking reflective, and said, 'What would he want to ask us questions for, though?'

'Well,' said Michael, 'in case we saw anybody trying to sneak Mr Biggs's . . .' He stopped short, for he guessed what might be in his sister's mind too. Television series had made her equally familiar with the hierarchy in Scotland Yard, and it was not difficult to jump to the conclusion that Detective Inspectors who had departments of policemen under them were not likely to concern themselves with cases of pilfering. 'Perhaps,' he tried again, 'it could be just the beginning. If there was a thief, I suppose they'd want to know before he started taking people's jewels and things. Well, anyway, I didn't see anything or anybody.'

'Neither did I,' Miranda agreed.

'I did,' Roddy stopped them both.

They stared at him in amazement, for he had not mentioned it before, and Michael quickly urged, 'Well, then you must tell the Inspector – and if they catch the thief perhaps you'll be a hero.'

The enquiry was conducted in the drawing-room of the Maitland flat, with the children's father introducing the subject with what Michael was pleased to see was the same evaluation that he himself had put upon the situation.

'Michael, Miranda and Roddy,' he said, 'this is Roger St Elmo, from Scotland Yard, who wants to ask you a few questions. There is nothing to be frightened about. But apparently someone tried to break into Mr Biggs's workshop and steal his tools. The police think it might have been someone in the building – perhaps one of the helpers – and want to catch him before he becomes more ambitious.' Then, realizing that the use of that word and its application to this affair might be too much for Roddy, explained further, 'Well, that he might try to enter somebody's flat. An ounce of prevention . . .' And then, turning to St Elmo, he asked, 'Isn't that about it?'

St Elmo nodded.

Dorothy Maitland was sitting up straight and grim, thoroughly hating the whole process, worried for the children, and prepared to jump down the Inspector's throat if he so much as brought a burnt out match into the conversation.

St Elmo did not make the mistake of patronizing any of the three. He proceeded to get straight on with his lie and his interrogation. 'You were all down in the basement yesterday with Mr and Mrs Biggs, weren't you? We know pretty well from them where you were most of the time, if not all. You, Michael, were with Mr Biggs until he locked up his workshop shortly after five o'clock. Miranda here was with Mrs Biggs making scones. Now after locking up his shop Mr Biggs went upstairs to talk to the doorman about one of the locks that was sticking. Where did you go then, Michael?'

Michael answered directly, 'I went to Mrs Biggs to collect Miranda. The scones they had made were ready, so we had some with tea.'

St Elmo nodded and said, 'Yes, that's right.' Then he turned slowly and asked, 'What about you, Roddy?'

Michael answered for him and before he could, 'He was playing "Blast Off".'

' "Blast Off"?' St Elmo affected not to have heard of this before.

Michael dutifully explained the game and how it worked, while St Elmo listened sombrely, and Miranda eyed her younger brother getting ready to speak.

'It isn't a game,' he said protestingly. 'It's real. The people come in and get into the capsule and wait for the countdown. Then I say, "Blast Off" and they go up to the Moon and stay there. Sometimes other people who have been on the Moon get in the capsule and come down – but I do all the controls.'

'Yes, I see,' said St Elmo, then added, 'Didn't you want tea and scones too?'

'He didn't know about them until we called him,' Michael again answered for Roddy. 'Then he came. I mean, when the tea was ready.'

'And after that, at about half past five, you all came upstairs again,' St Elmo continued. 'A little later, when Mr Biggs returned, he noticed the door of his shop was open and his tools had been taken down from their pegs and collected together, but nothing was missing. The thief had apparently been disturbed before he could make away with them. So that must have occurred during the time Mr Biggs was upstairs and you three were having tea with Mrs Biggs. When you had finished with your tea and were on your way back to your flat, did you see anyone or hear anything?'

'I didn't,' said Miranda.

'Neither did I,' said Michael. 'But when we passed Mr Biggs's workshop the door wasn't open. I would have noticed.'

Dorothy Maitland had a moment of swift panic, and thought 'Oh, dear. What have I done? I've started a lie going and there will have to be more lies. Perhaps I should have let the Inspector tell the truth.'

St Elmo was thinking the same thing, except his went, 'Damn women! Of course the door wasn't open. Now what do we do?'

It was Roddy who jolted them both back by announcing flatly, 'I did.'

'Yes? Did what?' asked St Elmo.

Michael and Miranda awaited the revelation with interest, unable to forget the bald statement Roddy had made during their earlier discussions of the conference. He had not elaborated then. Perhaps he would now.

'See something,' Roddy replied.

St Elmo, treading cautiously, said, 'You saw something? That's splendid. What was it?'

'A thing.'

'What kind of a thing?' St Elmo asked. 'A man? A woman? A boy?'

'Just a thing,' Roddy replied, then added evenly. 'It had horns.'

Michael interrupted here, and said, 'But, Roddy, we were all together. We didn't see –'

Roddy reacted with considerable scorn to his brother's stupidity. 'Oh, not then. Not when we all came up together. It was before.'

'When you were playing "Blast Off" before tea?' St Elmo asked.

Roddy nodded.

'Horns?' repeated St Elmo. 'And perhaps a tail?'

Roddy shook his head for a negative.

'No tail,' said St Elmo.

Roddy reflected and said, 'But it had blobs for feet.'

'Blobs?'

'Sort of like puddles. It slithered,' Roddy explained. 'It didn't have a nose or a mouth.'

'Did it have eyes?'

'I think so.'

'Where were you, Roddy?' asked St Elmo, leaning forward.

'At my "Blast Off".'

Michael interposed, 'That would be by the lift machinery, sir.'

'Thank you,' said St Elmo. 'And where was this . . . er . . . thing, Roddy?'

'At the end of the passage. It was dark. I couldn't see. I think it was bending over in the corner.'

St Elmo was thinking swiftly, 'What? A fellow in a stocking mask and rag-pads, or a child's imagination?' Then he asked Roddy, 'What did you do? Weren't you frightened?'

'No,' said Roddy, simply. 'I said, "Go away!" When I

dream things that are bad I wake up and say "Go away!" and they do.'

'And this one did too?'

'It slithered around the corner on its blobs.'

'What happened then?'

'There were people up on the Moon who were waiting to come down, so I had to work the controls – and then we had tea.'

St Elmo nodded gravely and said, 'Thank you, Roddy. You've been very helpful.'

Roddy looked pleased.

To himself, St Elmo thought, 'Children and their imagination! Back to Square One.'

When the three had withdrawn, St Elmo said, 'Thank you very much, Mrs Maitland. Thank you, Mr Maitland. I doubt if I shall have to worry you again – and I trust I didn't go too far, talking to the children.'

Dorothy Maitland looked as embarrssed as she felt, and said hastily, 'I'm afraid, as you can see, Inspector, Roddy is a highly imaginative child, given to the most bizarre dreams. I often have to go to him when he wakes up and comfort him.'

St Elmo smiled. 'I gathered that. Horns and blobs and things that go bump in the night.'

With a rush of guilt at the absurd inconclusiveness of the affair, Dorothy Maitland did not smile back, but instead said earnestly, 'Oh, dear. I do hope I haven't muddled things by refusing to let you tell the children about whoever it was trying to set fire to the block, but if they had seen anything or been worried or frightened I'm sure they would have said. If you'd like to talk to Roddy again – perhaps by himself – but I don't know . . .'

St Elmo shook his head and said smilingly, 'I don't think that will be necessary, Mrs Maitland. As a former student of "things", including those conjured up by my own children, I suspect that further questions will only tax Roddy's imagination to the augmentation of ears that flapped and several pairs of arms. I have only one favour to ask of you, and that is that you will not mention this to anyone – anyone at all. An arson investigation is one of the most difficult of all, and must be kept top secret. I should, of course, not have mentioned it to you, but for the fact that the presence of your three children in the basement at or about the time in question could perhaps have given us a little more to go on. It's still quite possible, of course, that whoever it was down there had been unaware of Roddy's presence by the lift shaft, and the child's sudden cry of "Blast Off", or whatever it is he says, frightened him away. Thank you both.'

Alone in the playroom, and well out of hearing, the children were conducting their own inquest. Miranda was troubled and introspective, Michael angry, and Roddy pleased with himself as having been the undoubted star of the affair, whatever it had been about.

'Why do they have to lie to us?' asked Michael. 'Such a whopping one, and stupid too. If we tell even a weenie one about something that doesn't really matter very much we catch it.'

'It was a lie, wasn't it?' Miranda queried. 'About the tools, I mean.'

'Of course it was,' Michael replied scathingly. 'And you know it. The door to Mr Bigg's workshop was tight shut when we left to come up. And anyway, if anybody had been mucking about with his tools he'd have asked us himself, or said something to me – did I see his door open or anything funny. Well, I didn't. And he didn't either.'

Miranda said nothing, but regarded Michael with troubled eyes.

'I know we're only children,' he continued, 'but why do they have to take us for such fools? I don't think for one moment that the Inspector chap thought we believed his reasons for being here.'

'What do you suppose the real reason was then?' asked Miranda.

Roddy answered first this time. 'The thing. He wanted to catch it.'

'That's right, Roddy,' said Michael sarcastically. 'He'll draw an identikit picture from your description.' He turned to Miranda again then. 'Something big, but I can't guess what. I don't think he's talked to anyone else in the block or we'd have heard about it. Maybe a terrorist trying to plant a bomb? There are Jews in the block, of course – Dr Bettauer, for one. Or perhaps it was the IRA – they don't care who they blow up so long as they're British. But why wouldn't they say so? My goodness, we read about it all in the papers every day or see it on television and aren't scared.' He paused for a moment, both furious and deep in thought, then, looking up again, said, 'One thing is sure. We won't be allowed to go down and see Mr and Mrs Biggs the way we've been doing any more. What do you think it was, Miranda?'

His sister looked once more into what was troubling her, and didn't want to say. She was very close to the truth and yet at the same time far from it, for the crime of arson and the threat of the firebug simply happened not yet to have been encountered by any one of them. They had been indoctrinated with the dangers of fire, matches, inflammables, and precautions that must be taken. It was just that neither in experience nor in their reading had they come across the deliberate or compulsive fire-raiser. Terrorism in all its other most hideous forms was the order of their day.

'I don't know,' said Miranda. 'It must have been something quite dreadful. Mummy was frightened, Daddy was angry, and the man – I mean, the Inspector – was being made to look foolish, wasn't he?' Then she turned suddenly upon her younger brother: 'Just what was it you did see down there, Roddy?'

Roddy was delighted to come up with it again with a few embellishments. 'A thing,' he said, 'with googley eyes. It was on its hands and knees, with horns, and when I frightened it away it slithered around the corner on its blobs, like I told you before.'

'Oh, for goodness sake, Roddy,' Michael cried in

exasperation. 'Don't be so stupid. There isn't any such thing as a "thing" with blobs. You saw that last week on television in one of those ridiculous cartoons. There was a sort of ghost. I came in while you were watching it. It was a fib you told the Inspector, wasn't it? Or just your imagination?'

Roddy looked up at Michael, and there was hurt in his eyes, though it was only Miranda who caught a glimpse of it. He said sullenly and half to himself, 'It *did* slither.'

'Oh, Roddy, you're the end,' Michael shouted. 'If you saw anything it had to be somebody, didn't it? You really didn't see anything, did you? You were just trying to be important.'

Roddy closed down for the day, at least on that subject. He went into one of those silences from which nothing could budge him, with his large eyes manifesting his resentment. Not to believe Roddy's imaginings was the highest crime of which his brother and sister could be guilty, and they rarely queried his tales of where he'd been, what had happened to him, and how he had triumphed.

Michael tried once more, even though aware of the futility. 'Come on, Roddy. Be a big boy.'

Roddy's lips remained tightly compressed, and Miranda thought she saw a tear gather at the corner of one eye.

'You've lost him,' she said to Michael. 'He'll never tell now.' And then to Roddy: 'Never mind. I believe you. And you were very brave to frighten it away.'

Roddy gave his sister a grateful glance, then turned firmly and went out of the room.

Michael was still angry, and said, 'Silly little baby. What do you do with a child like that?'

All the thoughts and confusion and worry within Miranda now seemed to crystallize, and she felt it was time to speak out. 'Michael,' she began.

'Yes?'

'Roddy did see something.'

Michael looked at his sister in shocked disbelief. 'Are you kidding? A "thing" with blobs? Come on, Miranda.'

'Not a "thing". A somebody.'

'How do you know that?' Michael challenged.

Miranda reflected. How did she know? Well, when it came to knowing as compared to thinking or suspecting, there was just no question. One did or one didn't. 'I can't tell you,' she said. 'It was something about Roddy that was different from his other make-believes.'

It was now Michael's turn to be troubled, for experience had taught him that Miranda would never insist that she knew something unless she did.

'You're sure?' he checked, lowering his voice. 'Maybe I was stupid and shouldn't have jumped on him so much. Could be if he did see something and didn't know who or what it was he saw down there in the half-light he had to invent – like what he saw on television. Ought we perhaps to tell the Inspector?'

Miranda shook her head in negation, and then, her voice dropping to a whisper, said, 'Michael?'

'Yes?'

'There's something else I know.'

'What?'

'Whatever it was that happened down there – and I don't know what, but only why – it had to do with us.'

Michael looked at his sister, genuinely startled. 'With us, Miranda? What do you mean?'

She regarded him gravely and said, 'Perhaps not exactly with us, but on account of us. On account of our House. The House.'

Michael stared at her for an instant, in confusion himself now, wanting to say, 'Us? Our House? You must be crazy.' But he didn't.

He said nothing at all, in fact, because he could see from the expression on Miranda's face that she wasn't thinking or guessing. She was feeling. And when Miranda felt something she was usually right.

CHAPTER XX

Metamorphosis

The rain, even though the Meteorological Office had ventured timidly to suggest 'some improvement likely later in the day', still did not let up. It simply varied in intensity between a drizzle, a steady downfall and a deluge, the last usually accompanied by winds and growls of distant thunder.

Miranda, gazing out of the window again, was pulling at her lower lip and thinking hard, as she seemed to have been doing for the last twenty-four hours, since the episode of the Inspector and the so-called attempt on Mr Biggs's tools.

Michael was lying on his stomach on the floor, surrounded once again by his drawings of the House, and checking off the by now almost complete set and location of tenants whose Melton Court flats occupied some part of the House.

Roddy, sitting cross-legged on the floor too, was silently watching his older brother, and busying himself with doodles on his own drawing pad in imitation.

Eyeing the blank spaces around him, Michael slowly announced, 'There's still 3E, a couple of flats on the second floor, and the people who live just along the corridor in 1C and 1E. But that's all – and I think they know about us – about the House, I mean. I should think everyone does by now. But we don't know anything very much about them. We could put their names in – I do know them. Mr and Mrs Aylott in 3E, a Colonel Ryder in 2C . . .'

'Michael,' Miranda interrupted, turning from the window and still tugging her lower lip.

'Mmmm?' he murmured, without looking up.

'Do you think we ought to stop?' Miranda asked.

Michael looked up now quickly enough. 'Stop what?'

'All this,' said Miranda, nodding her head at the plans all around. 'The – our House.'

'Whatever for?' asked Michael.

'Because of all that's happened since we started,' Miranda shrugged. 'It's had the weirdest effect on people, after all, hasn't it? Some seem to have been made quite unhappy by it, others plain angry – and it's all our fault, isn't it?'

Michael rolled over on to his side and nibbled at the end of his pencil, 'Oh, come on, Miranda. I thought we'd been through all that before, when Mummy and Daddy kicked up such a fuss. It certainly isn't our fault if some of the tenants have been playing up. Why should they, for heaven's sake? And anyway quite a few seem to be enjoying it all as much as we are. You *are* still enjoying it, aren't you?'

'Oh, yes, I think so,' said Miranda, uncertainly again.

Roddy looked from one to the other, his eyes growing larger and rounder and his expression faintly troubled.

'Well then,' Michael asked perplexedly, 'what on earth's the matter with you all of a sudden?'

Miranda sat down on the floor beside him, and looking at all the drawings said, 'Oh, I don't know. What with Mrs Potter dying, then the seance, and what happened in the basement . . . And probably a lot more things we don't even know about.'

'Now just a minute,' Michael looked and paused until he had Miranda's eyes on him. 'For a start, Mrs Potter would have died anyway – but she had a jolly good time with us before she did, didn't she? The seance was shown up for the farce it really was – and the basement business is out of our hands, whatever you say or feel about it. Surely, what we do in our House is a private matter, and nobody else's concern.'

What came to Miranda as something of a shock was not her brother's rather aggressive attitude but his easy use of the word 'House' when referring to their privacy. He might have said 'flat' or 'room' or 'home', but it showed how wholly he had adapted to her vision. They were no longer living in a set of boxes but a House for which each in his or her own way had longed, and which together they had brought into a kind of super reality.

Yet to Miranda even this in itself seemed a little frightening now. For the child in her was no longer and a young woman with a profound awareness of the effect that young people could have upon adults was taking possession. She wondered if she would ever think of this moment – this precise moment – when one day she would be a mother. She had grown up, and the realization, like the fact, moved and disturbed her. Something of her feelings came across to Michael as they sat communing silently and wondering together deep new thoughts. Almost without thinking, she said, 'I feel as though something awful might be going to happen.'

'What?' asked Michael. 'Who to?'

Miranda shrugged. 'I don't know. To the House. Perhaps to us.'

'Like being struck by lightning?' Roddy burst out as thunder rolled in the distance. 'And everything squooshed and us burnt to a frizzle? I don't like it.' And he looked as though he was about to cry.

'No, of course not,' said Miranda. 'You are always so silly, Roddy.'

The aggression was still in Michael's voice as he asked, 'What are you trying to do, though, Miranda? Scare him out of his wits? What's our House got to do with anything happening to anybody? I like it. It was you who saw it. Now it seems to me it's *you* who's being silly.'

Stung to near tears by her brother's rebuke, Miranda suddenly rose and rushed to the door, steadying herself with a grip on the frame as she turned and countered slowly, 'Silly, am I? Well, we'll see about that.'

Then, with a slam, all was blank and she was gone –
racing along to her own still room and flinging herself face
down on the bed, burying her trembling head in the pillow
in lonely worry and foreboding.

As Roddy scrambled up to follow her, Michael called a
curt, 'No.' But as he saw the sadness in his brother's eyes
he counselled carefully, 'She needs to be alone for a while,
Roddy,' doing his best to appear untroubled himself.

Then as a thunderclap burst over the block he cast around
for some immediate distraction, and suggested almost as if
there had been no thunder at all, 'Why don't we play
"Moonbase"?'

With the same thunderclap Miranda sank her face deeper
into her pillow, screwing her eyes tightly closed. There were
dancing kaleidoscopic sequins in the soft darkness at first,
then they slowed until they faded into unbidden sleep.

But in sleep, even more, far from leaving her, Miranda's
fears crystallized into a dream – a long, startling dream of
all her fears.

It began with a deafening, shuddering bang that shook
and flung Michael, Roddy and herself across the playroom
floor, and as they rolled over and up again their minds were
as dazed as their bodies. They looked desperately, speech-
lessly at one another, shock and bewilderment trembling
through them with the floor itself.

'Down!' Michael shouted as Roddy slid up on grazed
knees. 'Keep down!'

'But what is it? Where's Mummy? Mummy! Are you all
right?' Miranda cried out to her.

'Mummy!' Michael's and Roddy's chorus echoed in
Miranda's head.

Mrs Maitland needed no calling. She was there within
seconds, propping herself unsteadily but unharmed against
the doorframe, one ovengloved hand pressing her brow, as
her eyes urgently sought out her children.

Each floored head turned up to her as she gasped,
'Quickly! Quickly! Come on!'

Unquestioning, uncertain and as unaware as their mother

of the cause of the big bang, all three children clambered up and gathered around her.

Alarm bells started all about them, and rang and rang as they rushed with her out of the flat.

'Down the stairway,' Mrs Maitland directed. 'Quickly!'

The alarms were even louder in the corridor as they ran past the lift. Other doors were opening as they went. Other people were running before them and behind. Faces, faces, faces.

'What on earth's going on?' Miranda heard Mr Brant growl as he followed them.

'Outside! Outside quickly!' Mrs Maitland cried as they scurried down the stairs and into the growing clamour and confusion of the lobby, as everyone – everyone in sight – ran for the main doors and out into the street.

Mr Thompson and Tim Ryan held their backs to the open doors as they shouted and gestured sternly, 'Outside, everyone! Outside! Get right away!' over and over again.

'What has happened?' Miranda saw Mr Fraser asking no one in particular.

Mr Thompson answered him for everyone, 'We're not sure yet, but, please, hurry along while we check.'

'Sir! Down here!' Mr Biggs was calling from the top of the basement steps. 'Down here, sir! Quick!' as alone, in pairs or in groups – some carried, some limping, some screaming – everyone, as directed, rushed out and away into the rain, carrying the most extraordinary assortment of objects – jewel boxes, ornaments, bigger than themselves, pictures, books, fur coats and even coverlets and teddy bears – each treasured possession seized in a moment as instinctive as the dash for survival itself.

All traffic had stopped. Cars had collided, a van over-turned, and drivers and passengers alike ran, crawled and climbed in the disorderly rush.

'Over the road! Get right back over the road and right away!' still the voices were calling in Miranda's head.

Sirens joined the mounting chorus of alarms and cries as the crowd swelled, splashed and slid in the road and across it.

The rain, relentless still, was drenching everyone and everything exposed to it, yet almost unnoticed in the panic
and the turmoil that filled the crowded open air of Hallam
Road.

Over it all, Miranda heard the voice of Mr Thompson,
like a captain ordering 'Abandon Ship!' barking out to the
last few stragglers who plunged out and into the rain at his
command – while he, captain-like still, remained behind.

'What is it?' 'What's happened?' 'Did you see anything?'
the questions rang round in the jostling.

From all directions the impatient ringing of fire engines
and ambulances commingled with the wails of police cars
as they screeched and skidded and sprayed to a halt outside
the block of flats. Most of the crews dashed straight inside.
Others – mainly policemen – rushed to control and move
well back the shocked and terrified throng of tenants on
the opposite side of the road.

Glass suddenly shattered and fell through the rain on to
the front drive as a second and greater ground-wrenching
crash drew all eyes upwards.

'Look!' Mr Brant cried out in the retreating crowd. 'The
walls are going!'

The rain-drenched band stared up in silence at the huge
façade of Melton Court, as the lines of the building first
wavered and strayed off plumb. They were refusing to con-
verge. They took on a slant – vaguely at first, then gradually
more pronounced – as a cracked and crooked line of
concrete sections separated, crumbled and fell, exposing a
patchwork of interiors from the ground floor upwards.

Amidst screams of panic the crowd backed away even
more and clearer still from the plummeting debris.

And still Miranda's dream raced on.

Pleas, sobs and lamentations dinned the air as the
tenants strained and craned to scan the building that until
just minutes before had housed them. Their lives, their
possessions, their pasts, their futures were still in there.
Everything they had – all that they depended upon.
Outside and away – even farther away – they trembled

denuded by the unimaginable losses with which they were threatened so instantly.

Miranda, standing with her mother and brothers, stared on as one section followed another in a criss-cross of collapse, until, with one final toppling slab, the ground and first three floors stood exposed entirely, like an open doll's house.

Out of the clouds of tumbling mortar, Miranda saw a dark, familiar shape arising, with gables, chimneys and portico. 'Our House!' she cried. 'It's there! Our House! Do you see?'

Michael and Roddy looked. Mrs Maitland and others who heard looked. But Miranda knew, despite her cry, that only she could see anything more than the open, rained-in, girdered and beamed interior of the lower floors of Melton Court.

'She's hysterical, poor child,' a woman murmured, as if in warning, and in a pretence of control herself.

But Michael drew breath sharply as he noted and at once remarked to Miranda, 'It is exactly the size of the House. Just where it would be.'

'Exactly!' Miranda cried. 'It must have been straining to bursting point. But not any more. It's broken out – broken free – at last. Our dear House. It's there again. It's there forever.'

Miranda saw Roddy look up at his mother with anxious misgiving. He seemed frightened by Miranda's cries – and frightened all the more for her. As he buried his head in his mother's waist, Mrs Maitland shook the rain and the tears from her face and gathered all three children to her. And it was then that Miranda's eyes and heart registered the full horror in the crowd about her. She trembled and ached with sorrow for the loss mirrored in their frightened, hollow faces, and reluctantly even to herself regretted too late all that she had begun with the House that seemed to her to be at the very centre of the disaster they were witnessing. She longed to be able to help every one of the suffering families around her – worried for them, feared for them even – yet despaired that the House and its shattering epiphany now was more than anyone could check or control.

She saw Mr Murchison, nearby, look down in simmering silence at his wife, whose eyes were rolling in a frenzy of near-hallucination.

'The apocalypse! The apocalypse has come!' she was gasping. 'The evil that was within is bodying forth!'

In contempt he turned away from Mrs Murchison, snapping from his shark's jaw, 'Get a grip on yourself, woman. This is none of your sham. This is real – and ghastly. It's the end for us all.'

As he turned, Miranda watched as his eyes caught sight of Mr and Mrs Sinsavang kneeling in prayer behind him, with a group of shaven-headed men in orange robes dark-dappled in the rain, prostrate beside them, and he silenced himself abruptly in shared supplication.

Moments later the crowd of tenants seemed to gasp as one when Mr Biggs appeared following two police constables flanking a sunken-headed Mr Tringham. As he was bundled into a white patrol car and driven away at speed, speculation spread noisily through the onlookers, and when Mr Biggs passed through the police line to join his wife he walked into a virtual ambush of questions and guesses.

He held up his hands as if to ward them all off, announcing firmly, 'He has nothing to do with this. Nothing at all. He's been taken into custody on quite a different matter. No, not looting. Quite a different matter. Nothing at all to do with this.'

As he passed by Miranda, she looked up at him and queried, 'More to do with something in the basement, Mr Biggs?'

He stopped sharp, looked all around him, then down, with a nod and a confiding smile to Miranda. 'The basement indeed.'

'Do you mean he was –' Michael began.

But Mr Biggs cut him short. 'Yes. I found him there myself just before the first rumbling.' Then he shook his head in distaste. 'He was all set to have another go all right.

But he jumped like a scared cat when the ground shook. He dropped everything and tried to make a run for it – only this time he was cornered good and proper. He's a madman, that fellow. Must be. Kept shouting, "Infernal house! Infernal! Infernal house! Infernal!" when we nabbed him and his gear.'

Roddy seemed just about to speak up when a blast like dynamite shook the far ground-floor corner of the block.

And this time, as the dust cloud was dispersed by the rain, one collapsed ceiling and two caved-in walls were discernible in the frayed corner of the block.

'What was that?' 'Is it a bomb?' 'The whole building's going!' the cries came again.

'Good grief!' Michael pointed. 'That must have gone off just where old Mrs Potter had her flat. If she'd been in there now . . .' He shook his head and fell silent.

'She died peacefully before anything could kill her,' Miranda heard herself saying.

Just then, behind three thigh-booted firemen, Mr Thompson emerged, his face blackened, one trouser leg torn in a flap at the knee, and crossed the road alone.

'Are you all right, Mr Thompson?' Mrs Maitland was the first to ask. 'Whatever is happening?'

Everyone within earshot gathered around him for an answer.

'It looks as if there's been some flooding. That last bang, we think, was a gas pocket – though all main supplies were shut off at the first alarm, weren't they, Bill?'

'Certainly were, sir,' said Mr Biggs.

'But now what?' asked Miranda. 'What will happen to everyone?'

'We'll just have to wait and see,' Mr Thompson shrugged forlornly, then plunged his hands deep in his pockets and shuffled off.

'Oh, Mummy, we'll never go back, will we?' Miranda pleaded.

'I don't know. I doubt it,' Mrs Maitland shook her head. 'But the first thing we must do is try to telephone Daddy.

Let's see if there's a kiosk anywhere near that we can use.'

It was as the telephone was ringing in Flat 1A that Miranda suddenly awoke from her deep sleep – so greatly relieved to find herself safe on her own bed still. She could hear her mother answering the telephone in the hall quite normally. And yet she was drained by the dream, alarmed by the events in it all the more now, and convinced it had been a warning, the urgency of which the rain beating fiercely on her window only intensified. She jumped up and hurried out to the hall, but her mother, still talking, waved her quiet. She stood for some moments shaking with impatient fear, trying to signal to her mother but unable to catch her attention.

So it was that she decided to go back in to Michael and Roddy, whose shock more at her frightened eyes than her sudden re-entry turned to anxious concentration as she burst straight out with her dream and related everything that she could remember of it, in all its clearness and intensity, standing imploringly before them both.

As she finished, and sank exhaustedly pale on the edge of Michael's bed, Roddy asked hesitantly, 'You don't mean the flats are going to be flooded, do you? How could they?'

Michael then stepped forward, sat down beside Miranda, and as he wrapped a comforting arm around her spoke softly for her in reply, 'It can't be that, of course. But it could mean that after all this rain there's some sort of flooding underneath the building.'

There was clearly no thought or question in his mind of dismissing the dream, and Miranda hugged him and held on to him for that, her head firmly on his shoulder.

'Well, what do you think we should do?' asked Roddy. 'We can't tell anybody about a *dream*. Who would take any notice of that?'

'I don't think this was an ordinary dream,' Michael began slowly.

'It wasn't. I know it wasn't,' Miranda added forcefully.

'I think we've got to tell Mr Thompson,' he continued.

'Not only about the flooding but about Mr Tringham too. The thing is, how?'

As they puzzled and pondered, eventually Michael answered himself. 'By telling Mummy first,' he said decisively.

'You mean the dream or what?' Roddy queried.

'Yes – all of it. And then, surely, when she's heard the warnings she'll feel she must go with us to see Mr Thompson. She *must*.'

'It was Mr Tringham I saw in the basement, you know,' Roddy then half confided and half confessed.

'Well, why didn't you say?' Michael thrust forward. 'Instead of all that blob nonsense.'

'It wasn't nonsense. He was wearing sort of blobs – and a kind of head mask – but I could still tell it was him. It looked as if he was trying to make a bonfire. But he scares me – and I didn't want him to get his hands on me again.'

'Oh, Roddy,' Michael reproached. 'If only you'd said, then he'd have been arrested or taken in for questioning at least, and he wouldn't be on the loose still. So he could try something else any time – that is, again, unless we warn Mr Thompson first.'

When they heard the ting of the telephone receiver being replaced at last they all stood up together, and Michael, supportive and concerned as only he could be to Miranda, turned to her and said gently, 'Come on, let's tell Mummy.'

Mrs Maitland listened intently to all that Miranda had to tell – with a few promptings and reminders from Michael and Roddy – then nodded for time to collect her thoughts. She was disturbed by the account, though she tried not to show it, and concerned that the children now seemed to know more about the arson attempt than she thought they could otherwise possibly have done. It was this, above all, in fact, that convinced her that Miranda's dream was much more than that – and Mr Thompson should be told. She even suggested herself that they should go down together to see him.

Mr Thompson's smile at Mrs Maitland as she tapped on

the open door to his office dropped as he saw the three children filing in behind her. He was obviously vexed, too, at first, by what appeared to be still more childish imaginings coming from their mother this time.

But after the Tringham disclosure – at which he was clearly taken aback – he began to feel he simply could not afford to discount the dream entirely.

Saying no more than 'Sit tight a moment', however, he buzzed Mr Biggs and summoned him to his office too.

Mr Biggs listened from the first much more receptively as Miranda herself was called upon by Mr Thompson to recount her dream.

'Well I go to sea,' he gasped as she concluded. 'And, d'you know, Mrs Biggs has been complaining of a sort of dampness in our flat down in the basement for the last couple of days.' Turning then to Mr Thompson, he added, 'Of course, seeing as how the drains were all changed only last year, sir, they could certainly do with a check after the weather we've been having.'

Mr Thompson agreed, and, gesturing him to stay on a while with the silently seated Maitlands, proceeded to make two telephone calls as they watched.

The first was to Detective Inspector St Elmo, urging him to 'Get around here as soon as you can', explaining that 'We have reason to believe that Mr Martin Tringham in Flat 3E is probably behind the arson attempt' – the first time the term had been used in front of the children, who instantly looked one to the other as Roddy whispered, 'What's "arson"?'

Mrs Maitland signalled silence with a finger to her lips and a look that promised explanations later.

Then Mr Thompson made his second call – to the engineers' and surveyors' department of Truciman Estates. Again, he said urgently and with not a little self-importance he had reason to believe that underground checks should be carried out at Melton Court as a matter of some urgency. There was suspected flooding.

The second call over, Mr Thompson stood up to thank

Mrs Maitland and even the children this time, promising to keep them fully informed of developments.

They did not see Mr Tringham taken away for questioning – though taken away he was – but then nor did they hear when the Truciman engineers and surveyors had finished their first extensive foundation tests. The findings were all too positive: the underground watercourse was indeed flooding.

Land drains, well shafts and pumping equipment, the engineers explained to Mr Thompson, would have to be brought in almost at once, before eventual soil-stabilization could be effected. The Borough Surveyor's Department would also have to be alerted immediately – and Lord Truciman himself informed.

It was as a result of this that very early the following morning all tenants were telephoned or called upon by Mr Thompson's staff to assemble in the main lobby at 10.30 – adults only – for an important and urgent meeting to be addressed by Lord Truciman.

As people began to gather from just before 10 o'clock onwards there was a puzzled, grudging murmur of un-answered questions that increased in volume as the time set for the meeting approached. But when, at 10.30 precisely, the tall, impressive bulk of Lord Truciman emerged, nodding sagely, from Mr Thompson's office, with the Superintendent and a group of grim-faced Borough officials, and ascended the improvised podium prepared for him, all was soon chillingly clear.

Addressing them, none the less, in a deliberately con-trolled, no-panic tone, with nods of support and reassurance from the officials either side of him, Lord Truciman paused only to take breath before making his last important announcement. Since, to meet all safety requirements, Melton Court would have to be emptied for a week at least, while the work of draining, underpinning and land stabilization was carried out, he hoped very much that all tenants would accept and co-operate with his offer of free accommodation for that time at his newly completed Marlborough Hotel nearby.

Individual reactions blurred in the crowd, but amidst earnest expressions of gratitude and relief at the early discovery of the danger to the building Mr Thompson elected to speak for all when he rose to thank Lord Truciman for his generous hospitality in this time of emergency.

As he sat down again, to a chorus of 'Hear, hear', Mr Thompson could not help also feeling privately relieved that at least now the block could be emptied for the Sinsavangs' exorcism without the other tenants even knowing of their curious ritual.

Moments later, as the meeting ended, the Sinsavangs themselves quietly approached Lord Truciman to thank him for his extreme kindness but graciously to decline his offer of hotel accommodation, preferring instead to spend the necessary time away from Melton Court at the Lao Nam Embassy.

As the lobby was rapidly emptying of tenants, off to gather their thoughts and pack their belongings temporarily, Lord Truciman lumbered down to ask Mr Thompson to introduce him to Mr and Mrs Maitland, who had, after all, first brought the present emergency to his attention. Mr Thompson nodded obligingly, then hurried off as he spotted the Maitlands on their way to the stairs.

With formal introductions rather too formally managed by Mr Thompson, he then tactfully took his leave. Lord Truciman thanked them both more fulsomely than either felt appropriate in the circumstances. But it was, in fact, just as Mrs Maitland was attempting to explain that it was really their children to whom such thanks, if any, was due when she and her husband were silenced into disbelief almost by what Lord Truciman chose to call 'a gesture of appreciation'.

'If you will allow me,' he bowed as if for permission, 'I should like very much to offer you in straight exchange for your flat here in Melton Court one of the new town houses we've just built near Hampstead Heath. I'm sure your children would love it – I heard all about their passion for houses from Mr Thompson this morning – and it will be free for you to move in at the end of next month.'

Incredulously, both John and Dorothy Maitland could accept Lord Truciman's offer with no more than nods and smiles of thanks at first. But then, as Mr Maitland shook his hand in firm acceptance and sincere gratitude, clearing his throat to speak, a delighted Lord Truciman asked Mrs Maitland if he might meet their three children – and Miranda especially.

'The tenants here,' he nodded, 'have no idea just how much they owe to them – and this morning was not the best of times to tell them. Without your daughter, we could have had great structural damage – and even loss of life. But they'll learn. Believe me, they'll learn.'

An emboldened John Maitland readily agreed, 'Of course you shall meet them. But on one condition: that you, not we, tell them of your generous offer.'

'Well, if you wish,' Lord Truciman chortled conspiratorially as he ushered them both across to the now deserted lift.

Michael, Miranda and Roddy were caught quite off guard by the visit – and when the polished pate of Lord Truciman bowed in the warmest of greetings to each of them Roddy could not help watching the shine where his hair should be and puzzling over the reason for such an unbiblically bald Lord's title.

'We have much to thank you for – and particularly you, Miranda,' he declared. 'It's been a very difficult and rather frightening time for you, I know – but, by Jove, you've come through it all admirably.' He paused a moment, then went on, 'I had an opportunity, after our tenants' meeting this morning, to have a quiet word with your parents – and what I put to them they now insist I report to you. Namely, the offer of an exchange of this flat for a new house overlooking Hampstead Heath, as a token of my sincere appreciation of your alert behaviour in warning all concerned of the terrible dangers threatening this block . . .'

The children were so astonished that the rest of Lord

Truciman's thanks were drowned in their sudden whoops of ecstasy.

'Oh, how wonderful – isn't it, Mummy? Isn't it, Daddy?' Miranda beamed.

'It is exceptionally kind of you, sir,' Michael nodded smartly, then, with the beginnings of a laugh, added, 'I can hardly believe it.'

'Thank you, Lord,' Roddy ventured, trying the term for the first time.

He was not sure if it was because of that or just for sheer delight that they all suddenly burst into a whole scale of laughter.

But then, just as the revels calmed to smiles, Miranda more bravely than boldly affirmed. 'I could never forget our House here, though. I'll always remember it and hold it dear.'

'So shall I,' said Michael suddenly.

'And me,' Roddy added hurriedly.

Stunned to tingling by such accord, Miranda could only gulp as she whispered, 'Dear . . . dear old House.'

But it was in no whisper that Lord Truciman echoed, 'Yes, dear old House. Don't you worry, Miranda, my child. It will not be forgotten. In fact, I propose that Melton Court be renamed Melton House – in memory and recognition of The House That Wouldn't Go Away.'